Owldoll

(A Twenty-First Century Faery Tale)

by

Jerry Brooks

ISBN: 978-0-9980342-0-1
Owldoll (A Twenty-First Century Færy Tale)

Owldoll

(A Twenty-First Century Faery Tale

by

Jerry Brooks

Contents

Prologue

Good Reader of any Age, excuse my occasional need to provide an out-side comment on what you are about to read for valuable insight time might distort or alter before you ever see the words. This is the Twenty-First Century, a makeshift modern Age, where we live in perpetual impatience. You might think: how contradictory a claim the subtitle makes because færy tales are not contemporary. Yet what is modern today will someday be ancient history. Owldoll was derived from a local urban legend: a contemporary version of a fable, which was a tale, built on a moral framework. As such, this was a tale made of the stuff woven into a fable. But wasn't a fable from a bygone era the origin of old-time færy tales? The færy tale retold the fable with the moral framework left to the reader's imagination but allowed the storyteller, at no fault of his or her own memory or upbringing, to modify the original story. Our fable was fleshed out freshly by intensive interviews, dialog, and reflection with those whose character or characteristic were rendered nearly intact—a journalistic cryogenics—for what you are about to read. Listen up and hear this story where your imagination, Good Reader, advances an urban legend into a twenty-first century færy tale hundreds of years before the conformity and ordinance of time has made its transgression. After a brief introduction to the setting, the story starts at the beginning because that was where the story began. Any inaccuracies or gaps in this account are unintentional but are so slight you aren't missing anything. You'll pardon the inexactitude of my changing the name of the city to Midway—it was neither here nor there—because it was like a city near you and unlike that city at the same time. The similarities and differences would be so small you can associate it with the city you have in mind.

— Author

Daisy lived in a small city called Midway in an apartment building on a moderately busy street. Daisy had no sister or brother but she had a room of her own. In the room, Daisy kept a dozen, or so, dolls and teddy bears clustered together along the center of the wall right below the window. But this story really began when Deborah, Daisy's mother, was seven months pregnant with their first and only child, Daisy.

On a hot summer day, Deborah was walking in a part of downtown she rarely frequented with its funky little shops, cafés, and artisans. Across the street, she noticed a curious sign on an ornate dark purple and black trimmed building: Witchcraft Heights Potions. Deborah found the lettering style intriguing. So she crossed the street and went inside.

She looked around and only a few other people were in the store. A strong scent of sandalwood incense wafted under her nose and sunlight filtered in from a few skylights in the high ceiling. Around the shop were shelves of different sized bottles of various colors labeled by hand in neat calligraphy.

At the opposite side of the room, a woman with long, straight red hair walked through a doorway covered by black velvet curtains. Deborah and the woman made eye contact engaging the intimacy strangers develop spontaneously dissolving barriers usually in place.

As Deborah browsed around the store, she occasionally heard a tap-tap-tap, and then noticed a thin man wearing sunglasses with a walking stick on the other side of the store. His voice was barely audible: A new one. Y-esss? Y-esss? We'll see who wins the contest. Y-esss! Y-esss!

The man's yeses lingered like the smoke from an extinguished candle floating in the air; a presence of the past.

The red-haired woman half-smiled but her eyes focused sharply on the man as she answered him, "I have a solution for this dilemma...and you know it." They remained staring at each other, then she continued, "Time has come for you to go, hasn't it?"

He leaned heavily on the cane and said, "Y-esss. Y-esss? As

you know, if you reveal the spell to the one it will be cast upon, your Ilaç[1] won't work. Y-esss? Y-esss? Your Ilaç won't work. Y-esss! Y-esss!"

Deborah only heard the man mumbling something before he left that ended y-esss? And a short pause and; y-esss!

On the left-hand counter stood a cobalt blue bottle. Deborah walked over to examine it up close. *Even if the contents are of no value, it is a beautiful bottle: deep, rich violet-blue in a solid, high-hipped glass bottle,* Deborah thought.

"Welcome, I am Xhuljana Magjistare[2]," the woman announced. "You look familiar...not from here but from another time and place." Xhuljana's face glowed lightly like a soft-white bulb.

Deborah couldn't put her finger on where she knew this woman from. "I think I know you, too. Funny how that happens when you have a chance meeting.... We'll figure it out later. My name is Deborah. Nice...nice to meet you. Interesting bottle you have here."

Xhuljana said, "This is a special potion. One I should not have left out unattended. I had to go out back for a minute. I got involved and it took me much longer than I intended. I didn't mean to leave it out."

Xhuljana walked over behind the counter to where the bottle stood and Deborah moved closer to the bottle, too. She looked at Deborah a long while and said, "You mind if I tell you something I sense in you?"

Deborah nodded in agreement; half intrigued and half surprised by this personal inquiry from this exotic woman.

"I sense something very, very interesting about you. What I sense in you is an owl."

Deborah was taken aback. "You sense a what? An owl? The bird?"

Xhuljana smiled and continued, "I look into your eyes: their shape; the prismatic sparkles of grays, browns, and gold

---

[1] Eel-ah-shh

[2] Dg-hul-i-ana Mahg-ist-are-ay

radiating outward. But you're also like an owl in a mystical way, like the owl of Minerva, gifted seer of dangers hidden in the night. Funny, I was looking at something last night and it communicated to me about a union of two crossing paths.

"Your path and my path have crossed...here. Our destiny brought us to this point." Xhuljana pointed to an "x" pattern on a piece of leather draped over the counter. She winked at Deborah.

"Where two paths intersect is a special place. Just last night...I received a message.... Well, let me get it and show you instead of trying to tell you." Xhuljana spoke as she turned and walked to the opposite end of the store. She bent over, opened a cubbyhole door, and removed a wooden box with a carved top cover and other decorations.

"I want to show you this. I can just feel you'll make the connection. You'll get it," Xhuljana continued.

Deborah looked at the box Xhuljana had in her hands and thought, *What's that? Where have I seen this design before?*

As the red-haired woman got closer and placed the box on the counter, Deborah trained her eyes along the inlay and geometric design on the box. Xhuljana slid open the cover revealing a stuffed, silver-grey owl. Xhuljana removed the owl and stood it on its feet.

At first, Deborah was caught by surprise by its piercing hypnotic gaze. Tiny white feathers branched out to black feathers to silver feathers around the eye sockets. Deborah was drawn into their spellbinding attraction.

"Wow. I can feel the life being sucked right out of me," Deborah blurted out.

The owl locked onto her with oversized purple eyes with angular specks of green, gold, silver, and black angular radiating outward from jet-black pupils. Deborah felt embarrassed, like walking in front of an open window wearing just her underwear. The owl seemed to be calling her to come closer. As her fingertips stroked the backside of the owl's head, she felt a warm, low current, electrical shock. The energy resonated deep in her womb and the growing baby kicked with a little bit of excitement.

In her mind she heard a wordless voice. Deborah was unsure what the voice was saying. She blinked her eyes and refocused on the owl. The owl stared back like it knew the answer to a dark secret. Deborah rubbed her bulging belly where the baby just kicked as a loud car radio outside played, Who are you? Who? Who! Who? Who!

Deborah stepped a few steps along the counter. Xhuljana moved too and placed her hand softly on top of Deborah's left hand. Her touch was comforting to Deborah.

"Excuse me a moment. I won't be long," Xhuljana told her as she turned to go to another part of the store.

Deborah stared into the box and was mesmerized by the owl. She thought, *This owl looks so familiar.... Why? And Xhuljana, too. Where have I seen her before? Was it when I went to...*

"What!" Deborah yelled out. "You just blinked! But that can't...can't be. You're not...not alive!"

The owl seemed to be making eye contact and remained motionless at the same time. Deborah was unsure if she was imagining this but she thought she heard a voice speaking directly to her baby. She could not hear the words but the owl spoke to her baby in a slow, gentle voice, "W-issh. I will be your special friend. I will be your special friend. W-issh."

Deborah shook her head, touched the stuffed owl, and shook it for good measure. The owl didn't move but the baby did. The baby's tranquility rubbed off on Deborah, who might have been on edge by the sight of an animated stuffed owl.

It's my hormones going bonkers. They said to expect weird stuff. Now, I'm just imagining a stuffed owl is talking to Daisy and not to me! Phew!

She heard footsteps and Xhuljana came back. They both looked at the owl and the intricate wooden box on the counter.

"You see," Xhuljana began. "Last night, the owl communicated to me without words that we would meet again today. I knew you would cross over from the astral plane and come to my store."

Deborah looked puzzled—astral plane—and thought about just hearing a wordless voice, too.

Xhuljana explained, "We met at another time and place. In that secret dimension—the astral plane—where past, present, and future coexist, our spirits reunited and connected again. The owl was there, too. Did you think it was pure coincidence you came here today?"

Deborah suddenly remembered an exhibition she went to and asked, "Did you go to the William Blake exhibit three years ago? Is that where we met? Maybe that's where I saw you before?"

"Perhaps we did; Perhaps we didn't," Xhuljana laughed. "I'm not laughing at what you said. I did go to the exhibition... maybe twenty times: Blake was one of us. That is why we're attracted to his works. He lives on through them, don't you think? If you and I were together there, the power of the paintings would have blotted out any other forces. So we wouldn't have been aware of each other. When I said we met before, what I really meant was we met a long, long time ago during a different era."

This did not register to Deborah. Instead, she said, "I do remember the painting of the Owl."

Xhuljana's eyes opened wider, "That was the Hecate painting. Art critics have noted how the image of the owl—the constant companion that saw the dangers in the night for the goddess—eclipsed the image of the goddess Hecate." She took a slow breath and added, "Did you feel this about the owl, too?"

"Yes, I did," Deborah answered the way you nod in agreement when someone else nods. "I knew it was just a painting...I knew the image was not real...but I felt it reached out to me. I kept looking back at the owl as if it might say something. How did you know I liked that one? I thought about that painting for days and days."

Xhuljana brushed her long hair behind her shoulders. "When you feel the Spirits, your mind has walked in a new world. Those who have not traveled to these special places can't understand what those of us who have been there know."

Deborah detected the light pressure you feel approaching a burning fireplace in a cool room.

"Nothing to be afraid of," Xhuljana assured her.

Deborah faced Xhuljana but her eyes wandered back to the owl.

"Do you know the Owl Chant?" asked Xhuljana but did not wait for a response.

She sang a relaxing monotone:

Owl of blackened night.
Owl of second sight.
Guide me, show me, enlighten me, tonight.
Owl, grant me clarity,
As you have seen,
So mote it be.

Deborah immediately picked up the owl and pressed its face to her cheek. She felt a comfortable kinship she could not explain to herself. "Why do I feel this way?"

"You have made the connection through the Owl. It is part of the Spirit World we either possess or we don't. We can accept the mystery, and those who don't mock those who do." She leaned closer to Deborah. So close Deborah could smell cinnamon flavored toothpaste and noticed the brilliant whiteness of her teeth. Xhuljana giggled and her hazel eyes grew larger.

Deborah added, "This owl looks like the owl in the painting: How freaky."

"Don't say that," Xhuljana reprimanded. "Don't belittle your observation. You're seeing something most people never see. What we're talking about here is serious. Our raison d'être. You saw the image of the owl was even more powerful than the goddess. Not everyone sees this. You got it, or maybe you're right and the painting reached out to you. So, you got the meaning of the painting: The owl sees the hidden dangers in the night and is an essential companion...a mystical Being in its own right...there to help the goddess. You have a connection with the same mystical powers Blake gave the owl. It's there to save the goddess. Do you see it, too? That's what I meant when I asked, if you saw it, too?"

Deborah did not answer. She placed the owl on the counter and rubbed her hand down the backside of the owl's head and shoulders. Another jolt of warm electrical power surged through her. She couldn't tell how she felt but the baby moved.

Deborah looked away and saw the unusual bottle she noticed when she entered the store.

Xhuljana looked at the cobalt blue bottle that caught Deborah's attention and began, "I noticed you admiring this bottle when you first came in. You obviously have refined taste. Much of what we have here is for tourists, novelty or thrill seekers, or people posing as possessors of mystical powers. What they buy contain an innocuous solution: more or less colored water. What you have here is the genuine article."

She cradled it against the end of her arm and raised it to Deborah's eye level. Xhuljana read the label, "*Ilaç Magjistare*[3] : our family potion. Truly, a secret family recipe or mjeksi[4], it harnesses the powers within the feathers of the owl as in the legend of Shtriga[5] and the owl."

Deborah inquired. "I've never heard this story. What happened?"

Xhuljana placed the bottle back onto the counter and looked deeply into Deborah's eyes.

Xhuljana picked up where she left off, "Valbona was the mother of Rezarta, who became a much loved princess. Perhaps you've heard of them?"

"No, I don't think I've ever heard about Rey...Ra...Rapunzl.... Please, continue."

She looked back encouragingly. "Rezarta. Her name was <u>Rezarta and she</u> was the only daughter of Valbona. Valbona

[3] Eel-ah-ch mahj-ees-tar-ay

[4] Mag-ek-see

[5] Shhht-ree-ga

was part of the Court of Rozafa. The famous castle there was built in a mountainous area near two rivers. Shtriga—an evil witch—transformed into a moth. The moth sprayed an evil potion into the eyes of Valbona, sucked her blood, and flew away. Valbona was transformed into a witch and took another name. The potion made Valbona see what Shtriga wanted her to see. Shtriga and Valbona were defeated by the celebrated owl of the Rozafa Castle. The owl helped Rezarta end the evil curse on Valbona. So the owl earned an honored place in our history."

"I always wished I could perform magic," Deborah exclaimed. "I used to love stories like that when I was a little girl. I still do, I guess. Life can be so boring...."

Xhuljana noticed how detached Deborah appeared. She looked as if she was already in another land and was fixated on the blue bottle on the counter.

Deborah traced the letters on the label with her eyes pausing on the cedilla in *Ilaç*. She thought, *Even the words go together. Things happen for a reason. I didn't have to turn down this street, or walk through this door.*

Deborah looked up and saw Xhuljana. This set Deborah at ease.

"Please," Xhuljana asked, "take them both: the owl and the bottle. They belong with you. I get a very good sensation about this—almost like it was written in an ephemeris for today."

Deborah did not know what an ephemeris was but could not resist these gifts. So she blurted out, "Sure. How much do I owe you?"

Xhuljana had a small smile. "The *Ilaç Magjistare* is a gift. I insist. Its secret powers were created to end a witch's curse. Let's wait and see how you like the owl. It could take some time before the owl finds its place. When that day comes, we'll be glad you have this owl."

Deborah thought, *This woman is taking a big chance just giving these things to me. She doesn't know if I am an honest person. The owl and bottle might be valuable. I would never steal them but she doesn't know that.*

Then she got an eerie feeling and heard Xhuljana's voice in her mind, *I told you: Our Spirits were together before. It is an unbreakable chain. I am not taking a chance by giving them to you.*

When Deborah got home, she placed her new possessions on the kitchen table while a pot of tea steeped on the stove. The afternoon sun fell across the rugged blue bottle and Deborah marveled at its aura. She was absorbed by how well this bottle fit into her home: cobalt blue in the sunlight trailed by bluish shadows on the table reflecting onto the ceiling and floor as white curtains fluttered slightly.

"What a special day," she said out loud though there was no one else in the room. Her thoughts continued, *That woman, Xhuljana Magjistare. Pretty...a beautiful woman...a bit of foreign charm...a slight accent and that European je ne sais quoi.*

The baby kicked a few times in her womb. She rubbed her swollen belly. "Daisy, Daisy, be patient...just five more weeks."

Deborah heard the apartment door open and her husband called her name. She yelled, "...in the kitchen, dear."

Ricardo walked in smiling with a shopping bag in hand.

"Thought we needed milk, so, I picked some up. How was your day?" he said eyeing the bottle and unusual box on the table.

"Ricardo, it was a magical kind of day. I was downtown and was drawn by sign to a shop I had never seen before: Witchcraft Heights Potions. The shop owner took an immediate shining to me. In fact, she gave me this bottle as a gift. Actually, she never charged me for this...."

Deborah stretched toward the box and Ricardo pushed it closer to her. She drew it in front of her and slid the ornate cover open as the baby kicked again. She winced slightly as Ricardo caught the gaze of the silver owl.

"Daisy seems excited," Ricardo said.

"You know, Daisy gave me some feedback when I first held this owl. Weird. Xhuljana told me she had a premonition about her and I meeting and we have a connection with this owl. I don't know if you remember, the exhibit we went to a couple of years ago of William Blake's paintings and etchings? There was one of a goddess with a companion owl. The goddess depended upon owl to see dangers hidden in the night. I don't know... it's a long story."

Ricardo shrugged his shoulders and examined the owl in the box. He was a little leery about having a stuffed owl in their apartment. He picked it up, held it at eye level, and asked with a laugh, "Who are you? Hoo? Hoo."

"You'll never guess," Deborah said excitedly. "A car radio blasted that song while I was at the store. Who are you? Who? Who. Who? Who."

Ricardo looked at how happy Deborah was, the dark blue bottle on the table, the stuffed owl with oversized eyes, and he just smiled. "Okay. Okay. But would you not leave the owl out on display? I suspect some of our mousy friends will be intimidated."

"Mousy friends," Deborah chuckled. "Thank you, Ricardo. It could be part of being pregnant finding these things desirable. I'll probably outgrow it. The woman said I could bring them back. By the way..., do you know what the word a-femme-er-ous means?"

"Yeah. An ephemeris is a chart sailors used. It describes the position of planets and stars in the sky," he answered.

Deborah admired the bottle and asked, "You like it, right?"

Ricardo said, "The bottle looks nice: Good color, solid structure, and even the label looks artistic."

"She pronounced it: Eel-ah-shh mahj-ees-tar-ay: That's their family name. She said it was a genuine potion—not just colored water. I'll put it on the bookshelf in the other room and put the box in the bottom of my closet."

"You do that," he answered as he went to the refrigerator. "I'll start supper. Be careful with your magic solution.... You never know when it might be needed."

During dinner, Deborah told Ricardo more about her visit with Xhuljana. Some of the elements of the story seemed fantastical to Ricardo, albeit amusing. They continued talking when they went out on a stroll after dinner that warm evening. As they turned down a darkened side street, they heard a tapping like a poker on concrete and muffled voices.

"What's that?" Ricardo asked. "City dancin'? City plashin'?"

"Oh," Deborah sighed. "You know, that woman told me a old tale about an evil witch, Shtriga[6] and a magical owl."

They approached two men on the path ahead of them: one plump, bearded, and dressed in black, the other thin with wire-rimmed glasses wearing khakis and a dark red plaid shirt and black beret standing beside an old-fashioned camera with black bellows, a black cloth hood over the viewing screen, and mounted on a wooden tripod.

The rotund man spoke to Deborah, "Isn't it a wonderful evening? This could be your opportunity of a lifetime!"

Deborah hesitated to answer. There was something odd about these two.

"My friend here," the man continued, "is a professional photographer doing a feature for a national magazine.... I'm not able to reveal which one, I hope you understand. But he is looking for a pregnant woman. Just our luck you've walked by. Pure coincidence. Pure coincidence. Magnifique...très magnifique."

"She'll do, Vincent," the other man with the glasses said. "I can just tell. The magazine will love it: love it; love it; love it. Have them pose under the tree." He moved behind the camera and placed the fabric over his head. "Oooo...this is going to be perfect. Come along. Come along."

"Can't you see it? Your images immortalized," the plump one continued trying to usher them toward the spreading chestnut tree, "And what a fabulous surprise for your child! To be famous before birth! Just stand over here."

"Umm hum," Ricardo replied as he locked arms with Deborah and continued walking. After taking a half a dozen steps or so, they heard a swooshing sound behind them. It was difficult to make out what was on the sidewalk close to the two guys but it appeared to be a large piece of material with a fishnet pattern.

---

[6] Shhht-ree-ga

They heard another voice from the same direction as the two men saying, "Another failure. Y-esss. Y-esss. Do I have to do everything myself? Y-esss? Y-esss!"

Ricardo said, "Something just didn't feel right. I thought we needed to move on."

Deborah looked back. "I don't know. It could have been really cool to be in a magazine. You know...to be famous! Famous...for...Daisy. We could buy some extra copies, and frame the picture for Daisy. We could have...."

"How often does that happen?" Ricardo asked. "A magazine photographer in Playsteady Park...looking for a pregnant model...at night? I didn't see any lighting or a flash. Did you?"

Deborah looked disappointed and did not reply.

They continued silently and walked back to their building. As Ricardo reached for the doorknob, Deborah mentioned, "Funny, the woman at the store said owls can see dangers in the night."

"We could have used the owl you brought home tonight, it seems. Maybe you would have listened to the owl if it suggested those strange men were not who they pretended to be," Ricardo replied.

O O O

Good Reader, we are back at the beginning of the story of Owldoll and Daisy was nine years-old. It should be mentioned that the memories of a nine year-old may not be complete or accurate. A twenty-first century færy tale as you have noticed, Good Reader, does not begin with the obligatory Once Upon a Time but takes places in the here and now; although, here and now is a relative term in the scheme of things. When an important event or happening from preceding years is indispensable to the story, it will be interjected in my narration, or with another outside comment like this.

– Author

Daisy lived in a small city called Midway in an apartment

building on a moderately busy street. Daisy had no sister or brother but she had a room of her own. In the room, Daisy kept a dozen or so dolls and teddy bears clustered together along the center of the wall right below the window.

On a sunny afternoon as soon as Deborah put away the last clean dish she washed after lunch, Daisy ran in and said, "Okay mommy. You promised to bring me to the park right after lunch. And you know what Daddy always says: Our word is our bond. It is that important."

"I did say right after lunch. I didn't think you'd be so literal," Deborah paused. "Literal means taking the words in their precise meaning instead of a looser meaning or a more imaginative meaning. Let me do a few more things, then we'll go."

Deborah brought Daisy to the park. They walked around a while. Deborah said, "You see these flowers; the pink ones? Aren't they beautiful?"

Daisy picked a few flowers and smelled their sweetness.

"You see," Deborah continued, "just like you picked the daisies, I picked the daisies on a day just like this one. It was like the flowers were talking to me and I knew your name should be Daisy."

Looking up from the flowers in her hand, Daisy said, "That's a wonderful story mommy. I like knowing where my name came from. It makes it so much more special. I'll bring this bouquet home for daddy. We can tell him the story."

Deborah hugged Daisy and gently turned her from side to side. "He knows. He was with me that day, silly. He loved your name. In fact, he picked a bouquet of daisies that day...just like you did today."

When they returned to the apartment, Daisy put the flowers into a dark purple vase and left it on the table. She went to her room to play until dinner time.

Ricardo's eyes lit up as he approached the table and saw Daisy coming to the kitchen. "This reminds me of how we picked your name," he said to Daisy. "Mom and I were at Playsteady Park just before you were born. We hadn't chosen your name yet. We knew you were a girl from the ultrasound.

"The flowers were in bloom and the pink daisies...just shined their faces at us and Mom said what I was thinking, 'Daisy, that'll be the baby's name.' So, I picked a big bouquet just like this one. Boy, that brings me back." He looked at Deborah and then they both looked lovingly at Daisy.

"Daisy said, "So, it was as if the daisies saw you coming and sang out to you!"

Together Ricardo and Deborah sang, "Daisy, Daisy. Give me your answer do. I'm half crazy. All for the love of you. It won't be a stylish marriage. I can't afford a carriage. But you'll look sweet. Upon the seat. Of a bicycle built for two."

O O O

A day or two later, Daisy was in her room and had just put down her copy of Dr. Jekyll and Mr. Hyde and began playing on the floor with her favorite teddy bear.

"Chubby, what do you want to do today? I read this book before but felt like rereading it. Could you imagine inventing a medicine that changed your personality into someone evil?"

While she waited for the teddy bear to decide, a moth captured her attention. It was about the biggest moth she had ever seen. She felt creeped out.

"Look at that moth, Chubby," she blurted out and turned the teddy bear toward the window. "It has a pot-belly like it just ate a stack of pancakes. You're right, Chubby. I smell bacon. It probably ate a pile of bacon, too." The moth appeared to be looking at them and buzzed noisily. Daisy felt a light pulsation around her arms and shoulders that caught her off guard.

She heard a screeching woman's voice emanating from the same direction as the moth, "Just try and stay out of my way. Just try. I'll get you, my pretty, and your little dog, too." This was followed by cackling laughter as the moth flew away.

"What was she talking about, Chubby? I don't even have a dog."

Daisy stared at Chubby a while and wondered. She looked at the clock and saw it was close to one thirty. She went into the kitchen and called out, "Mommy, it's time to go to the park. You promised."

Deborah entered and exited the kitchen but not like usual. Her motions were repetitious and partially random. Abruptly, she did an about-face to the bedroom. Deborah pulled out a tubular off-white canvas travel bag with red roses, a long zipper along the top, and brown leather handles.

Almost behaving like a dinghy on unsteady seas, Deborah bobbed between closets and dresser drawers tossing clothes first onto the bed then into the canvas bag.

Daisy was uncomfortable with what she saw and went back to her room. She heard her Father asking her mother to stop, and think about Daisy, and to talk to him. She continued on her mission without another word. She zipped up the zipper and headed for the door. Daisy heard the door and came out of her room.

"Are we going to the park?" But Daisy received no answer. "Wait for...."

Deborah walked out, down the hall, to the stairs, and out to the walkway.

Daisy called again but her mother's eyes looked like concrete in December. Daisy pleaded, "Mommy, you promised to go to the park and play with me. You promised."

Roberto went after Deborah and Daisy followed. Everything seemed confusing. Daisy could not figure out if she was going to the park like she planned. Was her father coming, too? Why all the commotion? Why all the drama?

Deborah walked the three blocks at a steady clip and reached the stop as a bus arrived. She boarded it without looking back, or waiting in line like the other passengers. Daisy was in suspended animation at the front of her apartment building—neither here nor there—between a disappearing past and future.

"Daisy," Roberto whispered in her ear, "florita mia.[7]"

---

[7] (Sp.) dim. my little flower

Daisy watched the bus drive down the street and turn a corner. Then the sky turned dark, the wind picked up, and a bright flash of light came from between the buildings where the bus had turned. As Daisy watched numbly, a warm breeze blew across her shoulders and a humming vibration radiated through her.

O O O

A strange hush fell over the apartment. Daisy and her dad just looked at each other. Daisy got up, kissed her dad on the cheek, and went to her room. Outside, a steady rain banged and plopped a Gene Krupa syncopated rhythm on the awnings, leaves, trash cans, and ground. Mr. Villanova noticed the closet door was ajar, thought it odd, and felt drawn to look inside. He noticed a wooden box on the low-shelf at the back of the closet. The box had an elaborate geometric design, which he found curiously familiar. He saw the cover was opened and the silver-grey stuffed owl was not in the box. He remembered the owl's oversized purple eyes with green, gold, silver, and black angular specks radiating outward from jet-black pupils that locked onto him.

Oh, are you looking at me? That's what I thought the first time I looked into this wooden box after she went missing. Deborah brought this owl and the dark blue bottle with Albanian writing on it back from the funky store downtown. What was it called? Clockwork Heights... or something like that. Deborah was pregnant and started having vivid dreams and nightmares. She began to ask me about curses and ancient fables. Was it part of being pregnant? Is there a connection between these things and her disappearance? Nah. Maybe Daisy has it in her room. Ricardo pushed the closet door flush with the door jam and turned away.

Daisy was lying on her bed listening to the rain and staring at the ceiling. She heard a faint whooping, which she found disturbing. It was a noise she could not ignore. She stood on her toes and leaned across the pile of dolls to look over the edge of the window frame into the front yard.

A woman wearing a full-length raincoat stood in the middle of the walkway. Rain came down on the woman's face as she appeared to be looking right at Daisy in her unlit room. Daisy could not make out the woman's features but the water droplets were clearly visible.

Daisy's toes felt strained and she had to lean back to stand on her feet a moment. When she got up on her toes again, the woman in the walkway was gone.

O O O

Mr. Villanova was beside himself: Deborah was here and then out of nowhere she had packed a bag, fled down the stairs, walked up the street to the bus stop, and boarded the bus without ever looking back or acknowledged anything Daisy or he said to her.

He thought, *She never acted like this before.*

An unfamiliar knock came to the door and no one had rung the buzzer either. He inquired who was there but received no reply. The same unfamiliar knock again. He looked through the peephole and didn't see anyone. When he opened the door, Mr. Villanova found two tall policemen standing either side of doorway. "Oh. Hello officers," he said, "Please come in."

"Sir," one of the officers said. "You called to report a missing person? You claim your wife just disappeared? Like she disappeared into thin air? I believe those were the words the Desk Sergeant reported you used."

"Yes...I just cannot believe it," Mr. Villanova said to the two policemen. "I'm shocked."

One officer entered while the second stood in the hall face flush with the door jam and his hand planted on his service weapon.

"You can both come in," Mr. Villanova said matter-of-factly. "Deborah—my wife—was acting strange...all of a sudden. She had a bag packed and walked to the bus stop up the street. I called after her...at least I believe I called after her. But she just boarded the bus and didn't look back: she always waved to Daisy, our daughter, or to me...when she took the bus And she hasn't returned. Not a word from her either. It is so strange."

The officers did not introduce themselves. Mr. Villanova read their brass name tags: Budalla and Mizor. Officer Mizor entered with heavy footsteps and went directly to the master bedroom, stepped inside, stopped, stepped out, stepped back in again, and the sound of a single thud was heard.

Officer Mizor came back to the entrance and returned to the master bedroom. This time he went to a woman's shoe on the floor that was now visible. It was a gold leather, high heel, lucite wedge platform pump. He inserted a pencil under the tongue of the shoe, and lifted it. He snapped open a large manila envelope with EVIDENCE stamped in red ink on it.

"Excuse me, Officer Mizor," Mr. Villanova said. "That isn't my wife's shoe. I don't recognize it. She doesn't wear shoes like that. The sole looks like it's two inches thick!"

"I'll ask the questions," Mizor snorted.

Budalla talked to Mizor as he wrote on his pad, "Subject said something about the thickness of the sole." And they shared a knowing look.

"I'm confused: I called to report my wife missing. Isn't that why you are here? So, I can file a report?"

"Just answer the question," Budalla said. He jotted on his pad and asked, "When did you last see her? What are you hiding?"

"Gentlemen," Mr. Villanova said.

Budalla pointed to the door and said to Mizor, "He's not cooperating. Like in 67.2% of cases, the husband did it. Even if he didn't, he's bound to have done something."

They chuckled.

Mizor added, "We'll be in touch. Don't leave town." And the two of them left.

A few moments later he heard a familiar knock on the door. This time it was Mr. Harris, a neighbor from the fifth floor. He spoke with a distinctive southern drawl. "Ricardo, so sorry. I heard Deborah went missing yesterday: Any news?"

"Joel.... No, I haven't heard a thing. I just tried to file a missing person's report but...I think one of them planted a strange woman's shoe in our bedroom," Ricardo said. "It was one of those high heel shoes with a clear sole that was about two inches thick. Deborah didn't wear shoes like that. I don't get it. I called to report her missing and now I feel like...like I don't know what is going on."

Mr. Harris rolled his eyes and Mr. Villanova nodded his head. Mr. Harris said, "This cannot be easy for you. If it is any consolation, I do know a friend who went through something like this. He reported a disappearance of his wife and the two policemen who came to his house put him through the wringer, too. His situation turned out well. So, stay strong my friend."

Over Mr. Harris' shoulder came a familiar voice from another neighbor.

"O mon Dieu," Mademoiselle Lapin said in a voice whose accent was concerned and caring and understanding and perceptive and strong and comforting. "Our Deborah, where could she be? And your sweet daughter Daisy, she is okay, no? You need my help: all you need to do is ask."

Mr. Harris and Mademoiselle Lapin could tell Mr. Villanova was drained and needed some time alone. They excused themselves and went to Mademoiselle Lapin's apartment for tea.

Mr. Harris sat at the table and said, "This is rather unusual. Daisy is their only child and both Ricardo and Deborah fussed over her so. We have been like family—the Villanovas and you and me. I mean, we were closely knit like færy tale characters who embody the question and the answer without saying a word."

"Mais oui, Joel. But the question has taken Deborah away. And the answer about her way back is not so clear to see."

"Our dear friend probably tried to enlist the aid of our local constabulary. Another gentleman I know made a similar request...and he was engulfed in the circular illogic of statistical shenanigans: a virtual Catch-22 quandary where an appearance is assumed to fit a familiar form. Everything is seen as all cut and dry. How simplistic."

"You don't say," Mademoiselle Lapin replied.

"I do believe," Joel continued, "my friend told me about a Mizor and Budalla—the ones we saw leaving as we came—who have an attitude against minorities, especially Latinos and Blacks. They devoted all their efforts to try to implicate my friend. He had to hire Victor Answan—an urban legend in these parts. Mr. Answan is an investigator, who was able to unravel the mystery, exonerate the accused, and locate the missing subject through his unscientific examination."

Mademoiselle Lapin poured more tea for two and added, "Let us hope our friend's story turns out as well."

ооо

Good Reader, Midway is a tapestry of separate scenes amalgamated into a picture, of sorts. Like other cities, it has sections somewhat hidden from plain view peopled with unique individuals equally camouflaged to the casual observer like an illusion in an illustration. Here you are introduced to Ernest and Vincent, two gay witches, who were part of the urban legend from which Owldoll was derived.

As much as you, Good Reader, might not have seen them if you lived in Midway, they most likely would have shunned you out of their xenophobia and their instinct for survival. The legend provided a glimpse into this shadow world, which was fleshed out nearly intact through the same journalistic cryogenics you have been reading in Owldoll.

Vincent and Ernest plotted and schemed against Xhuljana, another witch, while an unsuspecting Deborah—eight months pregnant with Daisy—was drawn into their medieval world of sorcery and spells.
– Author

Ernest and Vincent each became lovers to a city engineer.

He was so enthralled by the situation, and subsequent ménage à trois, he used his position of power and influence in return. Ernest and Vincent were given a sweetheart deal on an old building located in a public alley near a fashionable neighborhood but was erased from all current city maps and the Registry of Deeds. Its tenants, like the building, had fallen through the cracks.

Ernest worked diligently in the kitchen frying up bacon, home fries, and thick buttermilk pancakes in lard and bacon grease. He had plastered and painted the kitchen to look like a cave. The textured walls were a gray-black coarse finish with painted veins of green mold and handmade papier-mâché lichen rosettes. Interspersed in the crevices and veins were portraits and cameos of females clad and unclad in relief and in fresco.

Vincent woke up after eleven when bright sunlight pierced through a moth-hole in the curtain and glared into his eyes.

Ernest stood at a black cast-iron stove with all the burners lit. Half of the burners had skillets cooking thick pancakes, and the other skillets had bacon frying with grease splattering and crackling. Occasionally, he'd siphon off some grease with a basting tool and drain its contents into the skillets with the pancakes and the skillet of home-fries.

"Phew," Ernest exclaimed as a pea-sized splatter of grease ricocheted off the brim of his tall pointed black hat to his wire-rimmed glasses. "A witch's work is never done."

He pranced to the cabinet and removed dinner plates and chafing dishes; then he began to pile the pancakes. "...fifteen, sixteen," he counted out loud. He grabbed some tongs and counted out the strips of bacon, "...ten, eleven, and twelve."

"Oh wretched daylight," Vincent moaned.

"Vincent," Ernest called out from the kitchen. "Come here. I've made a big batch of pancakes and a pile of bacon and, your favorite, home fries."

Vincent walked down the hallway: the only sunlit area in the living quarters. Two tiny windows located just below the crest of the cathedral ceiling sent rays of light weaving a web with specks of dust floating a configuration resembling the Van Allen radiation belts, which cast light down on the hallway. He stopped at the entranceway to the kitchen which let his big belly overlapping his black boxers precede him.

"I know who's there," Ernest coyly said.

"Gosh darn," Vincent snorted. "I wanted to sneak up on you. Bacon smells yummy."

Ernest took a flaccid slice of bacon, placed it into his mouth, and holding the opposite end while directing it into the cave-like opening in Vincent's black and gray beard.

They had chomped and slurped their way to a bacony kiss.

"I am quite famished—keep 'em comin'," Vincent announced in a bellowing voice and Ernest handed him his plate. Vincent polished the tines of his fork and the blade of his knife with a napkin. He inspected his teeth with the shiny knife blade. Ernest followed through as Vincent ate mechanically uninterrupted one plate-full after another.

"Mmm...nine, ten," Ernest counted as he delicately refilled Vincent's plate with pancakes. "And...seven, eight, nine, and ten strips of bacon: al dente just as you like it."

Vincent never broke stride: fork, knife, cut, mouthful, chew, chew, swallow—alternating between pancakes and bacon punctuating a chew to slide home fries onto the fork with his knife between the next chew—in a fast waltz tempo.

Then he picked up a black pitcher and poured a tumbler of orange juice to the brim. He raised the glass and poured the contents down his throat.

"Ahh," he added with a perfunctory belch.

"Good baby," Ernest responded.

"Oh, Ernest, pray-tell, what thought am I hatching?" Vincent asked after repositioning his belly with both hands. He continued without a comma, "We have been complacent..."

"Vincent, you wait a minute there, mister...er...exalted conjurer of noble lineage. You think we need another recruit—another witch to increase our fold. You always bring this up after a good bacony meal. Maybe it's the smell of rendered pig fat?"

Vincent looked sharply down the bridge of his nose, fluttered his eyelids, and blew Ernest a kiss. He added, "How right you are. It's been at least one hundred—one hundred twenty-six—years if I recall correctly since we added one. Xhuljana, Miss Goody Two-Shoes, converted Brunhilda to her clan back in Transylvania."

Ernest mouthed the word bitch and scratched the air with curled fingers.

"Ernest, guess what?" He asked rhetorically. "I cooked up a batch of serum for the occasion."

"You have someone in mind, don't you? You sneak. Tell me, tell me, tell me do," Ernest uttered as he brought a wooden spoonful if coagulating grease from the skillet to Vincent's eagerly open mouth.

After an audible slurp, Vincent said, "That woman we saw leaving Witchcraft Heights Potions a few years ago. I've had an eye on her since then. Xhuljana wants her but I think we can use her better. I spent the night concocting a batch of Shtriga's Serum just for her."

"Not that serum," exclaimed Ernest. "It is so powerful one drop in each eye...poof...an instant witch in the likeness of Shtriga."

"Even more delicious...she was pregnant back then and now she has a five year-old daughter. A two-fer! I followed her home and know exactly where she lives. I've hid in the shadows for years and know her every move. Now, her and her baby will be ripe for the picking, too," Vincent laughed deeply.

"Yippee," Ernest exclaimed. "We're gonna get a witch. We're gonna get a witch. And a pretty one, too. All those stereotypes of ugly witches with warts on their noses and ratty hair—oh, please."

Vincent stood at an angle to a large oval mirror with half-dollar sized brass tacks along the wooden frame enthralled with his image. He spoke in a loud voice, "Anyone who'd let themselves go like that should be called a hag—the word witch with its storied history is too good for them.

"Ernest, my dearest, recite the magic spell: the bewitching hour is upon us."

Ernest then pulled the brim of his pointed hat low over his brows, placed both hands palm down on the table, bowed his head, and repeated six times, "Syt i dalçin; Syt i plaçin"[8] then raised his eyes to look at Vincent.

Vincent picked up a dishrag and wiped around his mouth. He went into the other room and returned with a small black cauldron filled with a dark syrupy liquid.

He directed cunningly, "Ernest, my little witch, transfer some serum to a gelatin capsule while I recite the cursing chant."

Vincent crouched over as he attempted to assume the lotus position. He repeated a quasi-Gregorian chant six times, *"Möle keqe."*[9] There was a small explosion, followed by a gray puff of smoke, and he transformed into a big plump moth.

Ernest placed the filled capsule on the table. The moth picked it up between its six legs.

In a baritone mothy voice, Vincent said, "Ernest, off to our chariot. I'll be your navigator."

Ernest held the door of his lime-green Volkswagen Beetle for the moth then sashayed to the other side and got behind the wheel. The point of his hat crumpled on the headliner when he got in, so he flung it into the back seat. They drove down the street and the car sounded like a vacuum cleaner although it ran on gasoline.

"Take Canal Street toward Pleasant Street," Vincent said resting on the passenger's seat with the capsule held firmly between its legs flapping his wings to stay balanced. He gave Ernest very detailed instructions to avoid highly traveled roads along a serpentine route of darkened side streets and alleys to the one closest to the apartment building where Deborah, Ricardo, and Daisy lived.

"Ernest, pull over here. No, no, no. Right under the

[8] seat/eee/dan-chin, seat/eee/pla-chin
[9] mole-ay/ kek-ay

American elm...not the scrawny one...the one two car lengths from the corner."

The car bumped into the curbstone and knocked the moth off balance.

"You dim-witted ninny: Try to keep from making me drop the capsule. It'd make a better witch out of you, if it spilled," Vincent grumbled in a squeaky moth voice, panting, and nearly out of breath.

"So sorry," Ernest answered pouting "I was trying to avoid running over a dead squirrel. They get stuck in the treads of the tires and smell funny for a long time."

"Ernest, Ernest. We're witches not interior decorators."

"Sorry again, I'm wrong," Ernest replied. "Which house does she live in...? Get it: witch house?"

Vincent released his grip on the capsule and flew to the dashboard. He turned so he was facing to the right. "It's the building one in from the corner. I'll fly to the front side. There is a walkway and I'll fly up to the third floor. After a warm day, they'll have a window open. I know the window where Deborah's bedroom is located. Inside, I'll find a great spot. When she crosses in front of me, I'll put my belly onto the capsule for a direct hit."

"And before I go, rub my fuzzy belly gently."

Vincent flew back to the seat and stood up with the topside of his wings against the back of the seat.

Ernest ran the tip of his middle finger slowly up and down the moth's belly and Vincent giggled a mothy giggle.

"You're a dear," Vincent said.

Ernest got out of the car and went around to open the passenger door. As Vincent flew off, he said, "Be careful, my big, bad witch. There will be a treat for you if you snag us a witch for our very own."

He thought he saw a smile as Vincent flew from the front seat.

Some time later, the moth flew up to an open kitchen window, down the hallway, into the master bedroom, and lighted on top of a bureau. As Deborah came close, the moth pressed its thorax firmly on the capsule until one half shot off like a bullet with a trail of spray behind it. The moth watched with glee as a single drop of serum landed in each eye of Deborah.

"Ha, ha, ha, my little pretty, when the curse is upon you, your new name will be Angelina. We will see each other soon."

Daisy, in her bedroom, called out, "Aren't we going to the park?"

While she waited with her teddy bear, Chubby, a moth captured her attention. It was about the biggest moth she had ever seen. She felt creeped out.

"Look at that moth, Chubby," she blurted out and turned the teddy bear toward the window. "It has a pot-belly like it just ate a stack of pancakes. You're right, Chubby. I smell bacon. It probably ate a pile of bacon, too." The moth appeared to be looking at them and buzzed noisily. Daisy got a light pulsation around her arms and shoulders that caught her off guard.

Daisy heard a screeching woman's voice emanating from the same direction as the moth, "Just try and stay out of my way. Just try. I'll get you, my pretty, and your little dog, too." This was followed by cackling laughter as the moth flew away.

"What was she talking about, Chubby? I don't even have a dog."

The door to her mother's bedroom burst open and her mother stood with a flowered canvas bag in hand. Daisy called to her mother but her eyes looked like concrete in December.

Daisy pleaded, "Mom, you promised to go to the park and play with me. You promised."

The previous several minutes had stretched into hours. Now they blurred by in a fraction of a second as Deborah ran maniacally across the apartment oblivious to the pleas and cries from her husband and daughter. Deborah's eyes appeared to be fogged over by a film resembling a gray-green roe and her voice became a tough, hard to take, nonsensical shrill.

Deborah moved intently out of the apartment, and down the walkway. She walked the three blocks at a steady clip and reached at the stop as a bus arrived. She shoved past people waiting in line and boarded it without looking back at someone she knocked over. Ricardo and Daisy stood in disbelief.

Daisy watched mouth wide open while the other people aided the person get back up from the ground. The scene paralysed Daisy and Ricardo from moving as the bus drove down the street and turned a corner. Then the sky became darker, the wind picked up, and a bright flash of light came from where the bus had slid between the buildings.

As Daisy watched numbly, a warm breeze blew across her shoulders, and a humming vibration radiated through her.

O O O

Good Reader, the urban legend described a pivotal incident at school when Daisy was twelve years-old. Middle school became a confluence of everything: self-consciousness; selfishness; social awareness; independence; puberty. A time between here and there, and midway between childhood and maturity.

— Author

It seemed like an ordinary day except Daisy had a substitute teacher at school. He was a mild-mannered man and someone Daisy had seen at the school many times before. She'd seen him mostly in upper grade classrooms but he was in her class today.

"Good morning, I'm Mr. Brooks. Your regular teacher, Ms. Puffer is not in today. She left some things for us to do and it will be a fun day."

As Mr. Brooks took attendance a little girl went over to his desk. "I'm Peggy and my mommy died."

Mr. Brooks was silent. Before he could say anything, Peggy pointed to Daisy and said, "She's Daisy. Her mommy died, too."

"Peggy," Siobhan exclaimed. "That's just nasty. You know no one knows what happened to her mom. Look it, you're making her cry."

Tears fell from Daisy's eyes. "I miss my mommy."

A small girl jumped to her feet and shouted, "Peggy, you're sayin' that 'cause you're mad-ugly[10] ...'n'...nobody likes you."

Peggy stomped, "Na-ah. Listen shorty..."

Danny shouted out, "Salted[11]. Besides, your mommy isn't dead. You just wish she was."

Phyllis added, "Yeah, Peggy, why all the seventh grade drama? You can't stand not being the teacher's pet: Even if it means saying mean things about someone else. Sorry you had to hear this, Daisy. Just ignore her."

Peggy made a scrunched–up face and said, "Phyllis, you... you like Danny, so you're stickin' up for him: How pathetic."

Mr. Brooks spoke firmly, "Seventh grade settle down. Peggy, take your seat, please." Then he stood up and said, "Class, this isn't the kind of talk Ms. Puffer would approve of. I'm going to leave her a note and I'm sure she'll address it with you when she returns tomorrow. On the board is your homework for tonight. Please, write it down."

Mr. Brooks went over to Daisy and said, "It is okay, Daisy. Don't listen to someone who doesn't know what she's sayin'. If you'd like to take a walk, drink some water...g'head."

Danny said, "Sorry, Mr. Brooks, my bad. Daisy is my friend. She doesn't deserve it."

Mr. Brooks thought, *That's awful. I didn't see that coming. A seventh grader I never met before comes up to me and says her mother is dead. Then in the next breath tells me another girl's mother is dead, too.*

I feel terrible, poor little girl. It's a tragedy for a young child to lose a parent. What could I say? What could I do? Then another student in class tells me Peggy made the whole thing up. Peggy's callousness and disregard for others is very bad. I'll have to speak with Sue Puffer next time I see her.

ଠଠଠ

---

[10] *Mad:* Teenage expression modifier, equivalent to extremely, too, very.

[11] Teenage expression equivalent to *gotcha*

Mr. Brooks proceeded to the whiteboard and wrote: The Legend of the Gold-fish[12].

As the class took out their Social Studies folders, Mr. Brooks asked, "Who knows how the state of Massachusetts got its name?"

A boy in the back of the room shouted out, "It was named after Massachusetts in England."

"Nice try, but no," said Mr. Brooks.

Danny raised his hand and received a nod. "It was named after the Native American chief who saved Pilgrims the first winter in Plymouth."

"Good job, Danny. Ms. Puffer told me the class has been studying tales and legends of other cultures. Today, we're working on a legend passed on by the famous chief Massasoit, who Massachusetts was named after; as Danny correctly answered.

"After signing a treaty and smoking a peace pipe with English settlers like Miles Standish and John Carver..." he was interrupted by some laughter. He gave the class a look and continued, "Massasoit presented his storyteller, who wore a jacket made from an animal hide with long eagle feathers sewn along the bottom seam of the sleeves. He was called Speaking Eagle."

Mr. Brooks stood arms outstretched, stern-faced, and said, "Speaking Eagle told the gathered Englishmen one of the most famous Wampanoag legends: The Tale of the Gold-fish and the Wide Blue Crab."

He wrote the title on the whiteboard and the correct spelling of Wampanoag.

"This tale took place at an island off the coast of Massachusetts, which was connected to the mainland by a thin strip of land only accessible at low tide. Otherwise, the strip of land was submerged leaving just a big hill and a small hill visible. The Wampanoag tribe called this island Nahant[13], which bears the same name today."

---

[12] The children had already learned from Ms. Puffer what the Wampanoag called a Gold-fish was a mythical creature and not what we call goldfish. They learned squaw means woman, too.

[13] (Algonquin) "Two things united"

Mr. Brooks slowly brought his arms back to his side, went over to a white metal rocking chair next to the window, and as he sat down the children gathered around on the rug. His reading and storytelling voice was soothing and engaging.

"Speaking Eagle's story went something like this: A tribe of Gold-fish lived in the rocky waters in one of the little bays around Nahant facing Red Rock[14] long before the Wampanoag walked this piece of Mother Earth.

Gold-fish prided themselves for making a good life in the rocky waters of Nahant that other fish found too difficult. Gold-fish had a saying: Nahant is the only kin we've got. One day, a squaw Gold-fish swam silently to the clear, cool water at the far end of the bay marveling at the tranquility and admiring the vegetation.

"A rather wide blue crab asked her, 'Well, how do you do? Other Gold-fish shun this area but I notice you have a keen eye for the beauty of this part of the bay.'

"The squaw replied, 'I am well. And I did notice how nice it is here. Why is it, do you think, other Gold-fish shun this beautiful spot?'

"To which, the crab began his monologue, 'I am called Forked-Claw,' pointing with his snapping pinchers at a small crab on a nearby rock. 'My compadre-crustacean is called Feather Moccasin.'

"Feather Moccasin blushed and crossed his front pinchers."

The classroom erupted into laughter as Mr. Brooks did a pantomime of someone crossing his legs to control his bladder and some of the students found his pronunciation of Forked-Claw as Fork-Ed Claw amusing, too.

He resumed telling the scene, "Then Feather Moccasin asked rhetorically, 'Should we tell her our secret? Do you think she can appreciate the magic?'

"The squaw became motionless."

While recounting the Gold-fish Tale, Mr. Brooks noticed

[14] (Algonquin) The name of a neighboring town, Swampscott, means "Red Rock".

how it seemed to touch Daisy. The expression on her face and the look in her eyes telegraphed something teachers enjoy seeing in their students: a deeper understanding; a young mind participating in the world of ideas. At the same time, though, he sensed the sadness the story was unearthing in Daisy.

He noticed Danny, the boy who said salted to Peggy, was fully engaged in the story; Siobhan, another friend of Daisy, following along with a lot of interest; Amanda, the short girl who defended Daisy, looked fascinated as she occasionally looked out the window at the puffy clouds floating by; and Peggy, the girl who concocted the strange story about her own mother being dead and Daisy's mother being dead, too—How evil is that?— chatting away with anyone who'd listen about who-knows-what?

Mr. Brooks took a sip of water and carried on, "Forked-Claw side-stepped his way to a large flat rock seemingly made for oratory. He turned around thrice and bellowed out, 'On the other shore is a special place called Red Rock: Feather Moccasin and I have devoted a life-time of answer-searching[15] to the magical powers of Red Rock; and we have invented—if I may be so bold—an eye paint from a pulverized powder of Red Rock and special seaweed that gives the painted-one visions of beauty beyond the realm of earthly beauty: A Great Spirit's visual feast. Yes, a visual banquet fit for the Great Spirit.'

"Feather Moccasin added from his little podium atop a small rock teetering on top of another small rock, 'Do you think this squaw...this Gold-fish squaw has the insight to partake in the vision of visions? Other Gold-fish always swim away.'

"Before Forked-Claw could speak, the squaw spoke on her own behalf, 'I am considered a pretty good looker with eyes that see all they can see.'

"Forked-Claw snapped jubilantly elongating his large pincher dramatically, 'See, Feather Moccasin, do I know simpatico? Or, do I know simpatico?' Turning to face the squaw squarely, he spoke more deeply, 'You should return here the night of the

---

[15] Like all Native American languages, Algonquin was unwritten and transmitted orally. Colloquial expressions for research are approximated by this expression.

New Moon. You will transport us upon your back to the oppo-site shore where we will show you the visions of visions.'

"The next night—the night of the summer New Moon—the squaw Gold-fish swam silently to the far end of the bay to meet Forked-Claw and Feather Moccasin. They mounted her back looking like a creature from beyond the moon and stars. They swam across the bay to a hillside of Red Rock along the beach. Forked-Claw spoke to the squaw of the happy life seen through eyes he has painted with Red Rock powder. Forked-Claw told the squaw, 'We can all be beautiful in a world of beauty.'

"As they approached the sand of the shore, Forked-Claw urged the squaw to go onto the land. Gold-fish, like crabs, can breathe air and be out of the water for a spell.

"Feather Moccasin and Forked-Claw scampered sideways up the beach to the Red Rock hill jutting into the sea. Forked-Claw proclaimed, 'This is where Mother Earth separates from Father Sky and grinds out magic powder from Red Rock. I dis-covered...We discovered by painting a thin sheen of the powder with my magic claw over the eyes a world of beauty is laid out before you.'

"Feather Moccasin making a rhythmic click-clack flourish raced up next to Forked-Claw. He stopped and said, 'Do it, Forked-Claw. Paint the eyes of the squaw so she can see what we have seen.'

"Forked-Claw scooped out the pulverized Red Rock and seaweed mixture with his fore-claw, crab-stepping to his left up to the squaw, and smeared the iridescent granules over each of her eye lenses."

Amanda raised her hand, "Mr. B.? I thought Gold-fish could see into the future. You know, they had magic eyes. Why would a Gold-fish let a crab mess-up her eyes? That's so mad-cra-zy, right?"

Mr. Brooks answered, "Good, Amanda. Wampanoag leg-end had it that Gold-fish saw images in the sea: some predict-ing the future; some revealing the past. You're quite correct... Who'd want to let a crab mess with her eyes?"

Most of the class nodded no.

"The crabs held their breath undulating excitedly. It was as if the Great Sky and the Great Sea had ripped apart letting in all the light of the world shining on this spot and making it all beautiful. The squaw saw Nahant on the horizon outlined in shimmering crystals.

"They heard a long breath and the squaw said with a gasp, 'Everything is beautiful. Even old Nahant looks beautiful in the distance. Oh, but look at you, Forked-Claw...gasp...And you, Feather Moccasin...gasp...I have never seen crabs so beautiful... so shiny...so brilliant...so....'

"The crabs shared a moment and looked at each other longingly while Forked Claw smeared the mixture on Feather Moccasin's eyes and a hefty dollop on his own eyes. Then Forked-Claw spoke in a voice as low as the bottom of the sea; where everything sinks to its lowest, 'Even better than seeing old Nahant as beautiful...we are beautiful. It's my magic claw, you must admit it.'

"Feather Moccasin pirouetted with his pinchers held high, 'Don't you see? Don't you?' He lowered his pinchers and pointed them squarely at the Gold-fish, 'Beauty is in the eyes of the right beholder: Not just any old mollusk or clam. Pah-lee-ahs! I see we three in a beautiful scene. A setting where we are beautiful. Don't you see it? Chief Double Rainbow Crab, Powerful Hunter Moccasin Crab, and Golden Ruler Gold-fish....'

"The squaw swam a slow circle. Her eyes were covered with the mixture, and she had difficulty finding the crabs. When she did, she went closer to them and said, 'What a magic claw! What a world of beauty! How could I ever return to the plain world of Nahant?'

"Forked-Claw spoke louder, 'Enough about you.... If not for my magic claw.... So, it is here with us you will stay. You'll be ensconced in our world of beauty.'

"By Red Rock, the two crabs and the Gold-fish squaw talked day and night—day and night blend together in the world of beauty—about each other's beauty. Each new version each of them told became a more beautiful description than the previous one. This went on for many, many moons.

"Finally, the three embraced. But what the squaw expected was not there: instead she swam along the rough, gnarled shell of a crab not the luxuriously smooth skin of a Gold-fish. The squaw was perplexed. The Gold-fish squaw assumed the beauty she saw was truer than what she felt. This went on for many, many moons.

"Back in Nahant, a dark night followed without a moon to light the sky. The next day and night were covered with thick clouds, too. At first, the missing squaw was a concern but, after a while, many of the Gold-fish forgot about the missing squaw.

"Finally, the squaw swam back across the bay to Nahant. When she returned, no one recognized her: living with her eyes painted for those many, many moons has changed the color of her skin from the magnificent color of Gold[16] to a plain color of the earth.

"From that day forward, the squaw Gold-fish was not seen as a Gold-fish and swam, almost invisibly, in the same waters as her tribe. After several moons, the squaw Gold-fish sadly swam back to Red Rock and was never seen by other Gold-fish again."

Mr. Brooks saw the class was still thinking about the story. He asked, "Did you enjoy the legend of the Gold-fish?"

"Yes, Mr. Brooks. It was the bomb," said a girl sitting close by on the rug. The class agreed tacitly.

Mr. Brooks placed his hands on his knees, leaned toward the class, and asked, "What is the moral of the story?" He sat up straight and added, "You have learned legends and tales are built on a moral framework a society conveys through the story. So, for the next fifteen minutes, Ms. Puffer wants you to write a paragraph in your Social Studies Journal about the moral of the Legend of the Gold-fish."

"I know...I know," blurted out Peggy waving her hand in the air. "It's my turn: You haven't called on me...mmm, mmmm."

Mr. Brooks took in the looks of disapproval from around

---

[16] Gold is a metaphor for a precious stone, not necessarily silver or gold.

the classroom but his moment of silence did not discourage Peggy from insisting on being called on. He pointed his finger at her.

"You see," Peggy began, "the squaw Gold-fish was bored with the Gold-fish ways. So, she went to chill somewhere else. She found some cool friends and found the benefits of beauty and fashion." She stood and primmed herself. "She knew she was fly[17] and the other Gold-fish were mad-jealous."

Siobhan raised her hand and was called on. "What I think is the moral of the story has more to do with letting vanity run your life..."

Daisy raised her hand.

"Yes, Daisy," Mr. Brooks said.

Daisy said, "I think Siobhan is partly right but...the squaw Gold-fish was tricked. The two crabs were bad."

Mr. Brooks noticed a consensus, and added, "I like this discussion. Why don't you spend a few minutes more on this? Then we'll be working on Math."

The remainder of the day passed slowly for Daisy. There were little reminders bringing Daisy's mind to times when her family was whole: happier times.

Is mom like the Gold-fish in the story? Is she invisible to those around her?

Walking home with her friend, Siobhan, Daisy said, "OMG[18] , Siobhan. Know what I think?"

Siobhan answered, "No, what?"

Daisy continued, "I don't know why but I know mommy is not gone: I know she's somewhere. I mean she's gone but she's not gone-gone. Even before mom disappeared, I sensed something like this was going to happen: I'd always be looking around to be sure mommy was there; I'd have these dreams where I would be in an enchanted forest searching for my mom. When I'd wake up, I had to make sure mom was really there. Now, the nightmare has really happened; I wake up and

---

[17] Teenage expression equivalent to attractive, hot, sexy.

[18] *Oh my God* in text-speak

nothing is as it used to be. And I knew a day like today would arrive when I'd understand it was up to me to find her and bring her back."

Siobhan hugged Daisy around the shoulder. "Daisy, I'm with you. You're my bestest friend and you can count on me to help you."

Daisy looked directly at Siobhan and said, "Do you believe me?"

Siobhan returned her gaze and nodded her head slowly up and down twice. "Daisy, I get it...Like in a game of Tag, you're either It or you're Not It. And Daisy, you're It."

ⵔ ⵔ ⵔ

Daisy walked back and forth from the kitchen and to her bedroom from her bedroom to the kitchen pausing a few minutes in each room. Mr. Villanova walked into the kitchen from the den, saw Daisy standing next to the table toying with a teaspoon, and sensed uneasiness.

"You seem restless, Daisy," Mr. Villanova said.

Daisy replied, "Yeah, I'm fidgety. Why don't we go up on the roof? It is a clear night and there is probably a cool breeze. Please? Just for a few minutes? Could we?"

"I'm so tired tonight. Do mind if we do it another time?" he answered.

"Why don't I just go myself?" Daisy asked. "I'm going bonkers."

"I guess it will be alright," he said noticing her pent up energy. "Just be careful up there. Remember our Rule: Don't go past the low wall. Promise?"

"Yes, Daddy, I promise," Daisy said.

Mr. Villanova looked at her half-smiling, "And a promise is giving your word, right?"

Daisy nodded. She thought, *Our Main Rule: Our word is our bond. It's that important.* She continued, "I got to get something in my room first. Going up to the roof is probably a good idea.

It looks like a nice night."

Daisy quickly went to her room and took a pink rubber ball placed on tissue paper inside a small, sturdy, dark blue cardboard box from one of the small drawers in her bureau. She went out the door, down the corridor, up three flights of stairs, and over to the door on the top floor. The door creaked a little as she opened it then she climbed the five uncarpeted wooden stairs to the green metal door that led to the roof. She turned the large brass knob and stepped outside. She felt free like the cool wind on her face.

A gravel roof extended some thirty feet to a two-foot high wall with shiny sheet metal flashing that framed the cityscape. Her eyes followed the wall: a boundary her father made her promise never to cross. She felt safe within its confines and the cool night air was refreshing. Part of a billboard was visible with the words A Special Place.

Daisy began tossing the ball. On the first attempt, the ball got away from her. Daisy gasped and drew a breath of relief when it finally bounced against the low wall and came to rest. She thought, *Ooops, must be careful.*

Daisy heard a strange noise from just beyond the left-hand edge of the roof. It sounded like the wind had rippled and cried out in song. Daisy was so curious she hopped the wall and inched closer...so close to the edge and the darkness below. Daisy leaned over and was gripped with fear. She turned and rushed back to the other side of the low wall.

Daisy held the pink rubber ball her mommy gave her for her fifth birthday in both hands. It was special to Daisy: Mother told her it was the same color pink as the daisies in the park, which became her name. She and mom went to the park that spring to pick those daisies. It was a special memory for Daisy, who was deeply distressed by the loss of her mother. Everything happened so quickly: she was here and now she's gone. Her daddy did everything he could without letting on about his grief. The passing of time had dulled the pain Daisy felt but there is no explanation for the inexplicable.

Thinking about mom made her sad. Daisy began to toss the ball straight up and caught it over and over as she sang to the wind. Each time the ball made a smooth arc up and down then.... as if in the middle of a dream, the ball did not fall back. Daisy watched in awe as the ball followed a slow serpentine path through the night sky toward the edge. The ball stopped against a background of the night sky. It stood still in midair like a pink star in the painting *The Starry Night*: suspended, beautiful, mysterious. Then the ball plummeted down out of sight into the deep darkness beyond the edge of the building.

"Oh, no," Daisy swallowed. She ran after it, hurdled the low-wall, and stopped inches from the edge staring into the pitch blackness. She panicked over losing the ball. *How will I ever get it back? My pink rubber ball was so special—Mom gave it to me. Mom told me it was the same color pink as the daisies in the park; the daisies that grew into my name. Mom gave it to me. Please, come back...please, come back.*

Daisy looked out into the abyss, which was as empty as the hollow feeling in the pit of her stomach. Then she backed up as she knew she should.

She thought, *This is wrong. I promised never to go over the wall and close to the edge. What am I doing? I won't ever do that again. I could have fallen off the roof....*

The darkness was overwhelming. She turned to move back even further from the edge. Something out of the corner of her eye drew her attention to the top of the elevator shed. Under a clean white crescent moon, she saw a magnificent silver-grey owl. Daisy looked up into its oversized purple eyes with shards of black, green, silver, and gold radiating outward from pure black pupils. She was drawn to the owl and walked closer noticing how big the owl seemed compared to the stars.

Then the owl spoke, "W-issh. We are so small between the stars, so large against the sky. We are so small between the stars, so large against the sky. W-issh."

Daisy looked vacantly at owl amazed to hear what she just thought put into words but not totally surprised that this owl spoke to her.

"W-issh," the owl continued. "I can return your ball. I can return your ball. W-issh."

Daisy pleaded, "Come on, come on. Gimme my ball back. It's mine. Gimme."

Owl stood atop the elevator shed, a gust of wind lifted tufts of her feathers, and the moonlight drew attention to her alluring face.

"W-issh. Promise me this. Promise me this. W-issh."

Daisy looked back and assented without saying a word.

"W-issh. These things: Promise me this. These things: Promise me this. W-issh."

"Yes, I will," Daisy answered quickly. "You'll return my ball? What do you want? Tell me, tell me."

"W-issh. An owl can see things you cannot see. You cannot see what I can see. Promise me this: To trust what I say I can see. To trust what I say I can see. W-issh."

Daisy nodded her head up and down not wanting to waste a moment speaking. "It is true owls see in the night. I can't so that is true. Okay, I promise to trust what you see. Hurry, please, hurry."

"W-issh. An owl hears things you cannot hear. You cannot hear what I can hear. Promise me this: To trust what I hear. To trust what I hear. W-issh."

Daisy listened to the low rumble of street noises off in the distance and imagined the clarity owl heard. "Your hearing is probably better than mine. I will promise to trust what you hear, too. Please, even with your superior eyesight darkness has a way of hiding things. You've got to go get my ball before it's lost forever! We can talk about this later. Hurry, please."

"W-issh. Lastly, I am a good reader. Another gift I have is I read the words very carefully. Promise me this: You will trust what I say about what I read. You will trust what I say about what I read. W-issh"

Daisy answered slowly, "What a different request. Are we going to read books together?"

Owl looked into Daisy's eyes and Daisy felt a low-energy pulsation.

"Ah, so," Daisy said. "You can read some things better than I can. Maybe I won't see what you see in something you've read." Daisy thought a moment about talking to daddy about <u>Dr. Jekyll and Mr. Hyde</u> and how daddy helped her see words can have more than one meaning. "Yes, I promise to remember you can read the words very carefully. Now, please get my ball back for me. Okay, I will. But please, oh please, hurry, hurry, hurry," Daisy said with determination as if every second counted. She held her breath like she was submerged under water. Her heart pounded.

"W-issh. Your pink rubber ball is a clue. Your pink rubber ball is a clue. W-issh," Owl said under the crescent moon. "W-issh. Promise me this: To let me be your secret friend. To let me be your secret friend. W-issh."

Nodding rapidly to save time and convince Owl to fly after her ball. Daisy looked beyond the edge of the roof then gazed back at Owl, and said, "Yes. Yes, you will be my secret friend. I won't tell anyone, okay?"

"W-issh. Who'd believe you? Who'd believe you? W-issh."

She scuffed her feet on the loose gravel and smiled at the truth of the matter. Daisy felt the weight of sand sliding through a giant hourglass burying her pink rubber ball for eternity. "Yes. Yes, I promise. Now hurry, hurry, hurry get my pink rubber ball before it is too late."

Owl drew her wings back, leaped off the elevator shed, flapped her full-flung wings, and dove beyond the edge of the building making a sound like a roller coaster on its initial descent from the top of the first hill. Daisy stared into the impenetrable darkness.

After what seemed like an hour but was only a minute and a half, Daisy sensed a noise over her shoulder and she looked back at the elevator shed to see Owl lighting on it. Daisy walked closer and Owl stretched out her leg with the ball firmly in her craw. Owl released the ball and it floated to Daisy's waiting hands. The ball felt warm and was clean like it had rested on a fine down pillow—protected from harm while it was away.

Daisy was overjoyed and filled with relief. All she wanted was to bring the pink rubber ball back to her room and away from the world of darkness, which nearly captured it forever. So she bounced across the gravel roof and habitually closed the metal door behind her. Her feet barely touched the steps and the corridor to her apartment. Once inside, Daisy went directly to her room and jumped onto her bed with the pink rubber ball safely in her hands.

"You back?" asked Mr. Villanova.

"Yes, Daddy," Daisy said to the closed door. *I'll never take you to the roof again*, she thought looking at the pink rubber ball resting next to her on the bed.

Then a breeze passed over her and she looked to see Owl fly in the open window and perch herself on an upper shelf on the bookcase with eyes wide open with a piercing glare. Daisy was startled and a little frightened.

"W-issh," said Owl. "There is something that I see. There is something that I see. W-issh."

"I'm tired. Can't you go?" Daisy asked.

"W-issh. I see your pink rubber ball has been a link to your mother. Now it is a link to a secret friend. Now it is a link to a secret friend. W-issh."

"No! That's not what you see," Daisy said in an exaggerated fashion while flailing her arms.

"W-issh. You promised me this. To trust what I see. To trust what I see. W-issh."

Daisy pouted, "Yeah, yeah. It is a link to a special friend."

Owl stared at her long and hard. Daisy felt the intensity emanating from those oversized purple eyes.

"W-issh. I heard a mystery approaching. I heard a mystery approaching. W-issh."

Daisy shook her head. "How can you hear a mystery approaching? You're kidding me, right?"

"W-issh. You promised me this. To trust what I hear. To

trust what I hear. W-issh."

The sounds of breaking glass from an automobile accident came from outside. *Did Owl hear the accident before it happened?* Daisy wondered. A moment later, Daisy said out loud, "Did you hear that before it happened?"

Owl looked back steadfastly with a reassuring yet somewhat impenetrable countenance.

"You can hear much better than me. No question about it. You're right. Okay, what do I do?" Daisy finally answered.

"W-issh. Follow the words. I read the sign: A Special Place. Follow the words. A Special Place. W-issh," the Owl turned her head three hundred and sixty degrees. "W-issh. You must keep me in a special place. You must keep me in a special place. W-issh," declared Owl as she flew to the headboard.

Daisy thought, *Is Owl talking to me about the billboard I saw from the rooftop with the words A Special Place? But it is just a bill-board. It can't mean anything! But I did promise to trust what the owl read. Is owl telling me words are more than just words? Even so, how can I keep an owl in my room?* Then in a raised voice she spoke up, "No, no. How can I keep an owl in my room?"

"W-issh. You will trust what I say about what I read. You will trust what I say about what I read. W-issh." Owl said in a fairly firm tone.

Daisy clutched the ball closely and replied sharply even louder than before, "I only said those things to get my pink rubber ball back. I would have said anything. You have to go. You took unfair advantage of me. Go away, Owl."

Suddenly, the door opened and white light poured into the room. Mr. Villanova entered and approached Daisy. As he picked up the stuffed owl from the bed, he shook off a slight shiver he felt and stared a moment at the missing owl. It seemed to be staring back at him.

Mr. Villanova asked, "Were you having a bad dream? I heard talking." Then he noticed the stuffed owl felt warm.

At the same time, Daisy felt relieved the owl returned to being just a stuffed owl the instant the bedroom door opened.

How would she explain her secret friend—the stuffed owl her mother got from the red-haired woman—was a stuffed owl that magically came to life, and made her promise to be her special friend of all things? The best thing about a secret friend is it's a secret.

"I guess so," Daisy replied. "I was kind of upset about almost losing my pink rubber ball. I will never—I mean never—take it up on the roof again."

"That's probably a good idea," he agreed.

Daisy looked up and asked, "Daddy, if I promised Owldoll some stuff, but didn't really mean it, do I have to do it?"

"Daisy," Mr. Villanova replied. "Our word is our bond. It's that important. So the answer to your question is yes. You shouldn't have made a promise you didn't want to keep."

"I guess I already knew the answer," she replied.

Mr. Villanova turned to place the stuffed owl anywhere on the pile of dolls under the window. But he noticed a little footstool draped with purple felt against the wall. He moved it in front of the pile and carefully placed the owl there. The owl stood proudly in an almost regal stance.

"I like where you put Owldoll. It is a very special place like Owldoll is the queen in her throne room with her court assembled nearby. Look! They look like they are posing for a painting. Thanks, Daddy."

He bent over to kiss her forehead, and closed the door on his way out thinking, *She calls it Owldoll. How cute. Owldoll—owl... doll—is a secret friend like a doll and has an incredible sense of perception like an owl. I hope Owldoll will help Daisy see what she cannot see herself.*

"Owldoll," Daisy said to the inanimate owl staring back from the prominent place her daddy placed it among the other dolls.

Daisy had witnessed the transformation from a living, talking owl into the stuffed owl in that split-second before things get into focus. A fraction of a second with the intensity that grabs every synapse in your brain. Owl was the same owl her mommy had in the antique wooden box in her room. The mysterious box etched with hypnotic geometric patterns Daisy would trace with her fingers when she younger. Daisy was amazed by what happened, yet could have anticipated it. Daisy saw why there was something familiar about the wide-eyed owl on the rooftop, whose voice was soothing even if her words weren't clear.

Daisy knew from that moment she would call her secret friend Owldoll. "Look at that face: just look at it. You looked familiar and warm when I saw you on the roof. You are my secret friend. Good night, Owldoll."

Just outside the door, Mr. Villanova heard Daisy talking but could not make out the words. A jumble of thoughts raced through his head, *Just as I suspected; Daisy had the stuffed owl in her room. I wonder why Daisy is playing with it...? Is she making a connection with her mother? Is she too old to be playing make-believe like this? I can't deny her this, can I? She'll outgrow it soon enough, won't she? Of course she will.*

"Owldoll, you're going to help me find mommy, aren't you?" she yawned.

Daisy drifted off to sleep and the owl reanimated. Standing behind the window the owl was silhouetted by the bright light from the moon above the cityscape. The owl twisted her head one hundred eighty degrees and the owl's face was bathed in moonlight from outside forming a Technicolor image William Blake would have found captivating.

The owl spoke out loud, perhaps to no one or to her reflection in the window, "W-issh. Darkness comes in countless shades of blindness for so many. But darkness is my old friend and we have no secrets. To see is to have seen and the blinded are automatically precluded. Vision of what is hidden behind others' blindness is my solitary endeavor. Like Hecate, goddess of the night and magic, was predisposed to initially find no solace in the things I say, Daisy will have her doubts. And like Hecate, she will eventually understand my words then, and only then, see what was there before her all the time.

"Do you hear what I say I can see?" the owl asked rhetorically, paused, and quietly sang. "Daisy, Daisy, give me your answer do. I'm half crazy all for the love of you.

"W-issh. Follow this invisible road that leads you back home. Follow this invisible road that leads you back home. W-issh."

Shadows moved in soft focus gyration along a graceful arc against the smooth plaster of the ceiling: a bird flying and silhouettes of branches. Owl walked the floor inspecting the other dolls, abruptly stopped, turned to face Daisy, and spoke in a soft voice.

"W-issh. I've said too much. I must only use words that require thought. I cannot let my words reveal too much or they will unravel the magic. If Daisy keeps her promises, she will find the answers she seeks. W-issh."

Owl returned to her special place on her stage draped with purple satin before the dolls and teddy bears assembled on the floor. She turned her head to look back out the window, "W-issh. I have been given different names to fit my character. I accept this and it is my role. I will be called, Owldoll...for now. W-issh."

She twisted her head back to face the room, and transformed back to the inanimate Owldoll.

ϙ ϙ ϙ

Sue Puffer began her seventh grade Language Arts class, "We're going to review the Wampanoag[19] story you started when I was absent. What can you tell me about the Gold-fish Story?"

Peggy blurted out, "Oooo...oooo...me...me...."

Ms. Puffer scolded, "We don't speak out." She turned to another side of the classroom, "Amanda, what would you like to say?"

Amanda replied, "We learned gold meant something different to the Wampanoag, Ms. Puffer."

---

[19] Womp-an-awg

Ms. Puffer spoke softly, "Good for you. Who can tell me what it meant? How is it different than someone from our culture might think of Gold?"

"We learned," Amanda went on, "gold has two meanings for the Wampanoag...One is pretty and the other is...navee."

"Naïve," Ms. Puffer corrected. "The word is naïve. Do you know what it means?

Amanda answered, "Naïve means gullible or easily fooled."

Ms. Puffer acknowledged Amanda then called on Phyllis by pointing to her.

"Gold had two meanings," Phyllis began. "One was something that looked pretty but wasn't pretty on the inside and the other meaning was something that didn't know what it was worth, or thought it was worth more than what it was worth. Ya know 'n' stuff like that."

Danny raised his hand.

"Danny," Ms. Puffer called out.

"Someone who is naïve," Danny replied. "Gold symbolizes someone who is naïve. They thinks they are worth more than they really are."

Peggy blurted out, "Oooo...oooo...me...me...."

"Yes, Peggy," Ms. Puffer answered disconcertingly.

Peggy carried on, "To me, the Gold-fish was just doing what's natural: to get out of a small neighborhood and see the world. You know, bite the big apple. It must-a been kind-a exciting to cross the ocean to Red Rock. Maybe it didn't work out but at least the Gold-fish tried. I think that's the lesson. If you're stuck in the same boring place, take a chance."

Ms. Puffer added, "That's one view. Anyone else?"

Daisy raised her hand and stood after Ms. Puffer called on her. She stood with her hips turned slightly askew pointing to an imaginary spot in space. "I kind of agree and disagree."

"What do you mean by that, Daisy?" asked Ms. Puffer.

"Well...," Daisy hesitated a moment and looked around the classroom for eye contact from her classmates. "It was tragic... what happened to the Gold-fish but it was a cool beginning."

Ms. Puffer remarked, "Let's take a look at the two out-comes. Does anyone else think what the Gold-fish did was a cool beginning?"

Peggy bounced in her seat.

"Yes," Ms. Puffer acknowledged. "Peggy, you agree."

Peggy explained, "I said it first and Daisy is just copying my idea."

Ms. Puffer looked sternly at Peggy then called on Siobhan.

Siobhan began, "There is something else. The crabs were sinister...."

The class erupts into laughter and sidebar comments.

"Class! This is not third grade. You need to step up your game. Continue, Siobhan," Ms. Puffer exclaimed as she walked to the yellow table by the window. "Siobhan, sinister is a good word. Why did you say that?"

Ms. Puffer thought, *All this drama. Middle school girls: Old enough to have these feelings.... Not old enough to know where it's leading them or what to do when they get there.*

"Sinister was a Word Of the Week word you gave us last month," replied Siobhan. "You said sinister was eviler than evil: evil for evil's own sake. Well, the two crabs tried to scam Gold-fish. The two crabs knew what would happen if Gold-fish went with them to Red Rock and Gold-fish didn't know."

"I'm glad you are using a Word of the Week. But what did you mean by that?" Ms. Puffer asked.

Siobhan continued, "You see you got the two crabs. Well, the one named Forked Claw[20] seemed more sinister. I mean, they both were trying to deceive Daisy...I mean...Gold-fish..."

A collective gasp fell over the the classroom. Danny looked at Daisy, who became noticeably flushed.

"I meant to say Gold-fish. The two crabs were trying to de-ceive Gold-fish but Forked-Claw did most of the talking. Like the expression Mr. Brooks told us about: White man speaks with forked[21] tongue. It means he speaks lies."

---

[20] Mr. Brooks introduced the pronunciation: four-ked claw

[21] Mr. Brooks introduced the pronunciation: four-ked

The class chuckled a little.

Danny spoke out, "I agree. Forked-Claw was like the chief and Feather Moccasin was like a squaw." Someone in the class-room laughed loudly. "I didn't mean it that way...."

Ms. Puffer looked sternly at the boy who had made the dis-ruption and he cowered into his seat.

Danny went on, "Forked-Claw and Feather Moccasin have a codependent relationship."

"Let's get away from the psycho-babble," Ms. Puffer insist-ed. "Obviously, they're a team; leave it at that. Now, Phyllis, what would you like to say?"

Phyllis put her hand down and remarked, "Forked-Claw was very dramatic and tried to say the things that would appeal to Gold-fish. He tried to change the way she saw things. He wanted her to see a world of beauty."

Ms. Puffer nodded and added, "Very good. Take the next fifteen minutes and write in your journals about the story of the Gold-fish. You will get extra points use you use any of our Words of the Week correctly. Okay, take out your journals."

ণণ

After an afternoon in the cold sun, Angelina wandered lonely, hungry, and looked for a place to warm her feet as the sunlight faded. Maybe she could find another discarded doughnut like she had earlier? She noticed a street sign for the Leather District and instinctually continued in that direction. Angelina stopped to peer through the window of the Black Cat Gallery. A small crowd of people dressed in grays or in blacks mulled around an opening for a well-known local artist. In the center of the room was a table with crackers and cheese and crudités, which reminded her of how hungry she was feeling.

A tall, rotund man smoking a cigarette wearing a black tuxedo seemed to appear out of nowhere by the door. The two made eye contact. Angelina exhaled a visible breath in the cool air and the man puffed a string of five consecutive smoke rings: each through the center of the preceding smoke ring.

Angelina gasped, "I don't think I've seen anyone do that before."

"Well," the man gloated. "I developed this talent while I was attending university. Perhaps it accounts for the seven years it took me to graduate."

There was an awkward silence.

"My name is Vincent, by the way. Come into the gallery and I'll regale you with my encyclopedic knowledge of art."

"Of course," she replied. "I should have introduced myself. I'm Angelina."

"Charmed, I'm sure," Vincent lauded as he took her hand and kissed it while making a dramatic bow.

Once they got inside, the room momentarily became frozen as if everyone in the room was a part of an enormous painting on display in a famous museum. The silent, stationary patrons cast their gaze on Angelina but their eyes moved as if behind cutouts in the canvas. Vincent sauntered into the room unrepentant to the accusatory ogling they were receiving, which he seemed to enjoy.

"Excuse me, I'm famished," Angelina squeaked hoping no one could hear the rumpling of her stomach. She hadn't eaten since the previous evening; save for an abandoned third of a powdered doughnut and the end of a cup of coffee she found on an adjoining park bench when she woke up at dawn. She felt a little out of place wearing a discarded heavy woolen coat and stolen Salvation Army clothes she hadn't changed in several days.

Vincent replied, "Dear girl, let me put a plate together for you." He grabbed a plate and continued, "Some brie—the king of cheeses—and some water biscuits. Do you like cornichons?"

Angelina didn't know what he'd asked but feigned, "I...I'm, not sure if...I want...."

He picked out thirteen curvaceous but small dark green pickles. Then he scooped another handful and tossed them into his mouth. "Oh Mother! Or should I say: *Ma mère* as the old battle axe insisted. I remember being weaned on cornichons. It was that kind of household." He eyed some Stilton with a ripe blue vein and carved five wedges about an inch and a half thick and placed them on the plate. "I'll get us some Chardonnay. You take this and secure those seats over by the wall."

Angelina was relieved to find out *cornice shawls*, or whatever he said, were just those little pickles, and she walked to the seats by the wall.

Angelina picked a half-eaten piece of bread and some cheese left on a table they walked by while Vincent wasn't looking. Her mouth stung with the first bite but she persevered. She ate and ate not knowing when she'd have fresh food again. Vincent was consumed with the flavors of smoked fish, cornichon, watercress, cucumber, and pear he'd stuffed together into his mouth several handfuls at a time.

After eating some more smoked fish and watercress, he led Angelina to a smallish painting in the corner as he licked his fingers clean. The painting was mounted on a dark maroon fabric matting in an elaborate baroque style frame with tarnished gold finish. The canvas was covered in thick smears of oil paint using dark colors resembling a landscape of terraced hills, pruned cypress trees, and a stucco house infused with darkness.

A stylish young couple walked the exhibit perusing the paintings. The young man had a stylish haircut, wore an expensive looking suit, and the kind of shoes you wouldn't see at a discount store. The trim, young girl was practically decorated with diamonds and gold jewelry. Her multicolored evening gown was slit to just below her derriere. She had a fluorescent white smile and fire engine red lipstick.

The stares the young couple was making seemed to rip into Angelina's skin like running through thorned vines. The feeling intensified as the couple moved closer and closer. The girl sniffed audibly as she walked by Angelina and whispered, no doubt, an unflattering comment to her companion.

Angelina thought, *Did she say?:* Look at her smelly clothes; No true sense of what is hip or haute couture; And that bulky black woolen coat. Eww! *And wasn't that a cruel laugh she just made at my expense for others to hear? Better not meet up with me and my friend, Mary, in a dark alley, Missy. Who'll be a-laughin' then?*

Vincent was oblivious to the young couple. He was completely uninterested. For some reason, he was talking to Angelina and doted on her every word; he valued her opinion, or so it seemed. He turned his attention back and forth from Angelina to the small painting on the wall. He was almost expecting praise, or adoration. He waited impatiently, tapping his foot nervously.

"How handsome a farmhouse," Angelina finally mentioned.

Vincent replied, "Though it does look like a country house, the darkness hides some of the details of a noble villa." He paused flushed with excitement, fanned his face with his hand, and added, "I knew you could recognize real art. Can you identify this color?" He pointed to a particularly darkish rectangle.

Angelina answered quite slowly, "Err...not a purple or blue...Some...somewhere in between."

"Ah ha," Vincent acclaimed while raising himself slightly on his toes momentarily. "Tell me you're an artiste. Oh, you must be. What a soul. What *joie de vivre.*"

Angelina looked around the room feeling self-conscious.

Perhaps everyone was listening in and waiting for an opportunity to pounce on any misstatement she made. "I like the painting. You know, like everyone else."

Vincent looked sharply down, back to the last cornichon on her plate, lifted his eyes to Angelina, and pointed out, "No, no, no. It takes a fellow artiste or someone simpatico to appreciate art. Common people..." He made a dubba-da-dubba-da onomatopoeia from letting his jaw swing in quick oscillations. "Oh no, my dear. Common people never truly appreciate art. They may buy or collect it, hmmm. But only an artiste appreciates art as art. Don't you agree? Of course you do; of course you do."

"You don't say," Angelina responded unsure of the appropriateness of her off the cuff reply and she wondered if Vincent, who appeared wealthy and sophisticated, could tell she neither knew much about art or cared for the painting she initially thought was amateurish.

Pointing to the rectangular spot in question with his arm extended and pointing his index finger to resemble that of God reaching out to Adam in the painting by Michelangelo on the ceiling of the Sistine Chapel. "This paint is from my own formula in the style of the Renaissance Maestro Leonardo da Vinci. The Renaissance: what a great age. I enjoyed it so much."

Angelina looked at him inquisitively unsure of how to respond.

"I mean, I appreciate the greatness of the Renaissance. I could not possibly be that old, or could I?" Vincent snickered half sarcastically.

They shared a weak laugh but Angelina couldn't tell if she was the subject or participant of an inside joke.

He continued, "To achieve the rich color, I procured the lapis-lazuli stones from none other than Alexandra Rasputin; illegitimate daughter of Maria Rasputin—daughter of the Grigori Rasputin from the Court of Czar Nicholas II."

He broke into a chortle. "Now here's a story! Though she is a mere child of ninety-one, she has a regal sensibility for art. You must meet her."

A middle-aged man was looking to approach the table with the orderves. He politely spoke, "May I?"

Vincent exploded, "No!" He bodychecked the man away from the table, cornered the serving dish and grabbed the last four pieces of smoked salmon, a few sprigs of watercress, several black olives, and crammed them into his mouth triumphantly.

He didn't miss a beat and jeered, "You are not an artiste. You could not possibly fathom a simple charcoal sketch let alone a master composition like...say, that one on the far wall." He took a side step and hip checked the man further away with a curt, "Be gone."

Angelina was surprised but remained silent. The man only asked to reach for the food, which was for everyone. She took a small sip of the Chardonnay from the stylish plastic cup and waited for Vincent to continue talking about the ninety-some odd-year old woman.

Vincent resumed his narrative, "As I was saying before I was so rudely interrupted, she lives in our building. Rarely comes out of her room, poor dear. But when the Revolution came to Mother Russia, Maria—Alexandra's mother—was living in the French countryside and escaped the Bolsheviks. Grigori Rasputin, the mystic seer of the Imperial Court, had stashed a treasure trove of exotic minerals, gems, diamonds, rubies, and so, so much more in that country estate years earlier.

As a young woman in Paris, Maria was a tiger trainer at the circus by day and danced in the cabaret by night. While having a notorious love affair with Maurice Chevalier, Maria became pregnant with Alexandra. Maurice Chevalier saw playing around with cabaret and chorus girls as purely recreational and never learned, or inquired, about his illegitimate daughter. Maria tragically died of tuberculosis when Alexandra was nine years-old. The orphaned girl was raised by her mother's friends at the circus and the cabaret where she learned how to survive. Josephine Baker, one of her mother's friends, eventually told Alexandra about her family's history and her famous grandfather. Alexandra carried on the family traditions in the black arts and eventually brought the treasure trove to America. She keeps most of the valuables out in plain sight in her apartment. You should see it. Your head would do a three-sixty, Angelina. Oh, yes it would. I could go on all day."

Vincent's eye was then drawn to a well-dressed man a few feet away.

"Angelina...what a lovely name...I have been captivated by our conversation. However, I must depart for a previously planned engagement with my good friend, Dr. Perp. Forgive me. But we'll see each other soon enough. Oh, yes, soon enough." He took her hand, kissed it a long moment, and bowed.

Angelina stood stationary while he walked to the man. The two embraced and kissed on the lips. She didn't pay it much mind. Then they were joined by a third man, who was also dressed sharply in a double-breasted suit wearing wire-rimmed glasses. The three of them looked in her direction for a second like an audience at a play, turned around, and exited the gallery into the darkness of night.

Ernest led them to his lime green Volkswagen beetle parked under a fake gas street light. Once inside the car he asked, "So, who was the filly, Vincent? I haven't seen that one before. Are you trying to make me jealous?"

"The girl looked a bit of a vagrant...Y-esss? Y-esss? Probably eats out of garbage cans. Y-esss? Y-esss?" Dr. Perp added while he shook off imaginary germs from his hands.

Vincent cleared his throat and looked sternly at both of them. "For your information, she was the woman Xhuljana wanted. Hmmm. Hmmm."

"Oh," Ernest uttered with joy as Dr. Perp raised a hand delicately to his mouth silently saying the same word.

"Y-esss? Y-esss! Who needs Rev. Ravioli? We've found our Angelina. Y-esss? Y-esss." Dr. Perp concluded.

O O O

Good Reader, the urban legend of Owldoll was not a contiguous unfolding. It developed in bits and pieces, which roughly correspond to the order of the events you read. Time organized the parts of the legend into sections. Unlike the urban legend, this twenty-first century færy tale depends on the reader's imagination to ascribe the moral underpinnings, which will conform to what was envisioned. You should accept each scene as integral to the whole without discounting the smaller scenes as less important because you have the advantage of looking back from outside.

— Author

After school, Amanda and Daisy planned to meet at Siobhan's house. It seemed as though there were more rooms in her house than in Daisy's building. All the rooms were large and had high ceilings. Several long corridors with thick runners and there were a few dark wooden doors on either side that seemed to stretch endlessly. And there were even more rooms behind each door.

"Love your house, Siobhan," Daisy mentioned looking, back over the big front yard.

The girls went inside and crossed a large open room. Daisy looked down the corridor to the right and said, "It's so big. Every time we hang here, I see something new. See the pattern along the edge of the rug going along this wall? Looks like a long chain made from one letter S after another."

"The rug is called a runner," Siobhan corrected, "and the pattern is based on Celtic knots."

"Mad crazy, right?" asked Amanda bouncing up next to them.

Daisy added, "Know what's mad crazy was Siobhan sayin': The two gay crabs were trying to deceive *Daisy! El-Oh-El.*[22] Not so funny, Siobhan. You said those stupid gay crabs were after me...." Daisy felt the low-grade electric vibration again and thought, *Owldoll.*

Amanda thought Daisy seemed hypnotized, and she asked

---

[22] LOL is textspeak for laugh out loud

Siobhan, "She okay? It's like she drifted off to another world...."

Siobhan interrupted, "Let her come back on her own. You know, it seems to me like Daisy is still in touch with her mother, or makes a connection with someone who knows where her mother is hiding. Daisy keeps sayin' her mom's gone...just not gone-gone. That means she's feelin' her mom is somewhere, right?"

Across town at Daisy's apartment, Owldoll became animate, extended her wings, tucked them back against her sides, and glanced up at the reflection of the sky in the mirror on the bureau.

She wondered about the irony: *The gray clouds hide the blue sky and sunshine above until things clear.* Then she spoke out loud, "W-issh. Without the solution this spell never ends. Without the solution this spell never ends. W-issh."

The reflection in the mirror of a recurring pattern in the clouds caught Owldoll's attention and she continued, "W-issh. You're repeating a story that tells the story you're in. You're repeating the story that tells the story you're in. W-issh."

Across town at Siobhan's house, Daisy looked out the window at an overcast sky made of layers of clouds that drifted by and intertwined with each other. She wondered if it was a sign of things to come.

Siobhan pointed outside as she spoke to Daisy, "Look at the clouds. They're crisscrossing in the sky. The pattern looks like Celtic knots, doesn't it?"

Daisy mumbled incoherently half agreeing; half somewhere else.

"What's wrong, Daisy?" asked Siobhan. "What were you saying?"

Daisy shook her head. "Oh! That's not what I said. I said we might have stumbled onto the solution. You said the gay crabs deceived me but the story could be saying something about what we're looking for, too."

"I didn't say that," Siobhan protested. "I didn't say the story could be saying something...."

Amanda interrupted, "She didn't say gay crabs. You're just sayin' that 'cause Danny said the crabs were gay."

Siobhan insisted, "Just 'cause Danny said they were gay crab, doesn't mean they were gay crabs. Maybe they just talk funny. Hey, I just made a mistake, *kay*. I wasn't disin'[23] you."

"Yeah but maybe," Amanda grinned. "Maybe you really meant it. Remember what Ms. Puffer told us about a Freudian Slip? What you say is what you really mean to say, even if you don't think that's what you meant to say."

Siobhan made a face at Amanda and Amanda made a face back.

Daisy asked, "Why didja say the crabs deceived me? It was embarrassing. Shoulda seen the look Danny gave me. Thought I was gonna die."

Amanda giggled, "You like him, huh."

Daisy reacted, "Nah uh."

Amanda replied, "Yes, you do. Admit it...."

Siobhan interrupted, "Come on! And I just made a mistake. Chill[24]. I didn't mean it, Daisy."

"You did say: The two gay crabs deceived Daisy," Amanda insisted.

Siobhan laughed, "I don't think Daisy has met any gay crabs...or any crabs from...what's that place called...Nahant. It's in Massachusetts. And what is it the crabs could be trying to deceive Daisy about, anyway? A stash of secret seaweed?"

Daisy pondered a moment. "Maybe it really has to do with where my mom is?"

Siobhan looked funny.

"What's the matter? Did ya see a ghost?" Amanda mocked.

Siobhan confided, "Actually, I had a dream the night before last. In the dream, we were all in Playsteady Park and there were two shadowy figures behind some trees; a fat one and a skinny one. And they tricked Daisy to lead us to the swing set. You know with tales of sugar plums and candy...."

---

[23] K is textspeak for okay, or know
[24] disrespecting

"See," Amanda taunted. "Shadowy figures: you did see a ghost. You did see a ghost."

Daisy pouted, "Oh, Amanda. It's a dream and the two guys were in the shadows. Ghosts are make-believe...or made up for MTV."

Siobhan corrected, "Yeah, they were in the shadows but I meant shadowy guys like James, Victoria, and Laurent in the *Twilight* movies[25] . They got shifty eyes. They talk all funny and use words to deceive the Cullens. The guys got dirty necks and they are probably smelly, too.

"So in my dream when we got close to the swings, we could see the swings were all rusted and there was broken glass everywhere."

Daisy thought back about the woman in the black coat standing in the cold rain who looked at her from behind her eyes.

Daisy said, "I hate broken glass at the park. It's usually the hobos getting drunk in the park after dark and smashing bottles of booze 'cause they don't care about the environment."

Siobhan continued, "While we were trying to figure out what happened to the swings, the two shadowy guys were kidnapping Daisy's mom and putting her into a lime-green subcompact. Her mom was squeezed against the back door window because the fat one sat in back with her and crushed her up against the other side of the car. Her face was distorted against the glass. But she couldn't see us! 'Cause her eyes were covered with...I dunno...little white specs like what's on the skin on a toad. And moment by moment, more and more specs covered her eyes. Then the dinky car began to move making an electric hum as it drove into the darkness."

Amanda said, "That's one mad, wild nightmare."

Daisy stated, "It was like you were remembering the dream when you were talking about the Wampanoag story. The

[25] A best-selling series of books about a family of vampires (the Cullens) where one of their "teenage children", Edward, falls in love with a local teenage girl, Bella. The books and movie adaptations were immensely popular with teenage girls.

Gold-fish story was about the Gold-fish being deceived and having her eyes covered with a paste of crushed up sea shells and stuff so she could only see the world of beauty the two crabs wanted her to see."

Siobhan agreed, "But the Gold-fish story doesn't say whether the Gold-fish ever gets her vision back." She paused and thought this question out loud, "But maybe there's some connection with Daisy?"

"Maybe," Amanda added, "that's why you said the two crabs deceived Daisy? You were sayin' the Gold-fish was Daisy..."

Siobhan interrupted, "Nah uh. More like the Gold-fish was like Daisy's mom. Don't put words in my mouth."

Amanda pointed her finger at Siobhan, "You always say you have these dreams with heavy meaning, right? It's so not fair."

Siobhan said, "Funny thing is I usually don't dream."

"You're kidding," Amanda exclaimed. "Everyone dreams; I read it in a book."

Siobhan answered, "I'm so not kidding. I hardly ever dream. So to dream about Daisy and those two weird men was strange. I didn't know what to make of it."

Daisy added, "Yeah. And to make a Freudian slip during Ms. Puffer's class makes me think you were dreaming about the Gold-fish story. And your dream worked its way into this story."

Siobhan moved closer to Daisy and put her hand on Daisy's shoulder.

"Hey," Daisy shouted. "Let's get back to tryin' to find my mom. I know my mom left but she's not gone-gone." She smiled back at Siobhan. "What Siobhan said about her dream, the Gold-fish story, and the crabs tryin' to deceive me could be a clue. We gotta try to work with it."

O O O

Daisy and Amanda walked along the busy street and the hot pavement. They turned down a side street where the hustle and bustle of the main street seemed incapable of penetrating its isolation. City noises were okay and eventually became innocuous, yet ever-present like a completely faded advertisement on a wall. The buildings looked a little nicer with shrubs and manicured lawns. At the end of the street was the park: lush, green, with a pond, a large field, hills, baseball diamonds, basketball courts, swings, slides, jungle gyms, and sandboxes.

The entrance gate had a bronze placard: Playstead Park. Daisy always emphasized "play" and called it Playing-Steady Park when daddy took her there when she was three. Daisy changed the name to Playsteady Park. Inside, the park seemed a world of its own where everything was fun or beautiful or both.

The girls walked past the pond and beside a hill with flowers in bloom. A peculiar sound punctuated the picturesque park.

"That's a sound you don't hear every day. It sounds like a question: Who? Who? or Who? Who!" Daisy said to Amanda.

"Very perceptive," said a woman sitting on a bench underneath a spreading chestnut tree. The woman had very long, shiny red hair and wore a long dark dress with a lace border resting on her ankle-length black leather boots.

Amanda said, "I thought owls only said: hoo."

The woman continued, "The sound you're hearing is an owl rhyme. Owls are nocturnal creatures. That means they live during the night. Most people...most animals live during the daytime. It is this uncanny ability of owls that makes them special. Earlier fables told of owls that saw hidden dangers gods and goddesses couldn't see. So when you hear an owl in the day, it is warning you, if you can understand what the owl is telling you. Owls are known to speak in rhymes."

Amanda turned to Daisy and giggled.

"Don't you know owls speak in rhymes, or use metaphors?" the woman cautioned.

"They do?" Amanda replied.

Half-amused the woman chuckled. "Most owls begin and end a thought with a sound people tend to hear as who. It like hearing a foreign tongue: The jumble of sounds seems random—without a purpose. For those attuned to the language what is said, and unsaid, reveals the meaning."

Daisy spoke up, "Before Mademoiselle Lapin taught me some French, I thought *s'il vous plait* was *seal at play*."

The red-haired woman replied, "If you don't mind my saying, you have fascinating eyes. I look into your eyes: their shape; the prismatic sparkle of grays, browns, and gold radiating outward like a little flower. Your eyes are the eyes that transmit all they know."

As the woman got up to leave, she briefly turned back and said, "Little Fuzza,[26] listen carefully because I get the feeling you can hear what is being revealed in an owl-rhyme."

"So long, I'll try," Amanda said but the woman had already begun walking away.

Daisy thought, *farewell and thank you for speaking with us.* Then she faintly heard, "May the Owl of the Rozafa Castle watch over you, Little Fuzza."

Amanda answered, "She reminded me of Miss Luddy, our fifth grade teacher. Except, Miss Luddy is a real witch. I heard the red-haired woman say something about words that rhyme with owl. She was weird."

"Yes," said Daisy. "The woman said: May the Owl of the Rozafa Castle watch over you. Sounded like she knew something. I never saw that woman before, have you?"

"No. I thought you knew her," Amanda said. "I'm getting thirsty. Let's go to my house for some ice water, okay?"

○ ○ ○

Siobhan met the other girls at Amanda's house. They went inside and sat in the kitchen.

"Let's have some ice water," Amanda said as she opened the freezer door. Amanda brought the ice cube tray to the table and took down three tumblers brightly-decorated with gold painted wagon wheels and copper squares. She dropped several ice cubes in each glass. She stood looking bewildered as she stared

---

[26] When Daisy was a baby, she called a flower, "fuzza".

into the glasses.

"Something's wrong." said Daisy, a little unsteady on her feet. "Whoa. I have this strange feeling like I did when I found that old book behind your dresser. It feels like the vibration of a heavy guitar string..."

Siobhan broke into her conversation, "What up? Girl, you look pale.... You feelin' funny?"

Daisy appeared different: she did look pale; withdrawn; just not with it. The room emanated a pressure they all could feel. It was as if Amanda's bed was calling Daisy to lie down and she moved in its direction.

"Yeah," Amanda said. "Go lie down on my bed. S'okay."

"I feel like when you go up higher in an airplane and your ears pop," Siobhan said holding her ears.

Daisy felt overwhelmed and walked to the bed. "I feel real tired. I gotta lie down..." and she stretched out on Amanda's bed. The girls saw Daisy had greenish hue outlining her body and the pressure they were all feeling receded. The greenish glow seemed to absorb the pressure and encompassed the spot where Daisy was rapidly nodding off.

Siobhan whispered to Amanda, "I've never seen Daisy get sleepy in the middle of the day before. Hope she's not sick."

Amanda asked, "Should we call her dad?"

"No," Siobhan insisted. "She just needs to catch some zees[27] for a while. You'll see."

Amanda held the ice cube up and examined it like a test tube in science class. She moved it from side to side to get better light on it. As she turned toward the bed where Daisy was sleeping, she noticed the ice cube began to give off a dull yellow light.

"What do you see?" asked Siobhan.

Amanda answered, "Look here: there's something in the middle of the ice cube.... It's glowing!" As Amanda turned back toward Daisy, they both watched the ice cube glow a brighter yellow.

---

[27] onomatopoeia for the sound of snoring

"Go closer," Siobhan urged.

Amanda looked frightened and said, "Where did we get these freaky ice cubes, anyway?"

"Did you forget? We put those pieces of paper in the tray," Siobhan answered while tapping her foot.

Amanda shrugged her shoulders. "Actually, Daisy did."

"Gimme one of those...," Siobhan ordered as she reached into the tray but her grip slipped. The ice cube dropped to the floor and slid away, almost deliberately.

Amanda reached down instinctively but felt a vibration as her hand approached the ice cube. She uttered a gasp and shook it off.

"Pick it up and bring it here," Siobhan said. "I got an idea. Let's dig them all out. Maybe they'll help us? Ya remember the old book Daisy found?"

Amanda scrunched her nose, "No. What old book? I'm talking about the paper in the ice cubes."

Siobhan spoke to Amanda, "You don't remember the book Daisy found under your bed? You don't treat your books like she does: All of her book are in pristine condition. Just like they came from the store. You know what your books end up looking like...all dinged up and messy. You had a bunch of books shoved under your bed since preschool with old socks and other junk. Daisy found a really old book of stories from a long time ago: stories about knights in shining armor, kings and queens, fairy godmothers—or as Daisy used to say færy godmother and *merry-godmother*—and magic. The book had a cool drawing on the cover, remember?"

Amanda stared back blankly. Then her eyes brightened, "Daisy said there was a difference between a færy-godmother and a merry-godmother. A færy-godmother burned the kids in the oven and a merry-godmother helped the princess live happily ever-after."

"You've got it," Siobhan announced. "Daisy called them færy tales because they were designed to scare you. If you're not scared by a færy tale, you can understand the real story. Now do you remember the book Daisy found under your bed? The one where the frozen words came from."

Nodding her head, Amanda replied, "Oh, yeah, that one. When she picked up the book, it was as if the pages began to fly out of the book on their own like a waterfall. We thought it was kind of funny. Then Daisy said she saw special words on some of the pages: the words were calling out to her.

"Daisy put her hand on this one page she saw on the floor over by the bed.... It was like the word bunched up on the page, touched her hand, and begged to be torn out. Daisy tore the bunched up word from the page. An' that was weird. Daisy always treats her books better than anyone. So, she began tearing out these words. Then we helped trim the ragged edges, you know? So they'd be about the same size, remember?"

Siobhan looked at Daisy lying in bed dreaming with an intense look on her face: half angelic and half vulnerable. Then Siobhan continued, "Daisy went mad ballistic on those words. She began to shuffle the words: faster and faster—like a flip book but no picture formed. Daisy flipped them so fast we could feel heat. The words glowed and we were afraid the paper would catch on fire. Remember? The words began to glow like a weak flashlight. Then the words began to grow into creatures. I don't know about you but I was scared silly.

"Daisy placed each scrap of paper into a separate slots in the ice tray on the counter next to the sink and covered them with cold water to cool 'em off."

"Then I put the ice cube tray in the freezer later," Amanda said. "That seemed natural enough. You know, preserve them in time." She held out the glass to show Daisy like she could see them in her dreams and see the ice cubes glowing brighter as they got nearer.

Siobhan told Amanda, "Go closer to Daisy...go on. See, the cubes get brighter the closer you get to Daisy."

"Siobhan, the frozen words, we must free them." Amanda announced.

She held the cube firmly in her hand barely two feet from

Daisy. A bright light glowed from inside the ice cube and wandered around the room. As she walked closer to Daisy, the ice cube began to radiate from its center and the heat grew outward melting the ice cube away from the strip of paper. Eventually, the cube withered to a semi-translucent dodecahedron then to a clear sphere whose center is everywhere and whose circumference is nowhere. They watched the illuminated word come into focus and glow brighter from yellow to white. Amanda plucked out the strip of paper and held it in her open hand.

Siobhan and Amanda looked at each other as the three letters emitted noises like knuckles cracking as they grew into a crab-like shape. The word undulated slowly and blurted out "Ow-el" clear as a bell.

Amanda grabbed another cube and walked closer to Daisy. As the crackling sound of the letters quieted down, it said, "Dayn-jer."

Siobhan took a cube in each hand. When she got close to Daisy, the light was bright enough to cast shadows on the wall. The shadow appeared to be a woman and a flying insect buzzing around her head. The insect made several approaches to the woman's nose, barrel-rolled back at the bridge of her nose, and flew away. The silhouette of the woman changed: the outline of the hair got wilder, the shape of the face extended, and the nose became pointier.

As this was happening, Amanda drew Siobhan's attention to the shadows. They looked at each other in bewilderment and shock.

Meanwhile, the letters rumbled along and the girls heard, "Soul-looo-shun" and "Inn-soul-late" from the letters in Siobhan's hands.

Siobhan said, "What do you think that the images made by the shadow had to do with these words?"

Amanda held out her opened hands palms up.

"Me neither," Siobhan added. "But there is a connection. I'm sure as sure can be. We'll have to tell Daisy about this when she wakes up. It's a mystery: frozen words casting a shadow of a woman and a flying bug!"

The words stood in place making wave-like motions across the letters clicking like falling dominoes. A mildly intense electric shock radiated through the room, and the girls each felt it. Even Daisy seemed to react to this.

Siobhan stood with an ice cube in her hand. As the ice melted away, the letters purred and gave off a soothing glow. The vibration was comforting in Siobhan's hand. The girls heard a beautiful female voice say: *Spell*. Amanda looked on almost enviously. Even Daisy appeared to be looking at Siobhan wanting to join in.

"This feels so good," Siobhan said. "I could hold this word for hours."

Amanda rushed over. "Lemme try...."

Siobhan withdrew her hand and the word fell to the floor. It scampered away in a sideways direction.

Amanda pounced on it but missed. The word sped off toward the books under Amanda's bed.

"Help me," Siobhan yelled. "Capture the word before it gives us the slip and crawls into another book."

Siobhan stepped quickly between the word and the bookcase. The word halted and veered toward the wall. Siobhan held her ground and silently directed Amanda to sneak up behind the word. They moved in and cornered the word so close to the wall its shadow could be read from where each of the girls was standing.

Siobhan reached over and plucked it up. Then she walked to the table and placed it quietly next to the other words, which were remaining relatively stationary and making their clicking noises.

Siobhan told *Spell*, "Be a nice word and stay with your friends. You don't want a timeout."

Siobhan and Amanda held their breath then let out a gasp when the word *Spell* moved up next to the other words on the table.

Amanda said with her eyes fixed on the words on the table,

"The word *Spell* is so mysterious. But at least it is behaving like a good word."

Spell began to purr again, only louder. The other words followed suit by clicking louder. They got louder and louder building up pressure inside and outside the girls heads. The mysterious hum from *Spell* rang loudest like the penetrating amplifier feedback at a concert. The girls held their hands over their ears to no avail. An overwhelming sensation overtook them as the crushing sounds grew louder, and louder.

The powerful noises seemed to corrugate the air in the room creating a chronological maelstrom drawing Amanda and Siobhan into Daisy's dream: Where space-time took on a new significance. Everything looked sharper to Daisy, Amanda, and Siobhan. Yet three-dimensions did not account for the folded-space of the dreamworld: Light, energy, smell, touch, and sound were more intense. Time was different, too. Present, past, and future seemed to be together in a way none of them had ever experienced before. Perhaps it was why the air seemed corrugated; time and space, or space and time were melded in a nearly tangible way. When you were touching, you felt time; While you were looking, you saw sound; Where you were detecting sound, you heard what happened and what was going to happen. A dream being a dream made what seemed real a mystery.

Owldoll waited silently and beckoned Daisy to come closer. Daisy picked up Owldoll. A warm wave of energy ricocheted from Owldoll to Daisy. Daisy's hands warmed up and her grip loosened as Owldoll leaped onto the table. Owldoll looked more pronounced than before: She seemed larger than life, and more brilliant to the naked eye.

Daisy began to examine the wandering words on the table. Her eyes flitted from word to word: owl;

danger; insulate; hidden; darkness; reflection; solution; spell. The crab-like words began to move around the tabletop stepping laterally and changing positions. The word *owl* gained prominence like watching a constellation dance across the sky.

Daisy said, "*Owl* is symbolic. I don't take it literally.... *Owl* is either a subject or an object in this phrase."

"Or," Amanda added, "owl is a solution, right?"

"Very good," Daisy replied. "I didn't think about that. So, if owl is a solution, what is the subject? Hidden? Insulate? Danger? Maybe, Darkness?

Amanda looked at Daisy and said, "What danger?"

Daisy answered questioningly, "A hidden danger?"

After a pause, Amanda spoke up. "Owl in the darkness sees the solution to the hidden danger."

Then Daisy retorted, "We have two unused words: Reflection and Spell. Owl sees the reflection of the hidden danger in the darkness to spell a solution."

Amanda stood up, "Wow. We solved a mystery, Daisy."

Daisy answered, "But what is the mystery we solved?"

Siobhan and Amanda were suddenly back in the room. This magic moment passed: Amanda and Siobhan were left with only an inexact memory of the dream—the perfect context faded.

The girls had just visited a magical place. It was like a world without questions where everything made sense. Now they were back in Midway where things for a teenager rarely seemed fair, or followed any rules. Amanda and Siobhan were concerned about Daisy but not worried. She was safe in the dreamworld, or so they assumed. They both searched their minds for the details of the dream. Neither came up with much, even the colors and vivid images were gone. Both girls were about to say something—except Daisy spoke first and finished their thought.

Daisy's voice came clearly from her half-dream state: But what is the mystery we solved?

Amanda agreed, "Yeah, that's it. Now I remember! It's a mystery we gotta solve."

Siobhan walked over to the closet door with a full-length mirror and spoke to her reflection. "We were talking about the frozen words in the dream Daisy was having, and we were trying to understand what the words were trying to say. We have the words—They are right there in the ice cubes and on the table!—but the meaning is hidden. You know how Daisy always says her mommy is not really gone-gone...just hidden away like she's part of a mystery?"

Amanda continued, "A mystery for her to solve.... Speaking of a mystery, were you dreaming what I was dreaming? I mean, we were all there: you and me and Daisy. We were in a strange place where the air was folded onto itself. It was kinda like what happened was still happening and what was gonna happen was there, too."

Siobhan nodded in agreement. "What a strange place, huh? You know Daisy wanted to solve the mystery. She was trying to grab it out of the air! The answer seemed so close and so far away. But Daisy wanted our help so badly. It was like this is *our* mystery to solve, too. You know how you felt when your real mom went to jail. You needed us to be your friend. And we were there for you, right? We're still here for you. Let's promise to do our part for Daisy. An' jus' like her daddy always says about a promise: Our word is our bond. It is that important."

Amanda agreed, "Daisy is our BFF. We gotta help her solve the mystery to find her mother."

Siobhan looked at Daisy resting on the bed and back to Amanda. "When Daisy found these words, she said it wasn't by accident: it was as if these words chose Daisy."

Amanda looked at Daisy. "And we were chosen to help

Daisy."

"Whadda we waiting for?" asked Siobhan and picked out another ice cube. She brought it closer to Daisy and watched it glow brighter and melt. The letters oscillated as it grew. It squiggled and tickled her hand. The letters pronounced, "Hidden" and Siobhan tipped her hand to place the word on the kitchen table next to the others. They resembled a bunch of crabs walking from left to right.

Amanda grabbed the last two ice cubes and brought them close to Daisy. They melted and the words Insulate and Reflection barked out their names before joining the other words congregating on the table. Amanda and Siobhan stood mesmerized by the words they had unfrozen, and could no longer control.

The words seemed to have a mind of their own, and looked like they were working in concert with each other. They might conspire and escape undetected. Amanda and Siobhan were getting nervous. What if the words got away from them? What would happen if they lost these words?

Siobhan said, "Whoa. You forced it."

"No," Amanda replied. "You forced it. You told me to move words closer to Daisy."

Siobhan retorted, "No, you forced it. You took out the ice cube tray. I never said to move the ice cubes closer to Daisy. Now look what's happening."

The words bunched together and clicked even louder. The feedback screech pulsated; strong, stronger.

Amanda and Siobhan felt space vibrate wholesale and Daisy felt the dreamworld vibrate, too. Even the air and light moved in visible waves. Daisy opened her eyes and saw Amanda and Siobhan shepherding the crab-like words on the table. The clicking sounds diminished. This seemed to smooth the air and dull out the vibrations. But the vibrations shook Daisy from her dream. She sat upright, and took in the sight of the living words on the kitchen table.

"Look at these words, Daisy," said Siobhan noticing Daisy's eyes were open. "We melted all the frozen words."

"These words are mad alive," Amanda commented as though it were an everyday occurrence. "These are the frozen words. They've come to life. The words are talking and moving on the table and making noises!"

Daisy said, "I was just dreaming: Owldoll was there and she told me the words were part of a puzzle.... Owldoll said: Words don't only represent but they misrepresent, too."

"Look at this one," Siobhan interrupted and pointed to *Owl*, which had gone off by itself.

Daisy agreed. "Yeah. Owl stood out in my dream—I mean the word Owl. In my dream, I didn't put Owl and Owldoll together. Now, it's so obvious. Duh."

Amanda moved her face close to the word *Solution*. "This isn't obvious. A Solution is a solution, but a solution to what?"

Siobhan twisted about to get their attention. "The word Darkness looks like a shiny, black eel, don't you think?" As she asked the question, she halted. "Oh, look at it now."

The letters changed shading with a more geometric pattern like fish scales. The scales conformed to interlocking shapes with a cut-out on each side and a small rounded extension centered on its top. "Now, the letters really look like a pieces of a puzzle."

While the girls were trying to figure out how the puzzle went together, the words stopped moving. One by one the words became flatter, and fell back onto the table as the strips of paper they started out as. The girls moved closer; like someone with weak vision trying to read a blurred image on a page.

Amanda took the ice cube tray over to the sink and filled it with water. She brought it back to the table, picked up the individual pieces of paper, and put each in a separate section of the tray.

"Good idea," Siobhan insisted. "You never know if the words will turn back into moving words. Frozen words won't get us into trouble later. Yeah."

Amanda took the ice cube tray and put it back into the freezer.

Daisy said, "We gotta go online and look up the meanings of the words. If the puzzle is made up of words, then the answer is hidden in their meaning."

Amanda nodded. "Yeah, but.... I gotta go to my mom's friend's house for dinner. Let's do this after school tomorrow."

Siobhan added, "I probably need to go home, too. It is getting late."

Daisy said, "Okay, we'll do this after school tomorrow."

○ ○ ○

Daisy closed her locker and there was Danny's smiling face. They shared an awkward moment.

"Whatcha doin'?" he asked.

Daisy bit her lip. "Well...me and Amanda and Siobhan were talkin' and we were talkin' about the Gold-fish story. And a dream Siobhan had and said some interesting stuff. I was thinking, what if the Gold-fish story means something?"

"Duh," Danny mocked. "It does mean something."

Daisy stomped. "Mean something about finding my mom, doofus. You know, she's not gone-gone. There is a mystery involved and I gotta solve it. I think she left a clue at my house. I know it's there. Wanna help me look for it?"

"*Kay*," he impishly nodded.

They walked from the school to the apartment building. It was a warm, sunny day and they walked stride for stride with each other. Daisy was optimistic Danny would be able to help her find the clue she was sure was there somewhere. When they reached the building, they were met by two of Daisy's neighbors.

"*Bonjour*, Daisy," came the cheerful voice of Mademoiselle Lapin.

Daisy whispered to Danny, "These are good neighbors." Then in her outdoor voice, "Good afternoon...*Bonjour*, Mademoiselle Lapin and Mr. Harris."

Mademoiselle Lapin chortled, "Ah! *Un juene amour!* Oooo eees your leetle friend? He seems to be a nice boy."

"Oh, this is Danny. He's smart. Danny, this is Mademoiselle Lapin and Mr. Harris. They are the nicest people in the building."

Mr. Harris said, "You're too kind, Miss Daisy. Danny...it's Danny, right? Pleased to make your acquaintance."

Danny made a bowing gesture. "Thank you. Nice to meet you, too, Sir and Ma'am."

Mr. Harris observed, "How polite. Wasn't I just mentioning the deleterious diminution of common courtesy the other day?"

"*Mais, oui,*" Mademoiselle Lapin replied waving. "But we must be going. *Au revoir.*"

Mr. Harris paused, looked at Daisy and Danny, and spoke while turning away, "It may seem as though it is easy to put something over on us but there are usually clues all over the place for us to find."

Daisy waved as she continued into the building. She knew the French word *amour* meant love but couldn't be bothered with its implications now. "Come on...," she said to Danny as they entered the lobby.

Mr. Harris continued out of earshot, "I'm not sure if Ricardo is home. We'll mention this when we see him later. Don't believe he'd take kindly to Daisy having a boy over to an empty apartment."

"*Tout suite!*" Mademoiselle Lapin barked as she walked more quickly. "Don't be an old fuddy-duddy, as you say. To be young and in love...oooo la la!"

Danny and Daisy ran up the stairs making a muffled click-clack from their sneakers on the ribbed runners on each step, and the hard plastic mat on the landings. They half-skipped down the corridor.

Danny jumped ahead of her and faced the door in the middle of the hall. "This is it, right?"

"No," Daisy replied ignoring him as she walked past him to the corner apartment. "I live here: apartment number four three two B."

Danny sheepishly said, "Ooops. I thought you lived at four three NOT To Be."

Daisy smiled, "You goofball."

Daisy took out her key and opened the door. "Where to begin?"

"I dunno," said Danny.

She walked over to her room and over to the pile of dolls, teddy bear, and Owldoll. She picked up Owldoll and was immediately energized: she shot upright. Danny felt a tingle of excitement and began to see Daisy in a whole new light as someone other than just that girl who used to talk to him in first grade. He was getting a crush on her.

She spoke softly to Owldoll, "Where should I look? Help me find mom."

"Don't go all Dr. Doolittle[28] on me," Danny exclaimed.

Daisy hesitated, "I...I...am not trying to talk to Owldo... the...the ani...animals. I was just talking to myself, kay?"

Danny stared at Daisy. Daisy stared back at Danny. They stood silently a long while. Neither knowing how to end the impasse.

Daisy finally said, "Follow me. I wanna show you something."

Daisy thought out loud as she went straight to the den, *It's not that strange to talk to dolls....Boys! Uuuhhh!*

She stood in front of the bookcase and examined the ornate bottle her mother left there. She looked at it a long while admiring its rich, dark blue color before she reached for it. As her fingertips grew closer, Daisy felt a slight electric vibration: suddenly, she felt a presence familiar and distant.

Danny saw Daisy drifting off: mesmerized by the opalescent blue liquid.

"Do you feel it, too?" she asked as she looked over her shoulder at him.

"I think so," he uttered. "Feel what?"

She blinked. "Like when you get a shock when you touch

---

28 The Story of Dr. Doolittle Hugh Lofting (1920) is about a doctor who can talk to animals. Later turned into television programs and movies.

a doorknob but it continues like the noise through the floor when a neighbor plays their music loud."

"Yeah maybe," he agreed as he reached for her hand.

"Hey," she snapped as she withdrew her hand. "I'm being serious. I like you and everything but I'm trying to find mom. I feel these things. That's why I asked for your help. Because I thought you could...you could help me find what I was looking for...you know, this clue my mom left. I know she's gone. I know it but she's not gone-gone. And when I touched the bottle, I felt something. Guess you didn't."

Danny stepped in front of Daisy and picked up the bottle. As he drew it past her, she felt its presence more intensely.

"Weird writing on the label," Danny remarked and sounded out, "Eye-lack. Major-starr." He lifted the bottle up and down slightly, "This bottle is kinda heavy."

"Be careful, Danny. It's my mom's," Daisy implored. "I only have a few things that really remind me of her. She told me she really liked the color and the mysterious lettering. Sometimes, I look at the lettering and try to figure out if these words were why she bought it."

Danny asked, "What do you think it means? *Eye-lack. Major-starr.* It definitely is not English. Maybe it is written in Vampire? Where's Bella Swan[29] when you really need her?"

Daisy laughed. "Come on. Quit kidding. You think she's mad fly,[30] huh?"

Danny shot back, "You're fly, Daisy."

Daisy looked at him curiously.

Danny haphazardly swung the bottle this way and that, moving wobbly, and unsteady on his feet as he mocked dangerous moves with the bottle as he cried out, "Oooohhh...whoooaaa.... Lookout!!...oh, no-oooohhh!!"

Daisy reached for the bottle as he moved it behind his back. Their fingers touched and they were frozen: both holding the bottle; his hand touching her hand; her hand touching his

29 The local teenage girl who falls in love with the "teenage" vampire, Edward Cullen in the book and movie Twilight.

30 Urban speak for sexy

hand; Daisy's arms around him; Danny up against her.

Then the apartment door opened and in walked Mr. Villa-nova shoulder bag in hand.

Danny looked nervously at Daisy and she anxiously returned his gaze as they inched back from each other.

"Daisy," Mr. Villanova barked. "You know you're not allowed to have boys over when I'm not home."

"Sorry, Dad," Daisy said softly. "We were...I mean...I asked Danny...uhh...Oh, this is Danny. I asked Danny to help me find a clue mommy left. Well...she didn't leave a clue. We thought...I thought she left a clue...left a clue here...so I...So I...And Danny said...I mean, I asked Danny to help me. He's smart and I thought he could help me."

Mr. Villanova examined Daisy and Danny half amused by their innocence.

Daisy stammered as the two separated further, "I...I...I thought the bottle she bought had a mystic connection to mommy. And she...."

Mr. Villanova replied, "Deep inside your heart is in the right place, Daisy. Just be careful where you look because you never know what you'll find. I remember a saying from when I went to Hebrew School...Maimonides said something like: mysticism is fraught with peril."

"Umm...," Danny uttered. "That's kind of interesting, sir."

"Dad," Daisy remarked disapprovingly. "We weren't doin' anything. Geez."

Danny turned red. "I gotta go home, Daisy. See in school. So long, sir."

Danny began to walk to the door and slowed down as he approach it.

"Go see your friend out, *florita mia*," Mr. Villanova told Daisy as he gave her a dramatized stern look with a smile.

Daisy made a face back at him and said goodbye to Danny at the door. But before he left she whispered, "He didn't think we were fooling around. See you tomorrow."

He mouthed "Good" to her and smiled as he walked down

the corridor.

O O O

Syt i dalçin; Syt i plaçin.
Eyes that fall out; Eyes that explode.

Daisy, Amanda, and Siobhan were in Playsteady Park sitting on a park bench. Siobhan said, "Look over there..." as she looked to her left. "It's the woman we saw leaving the Witchcraft store."

"She was with the old lady that got into the weird taxicab," Amanda added.

"Oh, yeah," said Daisy. "The cab made a strange noise—like a spaceship or something—and zoomed off down the street. Let's follow her."

The girls followed the woman into the woods. After five or ten minutes, the girls lost track of her. They hesitated on the path and walked a little further until they heard a scurrying sound in the underbrush.

"I thought she went this way," pointed Siobhan.

"No, this way," Amanda insisted turned in the opposite direction.

Daisy motioned for them to go in the direction Siobhan indicated. They went a good distance and realized they were off track and doubled back. A short distance down the path Daisy noticed an illumination over a hill some fifty yards off the path. Quietly and carefully the girls climbed the embankment. The smell of burning pine needles filled their nostrils. They crouched down and peered over the top of the hill.

A short distance away was a clearing and the woman was standing in front of a campfire. She raised her hands and stood like the letter Y silhouetted by the light. The woman began to chant, "In the mutant night; Under the moonlight; Scare the children off with fright."

Burning logs blazed, sap underneath the bark hissed and

crackled, then a soft wind corkscrewed sparks skyward.

Amanda whispered as her nails dug into Daisy's arm, "I'm scared."

"Shhh," Daisy answered even more quietly as she patted Amanda's hand so she'd loosen her grip. "We have to stay put. We can't leave until she leaves or falls asleep."

The woman continued but what she uttered was not easy to hear. The words sounded completely foreign or disjointed. She repeated them six or seven times. Then the woman turned around and looked in their direction. The girls saw her eyes were covered with small, raised white dots. The girls tried to stay motionless unsure whether their cover had been blown. Each crackle of the fire, or shadow moving across the woman's face made the scene scarier. The mysterious woman finally turned back to the fire and began to shovel dirt onto it.

The girls looked at each other as the embers cooled and let out a gasp of air. Soon everything was dark. They heard an occasional snap of a branch break under foot and then rested quietly on the ground for a minute or so.

"Think we should check?" Amanda asked. "She's probably gone. The fire is out."

After another minute, Siobhan said, "I think we're alone now. It sounded like she was casting a spell. Could you make it out?"

Daisy nodded yes and said, "What I heard was: Shoot tea dance shin. Shoot tea play shin."

"That's what I heard, too," Amanda replied.

"Witches are supposed to talk in verses," Siobhan added.

"They recite an ancient rhyme and turn their enemies into slimy lizards," Amanda laughed as she made bug eyes.

"Be very quiet," Daisy said as she inched toward the campsite. She inspected the area intensely poking the leaves with a stick, looking behind a few of the trees, and sniffing the cold ashes of the fire.

"What did you expect to find a caldron and a pile of poisoned apples?" Siobhan chuckled lightly.

"I don't know what I expected. You'll have to admit there is something very odd about that woman standing before a fire trying to conjure up evil powers."

Amanda pushed her hair from her face and said, "Maybe she's just a wino cursing the husband and kids she's abandoned. You know, like Timmy and his sister on Garden Road. Their mom is a big wino. You see her behind the liquor store every once in awhile."

Daisy nodded and looked at Siobhan. They knew Timmy's dad was related to Amanda. His mother was a bad alcoholic: when the kids were real young, she used to leave them all day so she could hang out at an apartment in a building filled with weird people in the poor section of town and get drunk. And who knows what else? The mother ended up running away without ever saying goodbye three years ago.

"I'm with Daisy," Siobhan exclaimed. "This woman, the frozen words.... They're all connected. Reminds me of the witch project I have to do for Ms. Barry. I looked up Shtriga. Shtriga is a witch from Albania."

Daisy answered, "Wonder if what the woman said was in Albanian...or some other foreign language? What was it?"

Siobhan replied, "Shoot tea dance shin. Shoot tea play shin...something like that, right?"

Daisy agreed and so did Amanda.

✺✺✺

The bus made a right turn onto West Street. After traveling a short distance, the sky darkened suddenly. Deborah felt like she was in a tunnel but the bus was driving on a major street through downtown. The interior lights went on as the passengers looked around curiously with a sense of uneasiness. FLASH—lightning lit the interior so brilliantly passengers could make out each other's skeletal structure. Deborah was looking at two men standing up while holding onto the hand-straps suspended from a chrome rod when the lightning flashed again.

She viewed their skulls in x-ray silhouette suspended in midair. BOOM—a crashing sound like a ten ton giant falling onto a wrestling mat located a mile directly above the bus. BOOM—again a few seconds later, rattling the windows, and shaking the seats and benches.

Everyone, even the driver, was taken aback. There had been no signs of rain, and the forecast was for a mostly sunny, warm day. The weather made no sense and panic filled the bus.

"My ears hurt," yelled a man near the front of the bus. The man turned to the driver and pleaded for him to stop.

As the bus pulled over to the curb, the driver announced, "I'm stopping to inspect the bus. You should stay on the bus but I can't keep you here. If you'd like to get out for a moment, I'll let you get back on. We weren't struck by lightning but that was too close for comfort." Then he added, "Everyone's okay, right?" without listening for a reply.

One by one the passengers left and mulled around on the sidewalk silently, almost speechless. Deborah was dazed: everything looked different. It was like she landed in a new world Each minute her memories faded and were replaced by morsels of a new world: what looked this way now was all she could remember. Nothing looked familiar and the past was gone. She didn't know another person on the bus. She thought she recognized the city but couldn't recall its name or why she was there.

Deborah thought, *So different...so much the same. I don't know where we are. Where are we? I don't remember how I got here. I'm on a city street but how did I get here? The bus, the street, buildings, and people look foreign. It's like we're not where we were any longer. I'm neither here nor there.....*

A woman who sat next to her on the bus tapped Deborah on the shoulder. "That scared me. How about you?"

"Uh...yes," Deborah answered more from instinct than responsively to the question.

"I'm Kellie. I've never seen you on this bus before. What's your name?"

Deborah searched her memory and did not find her own

name. *I'm...I'm....* She heard: *Who are you? Who? Who! Who? Who!* She looked across the street and saw a taxi with a billboard for Angelina Carlton, Realtor and she answered, "Angelina...my name is Angelina. Sorry, I am not myself today."

"After this bizarre episode on the bus...I feel out of sorts, too. I didn't expect the sky to fall today," Kellie laughed. "Angelina is a nice name. It kind of fits you. Don't you think names mean something?"

Angelina replied, "Why yes! My name tells you all you need to know about me."

"You must be a little angel," Kellie agreed.

The driver got back into the bus. One by one everyone else returned to where each sat before. The thunder storm seemed to have passed and the bus traveled along its regular route.

Angelina began to see things differently. Her memories of what had been faded into forgetfulness: like waking up in a dream within a dream. Angelina felt as though other people on the bus were staring at her like she was out of place and got off at the next stop. She walked down the street and noticed her reflection in a large window. Her image—which seemed to be looking at her for the first time—seemed to be looking back inquisitively and moving independently. She didn't recognize the shape of the person in the glass. Her reflection was giving her the once over. *I thought I looked different than this image? Is that me? It must be...I'm looking at me.*

She saw she was carrying a tubular canvas bag and unzipped it. *Oh, there's clothes in here...some money...a toothbrush, hairbrush, matches..... Are these mine? Guess so. Maybe not? Don't look like they'd fit me. They don't even look familiar. Where was I going? Where should I go? Where am I going?*

A man using a walking-stick stepped up to her and said, "You seem a little lost. Y-esss? Y-esss? Not from around here. Y-esss? Y-esss!"

"Why no...I mean yes...I mean I'm not from around here," Angelina replied.

Pointing his black walking stick to a street a short distance

away, he said, "The Church of St. Alfonso is down that street.
Y-esss. Y-esss. They have a soup kitchen. Y-esss. Y-esss. You threw
the bums a dime in your prime, didn't you? Y-esss? Y-esss? And
nobody ever taught you how to live out on the streets. Y-esss?
Y-esss? Now, you're going to have to get used to it. Y-esss! Y-esss!"

Angelina looked where he pointed and saw the street was
not too far. She looked back at him but he was gone. *I'm going
to have to get used to it. I'm out here on my own. I don't know where
I am but I feel like I've been here before.*

ooo

Angelina felt the sands of time shifting in her head. A dust
of the new world replaced thoughts and memories: like col-
liding galaxies forming a new cosmos. The dizzying sensation
made Angelina feel awkward and self-conscious. She walked
down random streets without concern for direction or destination for a long time. Her eyes were eventually drawn to a store's
sign: Witchcraft Heights Potions. Its appealing calligraphy and
the building's purple and gold exterior attracted Angelina to
cross the street and go inside.

Angelina opened the door and a chime rang. The sound was
mesmerizing and seemed to awaken memories buried inside
her mind. Then they were gone and eclipsed by newer memories. Angelina walked into the store with wide-eyed amazement.
The layout, the glass countertops, shelves lined with beautiful
bottles with hand-lettered white labels, the broad board wood-
en floor, and intriguing people mulling about made the ambi-
ance alluring.

"Welcome, may I assist you?" asked a red-haired woman.

"Oh," Angelina said surprisingly and turned away not
knowing what else to say.

She strolled around and tried to feel at home. A tune played
involuntarily in her head: *Oh demon alcohol...sad memories I can't
recall...who thought I would fall, a slave to demon alcohol?* Every
time someone looked at her she felt out of place. She felt a

piercing sensation that made her feel even more uncomfortable. The red-haired woman seemed to be listening into Angelina's thoughts and appeared to be aware of what was going on in her head.

The red-haired woman moved by Angelina without stopping and said, "You might wonder why you heard that particular song? Is there a meaning it is trying to relate to you?"

Angelina said out loud, "How did you know what I was thinking?"

A man wearing a plain black t-shirt standing further up the counter held a bottle up to purchase. The red-haired woman motioned for him to go to the cash register.

She got the man's attention and called out with a slight accent, "*Keys To The Future*. Good choice. I'll be right with you." As she walked by she said to Angelina, "A key to the future is a key to the past."

Angelina walked across the room and stopped near a roly-poly, old woman with a sympathetic face.

"Excuse me, Miss," the old woman asked Angelina.

"My old eyes can't focus on such small words. Would you be so kind and read this for me?"

"Why not," Angelina replied and took the bottle from the woman. Angelina held it up to the light and read, "Good Luck Potion Number 9." And, "The price tag says three dollars and seventy-five cents."

The old woman's bent over posture exaggerated her loosely upholstered frame. Angelina lowered herself to hand her the bottle at her level. Angelina tried not to stare too deeply at the woman because her makeup was applied very heavily to cover up what might be described as facial hair, or stubble.

"Just what I wanted. Aren't you a dear," the old woman said. "Now don't argue. Pick a second bottle of this. I am going to buy it for you. I insist." The woman pursed her lips as she selected coins from her change purse.

She got a little closer to Angelina and spoke in a normal tone but put her hand next to her mouth like she was whispering a secret, "Sometimes, we don't feel our freshest, dear. I was a young woman, too, and I had days like this. Oooo, whooo."

Angelina thought, *Guess I haven't bathed in a while. Do I really smell bad?* And she sniffed the air around herself to no avail after she handed the old woman a second bottle.

A fly or a moth flew serendipitously past the counter catching all their attentions. The old woman and Angelina followed it with their eyes for a good minute. Then the old woman opened one of the bottles she just paid for and dabbed a few squirts onto her finger tips. As she flicked several droplets in Angelina's direction, she spoke in a distinctive monotone that sounded like *mole-ay keh-kay* twice and smiled a grandmothery smile at Angelina.

"Mmmm...nice," Angelina feigned approvingly even though the dark liquid smelled like pine pitch and vodka.

The old woman tugged Angelina by the sleeve and moved toward the door.

Xhuljana said while looking at Angelina, "Perhaps, I could show your granddaughter something more contemporary?"

Angelina looked into Xhuljana's eyes and felt a tingle down her spine she could not explain.

"She's not my granddaughter...kind enough for you to say, Miss. Just a nice young lady helping a ninety-one year-old woman read the tiny words on the label." Then to Angelina, "Could you help me down the curb? I am not as steady on my feet as I used to be."

"Yes...yes, of course. I'll be happy to help you," Angelina replied. She was curious why the old woman's voice had an odd modulation that bordered on sounding masculine.

"Please, come back next time you're in this part of town," Xhuljana said with a concerned look on her face.

Outside on the sidewalk, the old woman locked arms with Angelina, "When I was your age, I came to this place from France." She repeated *France* with a heavy French accent. Then she uttered Politics, and repeated *politique* with a French accent. "*La vie politique!* I couldn't trust anyone. Oh, you have no idea, my dear. But I found the streets in the Leather District the most comforting. Perhaps you will, too. And this store is a gem! A virtual oasis in the desert we call Midway. How drab! How ordinary...in the most uninteresting ways.

"We must meet again! You are such a dear to help a weak, old lady such as myself. Do come back. I frequent this establishment often. Like I said, it is an oasis. We must take tea! Thank you for being here to help me."

They stepped down from the curb to the street. A moment later a black taxi drove up. It resembled an English taxi. The old woman reached across, opened the door, pirouetted around on her toes behind Angelina, and out of her view. Then she continued moving like a decrepit nonagenarian and sat down in the back seat with a thud.

"Here," the old woman said as she handed Angelina the bottle wrapped in a brown paper bag. "Remember, Dear, we owe it to ourselves to be our freshest. Ta-ta!"

The woman closed the door and the taxi drove away making a humming electric sound. The cab moved at a much quicker speed than Angelina thought taxis drove. *Things come and go so quickly here.*

O O O

Daisy, Siobhan, and Amanda saw an eighth-grader, Danny, standing near the Pizza Pad. He came over and said, "I got ninety-five cents. Wanna pool some money and split a slice or two?"

"I'm hungry," said Daisy. "I got a dollar, I think."

Siobhan added, "Let's go in and see how much money we got."

Amanda whispered to Daisy, "You like him, huh? Don'tcha?"

"Quit it," Daisy murmured under her breath while giving Amanda a shove.

They placed assorted coins and two dollar bills on the shiny counter. Butchie, the owner and chief dishwasher, eyed their collection and said, "You have enough for two slices and two small drinks." He swiped the money into his other hand below the lip of the counter.

Amanda picked up the two paper plates with the hot slices of pizza while Siobhan grabbed the two drinks.

"Can I have a bite?" Danny asked eyeing the melting cheese.

"Yup," said Amanda.

Siobhan teased, "Y-e-a-h."

Amanda jibed, "Daisy, why don't you share your piece with Daannnnyy," elongating how she spoke his name as if to taunt Daisy into embarrassment.

Daisy snapped back to Amanda, "You think he's cute. Ewww."

Danny enjoyed their drama and winked at Daisy.

Vincent walked at a quick pace; almost skipping. He looked at Ernest and said, "Ev'rything's beautiful at the ballet...Music! Dance!"

Ernest answered, "Yes, so fine at the ballet. The Grand Hall, the plush carpets, the beautiful scenery...and the dancers. And what about the new dancer. Oh, what's his name?"

Vincent looked sternly. "Ernest, you know as well as I it is Raul. Raul...Raul...Raul."

Up the street, two homeless women sat on the sidewalk leaning against the bricks of a building. Mary wore a grease stained brown winter coat. A paper coffee cup with a worn-out discolored rim was placed in front of a cardboard sign lettered in black crayon: *Why lie? We need a beer.*

"Hey, get a load of these two," said Mary to the other woman, who wore a heavy black coat. Mary mimicked someone with an unsteady gait; her right arm extended; the back of her hand facing upward with four fingers jackknifed downward; swayed a seasick motion. "Wearin' a tuxedo on a...Monday...no, it's Friday, right? Yeah, Friday. Oh, and the fat one has a walking stick, a cape, and a monocle. I'll get some bucks if my name isn't Mary. Watch this."

At fifteen yards the women heard the larger tuxedoed man cavorting and spinning on his toes oblivious to his surroundings.

"Ernest, I'm invigorated. Raul, the new dancer, is so...so.... How shall I put this? Yum. I am reminded of the first time we saw Nureyev. He told me I had the makings of a dancer and how we were simpatico. Simpatico. What a lovely man. Well, this Raul is another Nureyev and almost as large. Mmmmm."

The thin man added, "Who knows when you'll see him again? Ballet dancers live a life on the road. At least you watched him dance this evening."

"Oh, Ernest," the fat man chimed in. "As you might have guessed, I've invited Raul to our abode next Tuesday. Be a dear and bake one of your famous *Schartzwälder Kirschtorte*. I'm salivating just thinking about the layers of decadent chocolate."

"Excuse me, Sir," the woman said in a fake in English accent. "You gents enjoy a pull on a jug dontcha?"

Angelina thought, *What's going on with the accent? Mary doesn't have an accent, right?*

"Ouch," Angelina said as Mary elbowed her in the ribs. Angelina attempted to look encouraging.

Vincent turned, batted his eyes, and returned his gaze to the woman. "I'd love to contribute to your noble cause. Lord knows, libations are the noblest cause in my life."

The woman continued, "Do you fine gentlemen know what is the best *nation?*"

Ernest and Vincent looked at each other baffled.

She quickly added, "It's the *doe-nation*."

Ernest guffawed, "A do-na-tion... Vincent, pay the woman. That was worth the price of the show."

Vincent pulled a twenty dollar bill dripping of gin from his pocket and waved it slowly before the women allowing the intoxicating aroma to be consumed.

The women wearing the black winter coat, who sat with her head lowered during the exchange, perked up. Their eyes locked.

Ernest faced Vincent and mouthed, "Angelina...." He snatched the bill from Vincent and dropped it into the cup. As the other woman grabbed the cup and stared deeply into it,

Ernest pushed Angelina's head back down triggering a momentary slumber. Meanwhile, when the other woman lifted her face back up from the cup, her eyes were crossed, and a Cheshire cat grin formed on her lips.

"Lady, I'd get while the getting's good," Ernest said pointing down the relatively unoccupied street.

The woman rose clumsily, stuffed the paper cup with the twenty dollar bill into her coat pocket, and trotted away hastily.

Ernest looked sympathetically at the huddled women, "Poor dear. Your friend, Mary, took her twenty dollars and she vanished in thin air." He turned to Vincent, who was standing behind the woman and taking a sip from a silver flask, and winked, "What's your name, dear?"

With a tear in her eye, she sputtered out, "Angelina."

Vincent added, "An angel of the sidewalk...."

Ernest asked, "Angelina, are you hungry? I mean...half of the money was for you."

Angelina looked up innocently with the slightest nod.

Vincent held out his hand to assist her to her feet and said, "Just a short distance from here is a fantastic place for Italian Cuisine—la cuccina italiana," with an exaggerated Italian accent.

Ernest and Vincent walked either side of Angelina. Vincent rat-tat-tatted and rum-pum-pummed his silver tipped black walking-stick as they sashayed an *off to see the Wizard* stroll down the boulevard toward the busier main streets ahead of them.

The ruckus from up the street drew Daisy, Siobhan, Amanda and Danny from the pizza to the sidewalk out front. When they looked up, they saw a woman dressed in a black winter coat locked arm in arm with two men in tuxedos high-stepping through the front of the Pizza Pad, which was completely open to the rounded street corner with several small islands of chrome rimmed tables with black or white Formica tops.

Ernest, Angelina, and Vincent turned back to the rounded corner where three streets intersected, made a few steps back to the street, turned back, and stepped in unison into the Pizza Pad. The air was filled with the wonderful smell of baking dough, tomato and oregano, sizzling cheese, and crisping pepperoni, which overwhelmed Angelina into an exhaustive euphoria.

Officer Budalla and his lanky partner, Officer Mizor, sat inside the Pizza Pad at a table off to the side with their coffee and doughnuts. They snickered as the trio entered the Pizza Pad like a troupe from a Broadway musical. Vincent waved his open hand left to right several times, threw his head back, and struck a pose for the boys. Officer Budalla holding a chocolate doughnut with sprinkles offered a pinky salute from the brim of his policeman's hat.

Vincent announced to the room and the cook, "The best pizza around. Right, Butchie?"

"Yes, Vincent," Butchie replied. "What'll it be today?"

"My good man, this young lady has never sampled your gastronomic delicacies..."

Butchie interrupted, "How many pies?"

"Sixteen," Vincent snapped back.

Butchie began to toss the dough in the air, spread it out on a board, ladle the sauce, and sprinkle clumps of cheese into pizza after pizza, then slide them into the baking over. Instinctively, he filled a jumbo sized cup with Coca-Cola without ice and placed it on the counter.

Vincent grabbed it, held the cup over his head, turned his eyes skyward, and emptied the contents down his open mouth. A moment later, he let out a gigantic belch.

"Good baby," praised Ernest.

Butchie sliced up the first four pizzas and placed them onto the stainless steel counter. Ernest carried them two at a time to the table.

Ernest said, "You better test these."

Vincent lifted the cape from his shoulders and draped it over the back of the chair. He pulled two slices—a quarter of the pizza—and folded it like a "V". He ate bite after bite after bite after bite replete with gnawing and grunting sounds as a red and yellow ooze dripped from the corners of his mouth onto his rose-pink ruffled shirt.

Ernest raced over with a mound of paper napkins and padded Vincent's mouth and chin. "If you did the laundry, you wouldn't eat like that!"

"Ernie-poo," Vincent said with pursed lips. "This is dry cleaned. So, you don't either."

Ernest noticed Angelina on the verge of collapse. He removed a slice, put it on a paper plate, and cut out a small helping. He put the cut piece on a fork and brought it to Angelina. "Here try a bite, Angelina."

Her dry mouth stung and the hot cheese burned a little. But the food felt good.

Ernest said, "There you go Angelina. Now you know who your friends are and where you belong."

"Please, sir, I want some more," she said weakly.

"*Food! Glorious Food!*" belted out Vincent. "*Hot sausage and mustard!*" He pivoted on his left toe while tapping heel to toe with his right. "*While we're in the mood, Cold jelly and custard!*"

Ernest looked disapprovingly at Vincent, then laughed behind Angelina's back mouthing, "Food! Glorious Food!"

Daisy, Siobhan, Amanda, and another classmate, Danny, sat at a table on the other side sharing some French fries. Danny looked at Daisy and raised his eyebrows. Siobhan nudged Amanda, who laughed at the sight.

Angelina opened her mouth and Ernest put another small piece of pizza on her tongue. The infusion of warmth, taste, and nutrients brought a temporary sparkle to her eyes that radiated momentarily with Daisy.

"Why are you laughing and acting mean to that old woman? I get this weird feeling she's looking at me...but not with her eyes," Daisy said.

Danny put his arms on the table and leaned toward Daisy. He asked, "You sure? She looks like a wino. I thought I've seen her and another woman wearing a ratty, brown winter coat passing a bottle over near Playstead Park the other night. They were laughing the way winos do."

Amanda added, "Mama told me to stay away from people

like that. Some of them hurt little kids."

Ernest looked on from across the room. He strained to hear what the children were talking about but he couldn't quite decipher their words over the ambient noises. His worried look caught Vincent's' attention.

"You're missing the point," Daisy said. "What I'm feeling is beyond what's here at the Pizza Pad. It's like there's something else going on that I can't put my finger on."

Siobhan moved closer and said, "Shhh. They'll hear us."

Everyone in the Pizza Pad grew quiet, almost in expectation, as a hard tap-tap-tap preceded a mysterious voice that spoke each word slowly and distinctly through his teeth, "Y-esss. Y-esss? Hot pizza? Hot pizza! Y-esss? Y-esss!"

Then a tall, pasty skinned, slender man wearing a black tuxedo entered the Pizza Pad and made his way to the table where Ernest, Vincent, and Angelina sat. He took a seat without acknowledging anyone.

"Would you like a hot slice, Dr. Perp? I'm going up to the counter to retrieve more pizza in a minute. Help yourself." asked Ernest cautiously.

Vincent muttered, "Mmmm. Mmmm," between bites, motioning toward two slices on a silver-tone aluminum pizza plate in front of him.

Daisy leaned across the table toward Siobhan, "It's like a parade of party-goers at the Holiday Inn. Maybe there was a wedding?"

Amanda spoke up, "I heard one of them say he was at the ballet. Check out those shiny shoes on the guys. The winos probably weren't at the ballet."

A fire engine stopped right in front of the open entrance of the Pizza Pad. Officer Mizor waved to one of the firemen in the crew section, who returned a thumbs up. A moment later it continued back to the fire station.

"That's my brother-in-law, Ronald. He flunked the patrolman's exam three times but I got him a job at Firehouse Four," Mizor said to Budella.

Ernest made his next trip to the counter and picked up the last three pizzas. Danny's eyes followed an imaginary trail of aroma from the counter to the table where three tuxedoed men sat with the hobo in the black coat.

Vincent picked up a single slice of pizza and inserted it into his mouth up to the crust. He snapped his jaw shut, took a bunch of bites, and loudly gulped it down. Cheese and tomato sauce oozed from both corners of his mouth.

After wiping Vincent's chin, Ernest looked into the Rorschach soiled napkins and said, "A red and yellow badge of courage. Our kind will always be put down and misunderstood."

Six high school boys wearing black NFL jackets bearing the logo of the Oakland Raiders—an eye-patched football player with crossed pirate swords behind him—pointed and laughed through a mouthful of curse words.

One of the boys mocked them to his friends, "Gaysically, a bunch of homos. Wearin' a tux to the Pizza Pad. Who's here to impress? Richard Simmons?"

Ernest shot back, "You silly boys."

"Ernest, you have to learn to ignore children," Vincent scoffed while staring right at them. "They're...They're...so... immature. Throughout the ages, it never changes. Back in the Dark Ages.... What a splendid time! Remember? Oh, yes! Children worked all day to keep a meager plate of food on the table. You could trade a smoked ham bone for a child: That's all they are worth. Frankly, I always preferred to keep the ham bone."

Ernest added, "Like Truman Capote put it: *All children are morbid: it's their one saving grace.*"

Vincent interjected, "That reminds me...about the time I had a fling with Truman. Mmmm. A year or two later, I ran into him in Greenwich Village. Know what he told me? Mmmm? He told me he based his character Randolph, who spoke that line in Other Voices, Other Rooms, from the many personal tales I regaled him about the time I spent with Oscar Wilde."

Dr. Perp grinned. He spoke at a tempo slightly slower than most, practically pausing between each word as if he was being paid by the syllable, and kept a running total in his head. "Y-es-ss. Y-esss. Vincent, you're a total vamp. How bland history would have been had you not been there. Y-esss. Y-esss? Mortals might not repeat their mistakes. Y-esss? Y-esss."

Vincent batted his eyelashes. "I did bring old Oscar over to our side. It was...how should I say...it? Delightful."

Dr. Perp corrected, "Y-esss. But Xhuljana redeemed Oscar Wilde to her side. Xhuljana gave him the magic portrait that kept him from aging. Her painting inspired him to write A Portrait of Dorian Gray. Y-esss? Y-esss. Of course, we had to destroy the painting. Y-esss. Y-esss."

"Damn her," Ernest cried out. "She completely abuses her magical powers. Every time we make three steps forward, she sets us two steps back. It's just like situations like this... "

"What's worse," Vincent whined, "is I can't just turn them into rodents and sent them running across the floor. It always has to be a secret...no one else can see."

Dr. Perp paused a moment. Perhaps for effect or to regain the spotlight. "Y-esss? Y-esss. *Surely, goodness and mercy shall follow them all the days of their lives....*Unless we cross their path. Y-esss? Y-esss? Nothing to worry about. Y-esss. Y-esss. Humans are destined to forget the past. Y-esss? Y-esss!"

Ernest and Vincent looked at each other silently then smiled.

"Y-esss. Y-esss." Dr. Perp returned the smile and laughed a Boris Karloff laugh again, "Humans: ha-ha-ha. They are unable to see their own destiny. Y-esss. Y-esss!

"Last of your pizzas, boys" Butchie barked out as he laid the last five steaming pizzas onto the counter.

"About time!" Vincent answered. He turned to Ernest. "Hurry. Go get 'em while they're hot. Mmmm...hot pizza. What do you think, Angelina? Is this all I said it would be? And more?"

Dr. Perp took a hot slice of pizza on a paper plate from Ernest. He raised it slightly examining it this way and that. He slowly put the plate on the table and picked up the slice of pizza in two hands. He turned the pointed end toward his mouth and brought it into his mouth at the pace of a spacecraft docking at the International Space Station. Then he bit off a tiny bite. He chewed a postage stamp sized bit practically in slow-motion. While Vincent pounded down another whole pizza.

"How elegant, Dr. Perp," Ernest remarked.

"Y-esss? Y-esss? Hot pizza. Y-esss? Y-esss? How plebeian. Y-esss. Y-esss. But it is good. Hot, tasty pizza. Y-esss. Y-esss? Enjoy slowly. Slowly. Y-esss. Y-esss." Dr. Perp said before taking a second bite. "Y-esss. Y-esss? What direction are you going, boys? What direction are you going with the new recruit? Y-esss? Y-esss?"

Vincent removed something wrapped in a blood red satin cloth and lay it on the table. He picked up a steaming slice of pizza and said, *"Möle keqe."* As the stream rose, it formed a dark cloud above their heads casting a shadow on the table and insulating the four of them from being seen or heard by the others in the restaurant. Ernest flicked his fingers at Angelina and put her into a trance. Angelina stared blankly, almost motionless.

Vincent opened the cloth revealing a set of tarot cards. "I will perform a reading here and now to confirm our direction. I have done seventy-two readings already and it is clear, at least it is to me, what is in the cards. All of my readings reveal the same Outcome."

"Do your magic," Ernest insisted. "Our destiny is to help destiny by getting there first."

"Why should we wander blindly through time?" Vincent insisted. "After all, we are descended from nobility and were freed from the humdrum ways of common people centuries ago. Tarot is how nobility sees the invisible world of destiny."

Ernest spread his hands over the black Formica table. The cards began to swirl like colorful leaves caught in a whirlwind. He closed his hands into fists and the cards fell onto the table leaving a black spot in the center resembling an armature behind a camera lens. Ernest pointed to one card and it moved to the center of the clear spot.

Dr. Perp looked at Butchie, who now appeared to be a wolf standing on his hind legs wearing a white apron. He knew Butchie could not see him. "Y-esss. Y-esss. It is a shame we can't predict a time when we won't have to hide using our powers. Y-esss? Y-esss?"

Vincent concurred, "I hate it, too. We know we're gonna win...at least most of the time. But the strength of our powers lies in the fact that no one knows they're there. By the time they figure out we have powers and they don't, they've been rendered useless."

Then Ernest pointed to four other cards seemingly beckoning him to free them from their places in the swirl. The cards moved forming a north, south, east, west pattern. The three men hovered over the cards awestruck.

Vincent looked over at the group of teenage boys and concluded, "They appear to be rodents and chipmunks fighting over a piece of cheese, don't they?"

Dr. Perp saw the same thing. The group of boys could not see under the shadow of the cloud at the other table, or what was in store for them.

"Y-esss? Y-esss. The tarot cards tell us the destiny of the future. Now, we can plan to capture Daisy. And now, we will have the mother and the daughter on our side. Wickedness is such a wonderful thing. Y-esss? Y-esss."

Vincent added, "Part of our destiny is to glimpse the future through tarot cards and follow the path the cards have foreseen. It is one of the sources of our power."

Ernest said to Vincent, "We should follow what your tarot reading foresaw: The little girl will walk home through the park and this will present an opportunity for us to bring her over to our side. That way Xhuljana won't get the little girl for her own."

Vincent rubbed his palms together and added, "How keen of you to remember. The center card was the Wheel of Fortune, a card from the Major Arcana, number ten. It displays the word *Taro* in English and *Torah* in Hebrew. According to A.E. Waite, it symbolized a moment of change is upon us." He turned over the center card: The Wheel of Fortune. "Ah ha! It means we are at a significant moment of change. When I...er..we cast the spell on Deborah it led to the change into Angelina and the next change will be when Daisy is under our spell, too."

"Y-esss. Y-esss," Dr. Perp agreed. "Arthur Edward Waite of the Hermetic Order of the Golden Dawn[31] . How he and Alaister Crowley[32] feuded over the true images of the tarot cards.... That's when Alaister traveled to Mexico where he claimed to coin the magical word *Abrahadabra*[33] . Y-esss? Y-esss."

Ernest rubbed his hands together in anticipation. "Abra-ha-debra. *Touché.* Just because you spent time with Arthur Waite and Alaister Crowley, don't be such a name-dropper."

"Y-esss? Y-esss," Dr. Perp sneered. "The Troth deck[34] does not have the profound symbolism. Y-esss. Y-esss. The Waite deck[35] is vastly superior in its imagery. Y-esss! Y-esss!"

Vincent presented both of his open palms either side of his face mimicking Crowley. Vincent shook his head vehemently. "Those vain references to The Book of Troth are just revisionist history. You know Alaister took the new spelling of the word from me. He was always selfish.... in more ways than one, mmmm. Well, Abra-Ha-Deborah."

"Speaking of Deborah...Angelina," Ernest insisted. "Let's get back to the reading. I know what's next: it's the good part! It's...it's...it's.... Do tell. I do love two-fers."

"You're right. I'll get back to the reading. The first card. The one to the right of the center card, the past," and as he turned it over, "the Five of Cups. It pictures a figure dressed in a long black cape hiding his, *or her,* face to conceal shame or sadness. He, *or she,* is looking at three cups overturned and he, *or she,* has left the two standing cups behind. The standing cups represent

[31] A society dedicated to Magick and Science in London (1891-1915)
[32] Member of Golden Dawn in Switzerland (1898-1899)
[33] Crowley suggests in his writings on magick and science the H is for Horus and Hermetic Order of the Golden Dawn
[34] A tarot card deck based on The Book of Troth by Crowley (1944)
[35] The Rider-Waite-Smith tarot cards (1901)

what was left behind. The fallen cups represent Deborah, who I...who we sprayed with the Shtrega Serum, Deborah became Angelina, and Angelina is joining us *not* Xhuljana."

Dr. Perp moved closer to the table scraping his chair on the floor, though the noise was inaudible in the Pizza Pad. "Y-esss. Y-esss. Not Xhuljana. Y-esss. Y-esss! Over the centuries she's been a royal pain in my.... Y-esss. Y-esss. Angelina is joining us... not Xhuljana.... Y-esss. Y-esss."

"A pain in my patootie too, Dr. Perp," Ernest snickered. "I haven't kept score but we need this one."

Vincent continued, "The two standing cups signify getting rid of the father and bringing Daisy into our fold. Then we'll be up two, Ernest. Let Xhuljana top that!"

Vincent continued without looking at the card as he turned it over, "The second card, the present, was the Five of Pentacles. It pictures a poor couple in rags in the snow in front of a bright stained glass church window with five large gold discs; each disc inscribed with a black pentacle. The man is on crutches and the girl is bundling herself in her ratty shawl. It's the little girl and her poor father. Their world has crumbled all around them.... We did do an awfully good job, didn't we?"

Ernest and Dr. Perp shared a giggle.

Vincent moved his head and overturned the card to the left of the center. He smiled, "The Queen of Wands. Her Majesty sitting on a golden throne in a flowing golden gown with two lions at her side. A six foot royal wand in her right hand and a sunflower in her left. And at her feet a black cat: the quintessential sinister embodiment of magic and evil. The Queen knows what she wants and, in our case, what we want is a two-fer. That is, the mother and the daughter to join us. I can just see it.... Xhuljana will have an absolute fit of rage. How beautiful."

Dr. Perp brought his hand ever so slowly to the card on the top. "Y-esss. Y-esss. The vision of the mystery. Like Michel de Nostradame[36] used to call it: The vision of what cannot be seen. The vision of what cannot be seen. Y-esss! Y-esss!"

---

[36] a.k.a. Nostradamus

"Won't you be pleased, Dr. Perp. Just what we wanted... ooh," Ernest gushed with saliva gathering in his mouth.

Vincent stretched his right hand, palm up above the card, and the card turned face up: The eight of swords. The three men looked intensely at the image of a bound and blindfolded young girl wearing a red stained robe standing imprisoned by eight long swords on soggy ground with a view of a castle on a hill in the background.

Vincent explained, "The blindfolded girl is young and beautiful. So it isn't Deborah, who...let's face it...is not young. The blindfolded girl has to be the little girl, Daisy! But you see, the eighth sword is providing an opening for her to choose the right path. You could also see the blindfold is loose fitting and she can probably see her way forward. Ah, the blindness of youth!"

Dr. Perp struck his walking stick on the floor smartly. "Y-ess? Y-esss? The leetle girl will make an important decision; and she will make it soon! Y-esss. Y-esss."

"Lastly...the *pièce de réstistance*..... THE OUTCOME," Vincent announced to the table and flipped the center card with a flourish. His jaw dropped. Then he feigned regaining composure. "The Death Card." He started to laugh like Boris Karloff just as Dr. Perp has done.

Officer Mizor looked over but he actually heard nothing. When Ernest looked at him, he had the head of a Minotaur but he was still wearing his police cap and eating a doughnut.

"You know," Vincent boasted, "this can only mean the death of childhood for Daisy and the transformation into an evil witch: the pinnacle of sorcery. Another witch! Oh...another witch! Oh...one like me...like Ernest and me...one like Ernest and me and, of course, you, Dr. Perp."

Dr. Perp responded, "Y-esss? Y-esss? I have to agree with you, Vincent. Y-esss. Y-esss. The Outcome is the leetle girl will be one of us. Y-esss! Y-esss!"

Ernest noted, "Good reading, Vincent, as usual. I just never get tired of your tarot readings. It makes the future so...just so...

manageable. Imagine how the ordinary people have to wait for fate. How uninteresting! While we deal ourselves our destiny. It's like cheating at cards. Truly, the only way to win. Oh my, cheating at tarot cards; how rich!"

Vincent looked at the last two slices. He asked rhetorically, "Should I leave these for you, Dr, Perp?"

"Y-esss? Y-esss? I've had enough, Y-esss. Y-esss," Dr Perp said with a dismissive stare, "you might fade away, Vincent. You haven't eaten in a long time. Y-esss. Y-esss. Fade away before our eyes. Y-esss! Y-esss!"

"You're a barrel of laughs, Dr. Perp," Vincent replied. "It's my metabolism: I'm quick, quick, quick. And you're slower than molasses." He grabbed the two slices and practically inhaled them.

"Vincent," Ernest said on cue as the dark cloud disappeared. "It's time to leave."

Ernest said uncovering a hidden pizza, "Angelina, this last pizza is all for you. Enjoy it. We really must be going."

Angelina eyed the pizza like someone set adrift on the open ocean viewing land.

As Ernest and Vincent were leaving, they both looked over and seemed to stare at Daisy for a second.

Ernest, Vincent, and Dr. Perp walked along the route they expected Daisy and her friends to take to Playstead Park. Ernest insisted, "Come along, Vincent.... We can find a great place to ambush Daisy."

Vincent replied, "It is not good for digestion to be jostling about. We had time for a latte."

Dr. Perp swiped at a rock on the sidewalk with his cane and it careened off a parked car into the gutter. "Y-esss? Y-esss? Your internal clock is one gigantic feeding schedule. Y-esss. Y-esss."

O O O

Back in the apartment, Mr. Villanova sat on the couch reading haphazardly. His mind was a million miles away. In Daisy's room, there was a pile of dolls and teddy bears under the window. Owldoll opened her eyes, rolled down the pile of dolls, and became animated before her feet touched the floor.

"W-issh," Owldoll spoke out loud to the room. "A word in the night. A word in the night. W-issh."

She slipped her beak under the slightly opened window, squeezed through the space, stood out on the ledge a moment, and then flew off into the deep dark night. Owldoll flew over Playstead Park. Owldoll lit onto a branch of a tree with a keen view of the park on an artificial island in the middle of an artificial pond, and spied Daisy approaching at one entrance and Xhuljana at another.

Xhuljana spoke to the wind, "*Syt i dançin; Syt i plaçin.*"

Owldoll flew to Xhuljana and said, "W-issh. Daisy will be here soon. W-issh."

Xhuljana replied, "Speak to her and give her hope. The sadness of the curse on her mother weighs heavily on poor Daisy."

"W-issh," Owldoll answered. "You can even see the words I am thinking from far away: the light is always on in your mind. You can even see the words I am thinking from far away: the light is always on in your mind. W-issh."

Xhuljana motioned with her eyes and Owldoll took off. A moment later, Owldoll gently landed on a branch of a tree overlooking a patch of pink daisies.

"W-issh. I can see dangers hidden in the night but my words don't show their meaning until a light turns on in someone's mind. I can see dangers hidden in the night but my words don't show their meaning until a light turns on in someone's mind. W-issh." Owldoll waited on the limb for Daisy to arrive.

"W-issh. I hope a light will shine on my words in Daisy's mind. I hope a light will shine on my words in Daisy's mind. W-issh."

A spreading chestnut tree was right in front of Ernest, Vincent, and Dr. Perp deeper in the park. The path forked to either side of the tree. The tree cast a heavy shadow around its base.

"See," Ernest shouted. "Here is our spot. You had several

tarot readings that predicted Daisy could come to a fork in the road, and the Outcome was the eight of swords! The picture on the card shows a blindfolded girl imprisoned by eight long swords: She will be trapped by the path she chooses! Our path!"

Dr. Perp agreed, "Y-esss. Y-esss. Daisy will be imprisoned by our spell. Y-esss. Y-esss. She will be on our side. Y-esss? Y-esss."

The three of them reached the spreading chestnut tree with a rat-a-tat-tat counterpoint between Ernest and Dr. Perp's canes.

The five teenage boys from the Pizza Pad came out from the shadows. The Oakland Raiders emblem with the eye-patched pirate looked threateningly at the three men. Three of the boys brandished broken tree limbs, which they smacked into their open palms.

The tallest, and most muscular, boy standing in the center challenged them, "Break with the bucks. Don't play stupid. Or we'll bump you up, if you don't hand it over."

The shortest of the teenagers announced loudly, "Get a load of Beetlejuice with the sunglasses over there. Hey, Pops? Why the shades at night?"

The three boys with the branches hooped it up like marauding monkeys.

"Y-esss? Y-esss?" Dr. Perp contemplated. "Are *they* trying to rob *us*? Y-esss. Y-esss. How amusing. Y-esss? Y-esss!"

Ernest guffawed, "B...b...boys, stop it. You're killing us. You want to wave some sticks to try to scare us? Now, run along and go home. We have serious business to do."

The tallest one scowled and turned to the boy to his right. "Dogg, show 'em we mean business."

He looked at the tall boy and grinned.

"Sure," the tall boy replied. He moved closer to the three men.

Dr. Perp took out a silver cigarette case and flipped it open. Then he plucked out a black cigarette, placed it into the holder, and began smoking.

Another of the boys stammered, "H..h..he..he didn't light up...he didn't light up! This is way spooky. It was already lit."

"Y-esss? Y-esss!" Dr Perp teased. "Hope you don't mind if I smoke. Y-esss. Y-esss." He continued to smoke indifferent to the boys.

"Heed my warning. We have hidden powers," Vincent informed them.

Their leader mouthed off, "Ooo what's next? Magic and stuff?"

Ernest giggled, "How perceptive of you...."

"Knock it outta his mouth, Dogg," the tall boy commanded. "Don't he know smokin' ain't good for his health. Maybe that's why he ain't got no color in his skin?"

The boy took three steps as he swung back his right arm, and on the fourth step he swung the black tire iron squarely at the black cigarette. S-M-A-S-H ! ! The metal rod shattered into thousands of pieces and the end in his hand stung like from a high-voltage zap. He screamed out in pain, "Ahhh!!"

Dr. Perp's cold stare could be felt through the jet-black sunglasses. One of the boys dropped his stick to the ground with a soft thud in the grass. Another started to turn to run but felt the roots from the spreading chestnut tree entangle his feet. He couldn't speak. He looked at his friends with a frightened look on his face.

"Shouldn't have done that...uh, uh. You'll be sorry," cautioned Ernest. "You were oh so brave at the Pizza Pad. Now look at you."

Vincent pirouetted four times to a spot equidistant from Ernest, Dr. Perp, and the teenagers. He pointed his left hand at the tall boy and his right hand at the boy who tried to knock the cigarette out of the mouth of Dr. Perp.

"Magic and stuff!" Vincent barked back with a voice which took on a booming, amplified quality. He contorted into an elastic-man wrapping his arms around his neck three times and wiggling his fingers at the boy. He grumbled, *"Möle keqe."*

A dark cloud floated over the two teenagers then descended over them. When it rose, they had been transformed into black and red chipmunks with pointy red horns on their heads.

"They're vampires," another one sobbed. "You just turned Ron and Billy into chipmunks. We've seen Twilight. Vampires can turn into animals."

Ernest stood incredulously. "There are only witches: No vampires. No monsters. No superheros. You have the genuine article—like us. Or the so-called Good Witches—like Xhuljana."

The short one crouched by his friend, "Ron! What happened? Look-it here....there's two red horns on the top of your head! You look like a little devil."

The teenager got nervous; almost paralyzed.

The boy continued, "Talk to me, Ron. Talk to me."

Ernest shook his finger, "Almost ironic, don't you think?"

"Y-esss. Ironic in the sublimest sense. Y-esss? Y-esss?" Dr. Perp took relish in the thought. "Y-esss. Y-esss. Ironic in the sublimest sense, in deed. Y-esss? Y-esss."

Ernest turned back to Dr. Perp. "They always portray the devil with horns and a long barbed tail. Ooooo, scary. Vincent, the curse you chose just plays into their old-fashioned stereotypes. Chipmunks with little red horns: how derivative. Since the devil is in a whole other league from how humans have portrayed him, let it suffice to say there is a resemblance. He is the complete incorporation of everything evil and pathetic and hopeless and hateful. Those likenesses doesn't do him justice."

"Ernie," Vincent countered. "When was the last time you heard of someone being turned into a chipmunk with little red horns on its head? Pretty original, I'd say."

Ernest conceded, "You're right, Vincent. It is original. Bet it scared the bejeezus out of them."

Vincent squatted down with his hand mimicking holding a pistol, and made bang-bang gestures. One by one the other teenagers turned into brown mice with little red horns on their heads.

"Now, scat," screeched Ernest and the chipmunks and mice scurried off into the underbrush.

"Y-esss. Y-esss. Somewhat ironic. Y-esss? Y-esss." Dr. Perp wheezed like a deflating bagpipe. "Y-esss....! Y-esss...! The one they called Ron. What a larf: *Knock it out of his mouth.* What fools these mortals are being. Y-esss? Y-esss."

"Oh, you made a funny, Dr. Perp. But, really...." Ernest corrected, "Shakespeare wrote: *Lord, what fools these mortals be.* It's from A Midsummer Night's Dream. You remember him in Stratford-upon-Avon. Boy, could he drink."

Dr. Perp looked back seriously. "Y-esss? Y-esss? I remember Xhuljana convinced him not to listen to us. Y-esss. Y-esss."

Vincent shrugged, "Ah huh. And Shakespeare would not have been bothered by your misquote, Dr. Perp. He was always sauced. Xhuljana won him over even before we tried. She probably plied him with liquor. Remember? We were at some god-awful peasant pub drinking horribly rancid alcoholic beverages... cheap, disgusting...eeww. The stuff Shakespeare liked to drink was absolutely vile." Vincent made a contorted face. "That's where he came up with the lines for Julius Cæsar. Shakespeare jotted down those lines as he recited them out loud so all those drunken peasants would laugh at us. He made a dramatic look skyward then looked at us.

He then unto the ladder turns his back,
Looks in the clouds, scorning the base degrees
By which he did ascend.

Xhuljana and he had a big larf. Xhuljana knew we couldn't use our magic in public. And the whole pub was laughing at us. And our ambition to win Shakespeare over to our side. Who loves to drink more than us?"

Dr. Perp looked a little sullen. "Y-esss. Y-esss. Always chasing the big fish, Vincent. Y-esss? Y-esss?"

Ernest sprang to his defense, "Now stop that. You know as well as me all mortals are *not* created equally. Don't pretend you feel differently. You felt the sting of the defeat as much as Vincent or I did. Could you imagine if he had written for our cause? How would our names have been immortalized?"

Vincent announced, "He'd have written foldly of me.

Remember how he looked at me? Hmmm?"

Dr. Perp pointed his index finger up and put his other hand up under his nose to muffle his voice. "Y-esss. Y-esss. Daisy and her friends will be leaving the Pizza Pad soon. The leetle girl could be very close right now. Y-esss. Y-esss. To the shadows, boys. To the shadows, boys. Y-esss. Y-esss."

They moved silently into the shadows of the spreading chestnut tree and waited.

O O O

Daisy, Siobhan, Amanda, and Danny got up from their table at the Pizza Pad and walked around the corner to the tree-lined streets and neighborhoods where they lived. They turned on Elm Street and the city noises diminished more and more with each step.

Daisy looked back at the Pizza Pad and locked eyes with the woman in the dark coat. Daisy sensed a mystery, or an unanswered question, which intrigued her nonetheless. She walked looking backwards and eventually turned around to keep up with her friends.

"That was weird," said Danny. "You don't see a bunch of guys in tuxedos at the Pizza Pad like they just stumbled out of the Algonquin Club and needed a quick slice before their limo took them to their mansion in the 'burbs."

"Yeah," Amanda joked and pantomimed. "A bunch of dancing guys in tuxedos and the starving wino, who danced for her dinner with them."

Daisy appeared saddened by these comments and she looked tenderly at the woman in the worn out black coat again.

"It's okay, Daisy," Siobhan added. "No one was making fun of the woman over there. K?"

"When she looked into my eyes, I felt something," Daisy said staring into space as they walked a little further and reached the entrance to Playstead Park. "I'm gonna cut through the park to go home."

Amanda admitted, "Didn't say it to be mean. Sorry, Daisy."

Daisy, Danny, Siobhan, and Amanda reached the entrance to Playstead Park. Daisy veered off toward another path as she started into the park.

"I'm going this way," Daisy hollered back. "It's faster. I'll see yous tomorrow."

They waved to each other. Danny, Siobhan, and Amanda continued down the street and Daisy walked into the park. Several steps later, Daisy noticed a patch of wild flowers.

These are the daisies that I got your name from, she heard in her mother's voice. The wind rustled some leaves. Up on the limb of a tree sat an owl with very large and luminous purple eyes. The limb swayed slightly in the breeze.

Daisy said, "Owl? You have a very kind face. When I look in your eyes, there's a feeling inside...." Suddenly, she felt her mother was nearby and she cried out, "Mommy."

The owl stared back in way that was comforting to Daisy.

"You know, owl," Daisy admitted. "My mother is gone. I don't mean she *gone*...not gone-gone. It's like when you think about someone really, really hard. And it's like she's here. But I know she isn't. It is like I'm in a bad dream but I can't wake up."

"W-issh," the owl spoke. "Listen to your heart. Listen to your heart. W-issh."

Daisy responded, "I want to listen to my heart but everything is a giant mystery to me. There are missing pieces."

Owl stated, "W-issh. Part of your puzzle is because the words are frozen. Part of your puzzle is because the words are frozen. W-issh."

"We're going from one mystery to another," Daisy suggested and she heard a flutter above her.

"W-issh. You're beginning a mystery. You're beginning a mystery. W-issh," came from over Daisy's head but not from where the owl had been a moment earlier.

"A mystery? What do you mean: a mystery?" Daisy asked to the darkness.

"W-issh," said the owl looking at Daisy from a limb on a tree on the other side of the path. "The mystery you find is the mystery that's chosen you. The mystery you find is the mystery that's chosen you. W-issh."

Daisy stood for a moment then asked, "The mystery of finding my mother? Or the mystery of finding the wino who looked at me?"

"W-issh. The mystery you find is the mystery that's chosen you. The mystery you find is the mystery that's chosen you. W-issh." The owl spread its wings and folded them again, "W-issh. The mystery is a puzzle. The mystery is a puzzle. W-issh."

The owl suddenly flew off. Then Daisy heard footsteps behind her. She saw the silhouette of a tall, slender woman, The woman wore a long coat and her fiery red hair hung past her shoulders.

"Oh, excuse me," the woman said when she saw Daisy in front of her. "Didn't mean to startle you. I usually don't see many people in the park at this hour."

"Me neither," answered Daisy. "Did you see the owl that just flew off?"

"Why, no. Owls are fascinating creatures, don't you think?" the woman asked. "I must have been off in my own world. Sometime, you don't see what's right in front of you."

"You're right," Daisy agreed. She thought, *Sometime, you don't see what's right in front of you.* "Because for us kids, almost everything is a mystery."

The woman had a kind smile. She asked Daisy, "Don't you feel like the mysteries we find are mysteries that have chosen us?"

Daisy gasped, "You're not gonna believe it.... I just had that thought a couple of minutes ago."

The woman laughed a little. "Just like I said: The mysteries we find are the mysteries that have chosen us. I guess it was a good thing we ran into each other tonight."

They walked along together for while each in their own

separate space. When they came to a fork in the path, the woman went one way and Daisy went the other.

"Good night, little girl," the woman said pleasantly.

"Good night," Daisy replied. She waved to the woman and continued on her way home.

When Daisy and the woman were well out of view, the three men stepped out of the shadows.

"Well, Miss Goody Two-shoes ruined another one for us," Ernest snarled.

Dr. Perp agreed, "Y-esss. Y-esss. No point in confronting Xhuljana in front of the leetle girl. Y-esss? Y-esss."

"Should have listened to me," Vincent protested while stomping his feet. "Xhuljana would have backed down. It is as much a disadvantage for her to reveal herself as it is would be for us."

A heavy flutter passed overhead and the wind bent the branches of the spreading chestnut tree. "Y-esss? Y-esss?" Dr. Perp questioned. "There will be another time. Y-esss. Y-esss."

Vincent concluded, "Let's go back to our lair. Ernest will make fettuccine Alfredo with buttermilk, butter, and cream. Yum. Dr. Perp is correct...as usual. I'm left positively famished by this giant disappointment."

O O O

Daisy said, "Owldoll, I guess what you're trying to tell me is important. It must be. And I know you're trying to help me find my mom. Why can't you talk *normal?* But why do you talk weird? Why do you always say wwwwiiiisssshhhhh?" Daisy mimicked Owldoll bobbing her head to attempt to make herself sound authentic.

Owldoll replied, "W-issh. You promised me this. You promised me this. W-issh."

Daisy plead, "I know I promised. And I know my word is my bond. It is that important. Got it! It would be way easier if you'd just come out and say it. Please, just tell me...."

"W-issh. But the words I choose are important for you to hear. But the words I choose are important for you to hear. W-issh."

Daisy said, "Owldoll, I'm sure each word is important. Words can have more than one meaning.... I get it, ya know. But why does everything sound so confusing?"

Owldoll replied, "W-issh. I can only say what I can say. I can only say what I can say. W-issh."

Daisy plead, "Come on...Come on. You could tell me, if you wanted to...You're as free as a bird." She looked into Owldoll's oversized purple eyes hoping to coax the words out.

"W-issh. But the words I choose are important for you to hear. But the words I choose are important for you to hear. W-issh." Owldoll paused. "W-issh. You'll understand the answer to your question when the time is right. You'll understand the answer to your question when the time is right. W-issh."

Daisy grumbled, "Shoulda known...it's always you'll understand when you're older. Adults never think kids know anything."

Owldoll looked deeply into Daisy's eyes. "W-issh. You will understand when the time is right. You will understand when the time is right. W-issh."

Daisy answered, "Oh, Owldoll...I'm upset 'cause I don't understand the things that have gone on in my life: Mommy just up and went off like she was swept away helter-skelter—trapped by the winds of war—caught up in an undertow. *Kay?* Mom wouldn't leave me...she wouldn't deceive me. My mom didn't just disappear! She's gone...but she's not gone-gone."

O O O

The flea market was already awake beneath a pre-dawn Pepto-Bismol, grape soda swirled sky. From a distance, the structure resembled the two eyes and outline of a crocodilian creature protruding from a cratered concrete cay waiting for its prey. This football field-sized aluminum and tin behemoth sprawled along a wooden wall of mismatched scraps of railroad ties and lumber. Its structure looked like two halves of an enormous corrugated metal pipe whose rust-colored paint was splotchy and faded. A dented fifty-nine International Harvester Pickup approached the Midway Flea Market with canary yellow headlights ricocheting off the potholes of the parking lot and pulled up to the illuminated merchants' entrance like an Egyptian plover ready to feed from an alligator's open mouth.

"Johnny, where you been? Missed you last week," asked Ralphy, the Clock Guy. "Got a load of Batman clocks made outta old vinyl LP records[37] cut to look like the bat symbol[38] . They're makin' a come back, I'm tellin' you. We'll make a killing. You better talk to me later."

"I was outta town, Ralphy. Went to an estate sale up country. I'll get back to you about those Bat Clocks real soon," replied Johnny coming around the front of the pick-up. He took a long, hard look at a platinum blonde standing with the other flea market dealers under the electric light by the door. Her parabolic features were outlined by her skin-tight, electric blue, mid-thigh length, knit dress. "Lucy. I missed those million-dollar tits. Glad I came back."

Lucy laughed and spoke with her Ukrainian accent, "Joeknee. You really knows how to dreet da ladies."

"Ralphy, How many in a box? Dozen clocks? Gimme a box. I'll see what I can do," barked a short, muscular, man with buzz cut salt and pepper hair.

Ralphy thought about it a moment and replied, "Sure thing, Mac." He took an open cardboard box from a dolly of items he was going to wheel into the flea market and handed it to Mac.

"Hey, 'nuff small talk, got some business to attend to," Mac stated and turned to Johnny. "Mr. Funk, you wanna make a quick C-Note? I met these guys—I am using the term *guys* loosely—and they want to hire a chauffeur this afternoon for a couple

---

[37] LP for Long Play analog sound storage system on 10" or 12" typically black polyvinyl chloride discs.

[38] Batman was summoned by a large searchlight with a silhouetted bat symbol blacked out in its center.

a three hours. You in?"

Johnny did a double-take. "You serious, Mac?"

Mac replied by pointing to a Rolls Royce parked nearby.

Johnny ogled the prestigious vehicle and rubbed his chin. "Let me see....Johnny Funk as a chauffeur. Baby, I can drive their car. Their car..? A vintage Rolls Royce Silver Shadow. What a sweet ride! A C-Note? Two o'clock...Drive their car... three hours.... Their car...CASH...a crisp Benjamin...a C-Note[39] in CASH...." He snapped his fingers on the first and third beat in four-four time and broke into his Mr. Funk song voice, "*If you wanna go and take a ride wit me / We three wheelin' in the Four with the gold D's / Oh why do I live this way?*"[40]

Lucy and Ralphy chimed in the chorus as Johnny's finger snapping continued, "*Hey! Must be the money!*"

Johnny began the next line, "*If you wanna go and get....*"

"Can the midnight choir!" Mac interrupted loudly silencing them immediately. "Hey Johnny, you want me to ask someone else, or what?"

"Done, Boss." Johnny turned to Mac and bowed, "Johnny Funk, Flea Market Chauffeur, at your service."

"Okay," Mac held out something dark in his hand, "They want you to wear this here chauffeur's cap; these here sunglasses; and drive this here Rolls Royce to the Church of Spirituality at two o'clock. They'll tell you the rest when you pick them up." Mac handed him the black chauffeur's cap with a black vinyl bill and double dark wrap-around sunglasses like those worn by Kato[41] from the Green Hornet.

"How'll I know these guys?" Johnny asked Mac as he donned the cap and sunglasses.

"You'll know 'em when you see 'em," Mac said with a half smile. "There are three of 'em. A fat one who don't stop talkin': he goes on and on and blah, blah, blah. He'd talk a dog off a

---

[39] C equal 100 in Roman numerals; Benjamin Franklin appears on the face of a hundred dollar bill.

[40] "Ride Wit Me" by Nelly (2010).

[41] Comic book character portrayed on television by Bruce Lee, martial arts icon, in "The Green Hornet" (1966-1967).

meat wagon. And there's a thin one. He don't talk that much. He follows the fat one like a puppy. And then a tall, thin one who stands about six foot four, his skin is the color of plaster, he uses a walking stick, and wears sunglasses day or night. He seems to be the guy in charge and he talks...," Mac began to say one word at a time with a pause between them, "like...this.... It...takes...him...for...ever...to say...any...thing." He took a deep breath. "You can't miss 'em. And they got money to spend."

Ralphy chimed in, "They just happened to be coming along at the right time, ay Mac? Remember: a fool and his money is soon parted.... "

Mac was examining one of Ralphy's Batman clocks and snapped it in two in a fit of laughter. "Haw, haw, haw...that just caught me right, Ralphy. The rhyme goes like this:

> *A fool and his money,*
> *Be soon at debate:*
> *Which after with sorrow,*
> *Repents him too late.*"[42]

"Awl-wayz dee in-dee-lek-too-awl, ain't you, Mac?" Lucy added.

Mac said, "I remember learning that rhyme from me mother."

Johnny surveyed the lot, looked at the black and silver Rolls Royce, and confirmed, "Mac, toss me the keys. Gonna run a few errands first 'n' check this limo out."

Mac fished through his pockets for the keys and said, "Johnny, go to the Church of Spirituality. Be there right at two o'clock sharp. These guys are a little funny, if you catch my drift." Mac rolled his eyes as he dangled the key chain above his head. "So be there on time! Not ten minutes early. Not ten minutes late... be there at two o'clock sharp!"

He moved close and confidentially spoke into Johnny's ear, "Sounded like there's a bonus in there, too. And if they do, you

---

[42] Thomas Tusser, 1573

cut me in for thirty percent, *capisce*[43] ?

"Johnny, I wanna teach you 'bout the business: Didja see what I did with the Bat-Clocks? That's the secret: Never pay nothin'! Never pay nothin'! Next time, I'll trade a box of some *chazirai*[44] I paid nothin' for to Ralphy for more cases of Bat-Clocks!"

Johnny shot him a look. "Mac, you're the king of the flea market. You'll get your cut."

Mac continued, "These guys burn through money like it's going out of style. They bought these here sunglasses and a chauffeur's cap." Mac laughed a belly laugh, "And they paid retail...they paid retail at the Midway Flea Market!"

"That's gotta be the first time...ever," Ralphy laughed along with him. "Well, sometimes you get a tourist who gets intimidated by our squalid conditions, pays the asking price, and just wants to get out of Dodge."

Mac, Johnny, Lucy, and Ralphy had a big laugh together.

Mac tossed the keys to Johnny. "Remember: two o'clock sharp."

Johnny took the keys: a copper skeleton key encrusted with acne-shaped growths that felt sharp to the touch. The key chain looked like a large, cherry red lozenge with a silver pentacle etched in its center and black metal ring for the key.

Lucy smiled, "Joe-knee, you takes me for a ride? You has all dee morning before you goes to dee work, no? You say yo-kay, Joe-knee? Yes?"

Johnny answered, "Baby, let's take this hot rod out for a spin," then Johnny, always the gentleman, opened what he assumed to be the passenger door for Lucy.

"Joe-knee, look see here. Dee steering wheel ees here." She reached in and tapped the steering wheel with her hand a few times.

Johnny opened his eyes wide, "It is an English model with a right-hand drive. Well, blow me down!"

[43] (Italian/Sicilian) Do you understand?

[44] (Yiddish) junk. (Yiddish כאַזעֶר, from Heb. חזיר "chazir," pig) Pronounced with guttural "Ch" like Chanukah.

Lucy screamed, "Joe-knee!"

"Lucy!" he reacted. "It is an old English expression."

"Oh...oh. Dare weel be dime for dat later," she uttered as she sashayed to the other side of the car and climbed in.

Once inside, he didn't notice a place for the ignition key. As he kept looking, the Roll Royce started up with the vibration of an electric buzz. He didn't recall touching the accelerator, though he recalled thinking it looked more like a plank, and he didn't see a brake pedal. The car shifted itself into drive, sprang forward with what looked like head-jerking acceleration, but movement was virtually undetectable. The limo spun around in a tight circle spraying out dirt and gravel pinging off the building and other cars in its trajectory.

Johnny enjoyed the oscillations of her double-E's as they matched the Silver Shadow's bouncing path across the uneven parking lot, and slow-motion dip when the tires met the pavement of the road in a screechless arc as they banked off to the left. He held onto the steering wheel for balance and realized he wasn't steering the car; not really. He'd turn the wheel habitually but the car went where it wanted to go.

Lucy arched her back while she pushed her shoulders into the Burgundy red leather seat and purred as she parted her lips, "Oooo Joe-knee. Me likes dees."

O O O

Vincent, Ernest, and Dr. Perp stood in front of the Church of Spirituality: a black building with its three knurled black spires tapering to antennae-like ends flexing to the heavens divining the exact time and place listed in an encyclopedic ephemeris marking planetary positions for the births of the next three preordained future mystics, and safeguarding the secrets of spirituality behind a heavy black metal door outlined in barbed wire.

Ernest asked Dr. Perp, "What time did you tell the chauffeur to meet us here?"

Vincent interrupted, "I was the one who told him. And I implored the rugged hunk of a man at the flea market to have the chauffeur here at two o'clock sharp—not ten minutes early—not ten minutes late! Although, the Silver Shadow will assure his punctuality. Hmmmm."

"What about Xhuljana, Dr. Perp? What can we do?" Ernest asked anxiously. "I'm so nervous."

Their attention was drawn up the street to a silver and black Rolls Royce approaching at breakneck speed with an electric hum trailing it by a second or two. The car came to an abrupt halt right in front of the three men almost purring with barely perceptible inhalation and exhalation.

"You know the Silver Shadow prides itself for having on-time arrivals. You'd think it alters the forces of nature...," Vincent chuckled.

The driver's door opened on the sidewalk side and Johnny sprang out. He was wearing the chauffeur's cap and dark wrap-around glasses from the flea market, his curly gray hair spilling outside of the sweatband of the cap. Johnny stood silently in ripped dungarees, an orange plaid shirt, and a Boston Red Sox jacket from the 1940s.

Ernest stepped forward slightly, "You must be the chauffeur the fine man, Mac—yes, he is a fine man—Mac from the Flea Market told us about. I'm Ernest. You look so...so...I don't know...so *chaufeury*. This is Vincent and this is Dr. Perp. And you're right on time. Punctuality is so...so important. Don't you think?"

Johnny examined the three men disputatiously while almost dazed. "I'm Joh...Johnny...Johnny Funk...at your...service."

Vincent whispered audibly to Ernest and Dr. Perp, "Oh, he'll do." He turned to face Johnny with a counterfeit smile. "Pleased to meet you. My name is Vincent. I'm a man of wealth and taste. So tell me, how do you like our Rolls Royce? Nice ride, huh."

Johnny opened the rear door for Ernest but felt miffed by the condescending remarks. He then challenged the big man,

"Why are you wearing that Army surplus, black muumuu, bivouac outfit?"

"Y-esss? Y-esss?" Dr. Perp spoke in his unhurried, elongated style, "Did this insolent chauffeur really say his name is Johnny *F u n k*? Y-esss? Y-esss?"

"The name is Funk.... Deal with it!" Johnny snapped back.

"Don't be an old fuddy-duddy Perpy, old man. This is amazing. He is obviously an unrefined commoner. Let me illustrate—dare I say, educate a heathen." He turned to Mr. Funk. "My good man. This is an authentic ceremonial robe from the Shang Dynasty[45] . The purpose of these billowing...billowing... billowing sleeves...." Vincent flapped his arms catching the breeze into the cone shaped cuffs that opened up large enough to engulf a toaster oven. "Because, Mr. Funk, they were made for the transportation of the regal dogs of the Shang Court."

Following suite at a snail's pace, Dr. Perp complained, "Y-esss? Y-esss? Why do you boys always insist on a driver? The Rolls Royce drives itself impeccably without any outside interference. Y-esss! Y-esss!"

Vincent reached into his sleeve and produced a red lacquered box with jeweled and gilded trim. He removed a satchel hung around his neck from inside the robe that held a golden key, which he inserted into the lock. The top lifted off the base and revealed a small brown-black dog with a scrunched-up face, two milky-white, disc-shaped, glazed eyes, and a panting grayish, orangery tongue with black spots outlined by broken teeth.

"The pug was bred for royalty. They are extremely, extremely intelligent...*trés intelligente*. And they were bred small, so they'd be out of the way and only make little...teeny, tiny poops." He laughed like a schoolgirl.

"Nice Gup. Nice Gup," Ernest cooed as he moved close to the dog's face. As he got closer, his face contorted, "Ewwww, baby. Vincent, a mint for Gup. Please...quickly!"

Vincent took a peppermint patty from a pocket, unwrapped it, put it between his own teeth, and brought it up to Gup.

---

[45] 1766-1122 BCE

"Grrrr....ruff...ruff," uttered Gup as he bit at the strong peppermint smell wafting by.

Vincent turned his head from side to side in a game of hide and seek. Finally, he let Gup take the patty, save a corner lodged behind his teeth.

Ernest said to Mr. Funk, "Poor Gup. He's blind. It's another reason we have to carry him."

Vincent quickly added, "But he reads Braille. See....," He took out a small book. Its cover was hand-painted in a childlike style of watercolor flowers and cameos of coiffed women with gray-green skin and long noses looking slightly to one side. Vincent turned the stiff cover and began dragging the dog's front paw along the raised characters. He used a Brooklynese accent for affect, "My name is Gup. Just like Dog spelled backwards is God; Pug spelled backwards is Gup. I come from a long line of royalty dating back to the Shang Dynasty. I have a refined pallet: I never eat dog food—Don'tcha try to feed me plebeian swill or I'll immobilize ya! Only feed me filet mignon, jumbo shrimp, or rack of lamb trimmed from the bone with a silver knife. That's all I'll eat! Unless you has Italian pastry. See?"

Ernest continued, "So you see, Gup is a special member of our family."

Vincent made a coquettish woof-woof while dragging the dog's paw over the bottom of the page, and closes the cover with the topside of a rear paw.

"Y-esss! Y-esss!" Dr. Perp spoke impatiently as he tapped his foot on the sidewalk. "Gup learned about food from Vincent. And years of Italian pastry have reduced Gup's incisors and canine teeth to fractured stumps. Shall we depart? Y-esss? Y-esss."

Johnny Funk, Flea Market Chauffeur, opened the rear door. "Your chariot awaits."

Vincent announced, "How regal! Mr. Funk, you are a picture of perfection for our soirée. What's a limo without a chauffeur? Hmmmm? After me...."

Vincent entered first and the car swayed like a waterbed. Ernest and Dr. Perp followed. Johnny closed the heavy lead-lined door with a thud.

Once inside the Rolls Royce, they saw Lucy in the front passenger seat and she acknowledged them with a friendly smile. Lucy batted her eyelashes, beamed her décolleté proudly, and waved at the three men who ho-hummed the gesture.

Lucy spoke with her heavy accent, "Hallo. You see, I iz Joe-knees friend, jes. It dis yo-kay for me to bees wid Joe-knee, no? Goot. Zo nice an meets yous fancy gentlemans."

Dr. Perp cupped the heel of his walking stick and shifted it in her direction. "Y-esss? Y-esss? Are we in Olde SoHo for a stage show with the buxom sidekick? Y-esss? Y-esss!"

Vincent rested his chin in his palms and uttered, "Meow, meow, meow, meow. Meow, meow, meow, meeeeowww," as if it made perfect sense.

Lucy laughed, "Oooo, Joe-knee. He makes the pussycat noises."

Johnny spoke loudly toward Lucy, "It's the jealousy of a pussycat poser. Oh, pussycat...up yours!"

Ernest interjected to Vincent and Dr. Perp, "It is quite alright. We can just close the partition window and we'll have total privacy."

"Yes, Mr. Funk," Vincent chimed in with an overstated wink. "We don't mind if you brought along your little friend."

Johnny reached along the seat and squeezed Lucy's ass. "The pleasure is all mine, I'm sure. The pleasure is all mine."

The glass window rose from between the driver's seat and the passenger's compartment as Lucy joyously giggled.

Ernest agreed, "The chauffeur just gives the scene that certain *je ne sais quoi*. Oh yes, he does! *Trés, trés, trés élégant!* And the blonde with the big nay-nays and conspicuous hey-nani-nani.... Absolutely perfect."

The Silver Shadow drove away from the curb on its own accord. Buildings, pedestrians, lamp posts, and trees were moving by faster and faster as the solid Rolls Royce made an electric noise like something from *Star Wars*[46] with a cushioned ride which felt almost like sitting on a stationary sofa.

Johnny saw the space of the front passenger compartment bend independently like a sheet of rubber being twisted in Gaussian lens formula[47] variations. He and Lucy would practically be knee to knee one moment then without shifting positions be sitting back to back the next moment. The windshield would warp like a Möbius strip[48] displaying an outside view swirling by upside up changing to upside down and pop back as if nothing had happened.

"Ooooo, Joe-knee," Lucy uttered. "Me worried. Iz you? Iz like Morozov[49] story where the world is all make-ed upside down."

As the passenger compartment sank half a foot, the long hood with the silver nymph over the grill flexed toward them revealing a view of the cloudy sky from above the treetops. The seat lurched and they were drawn closer to the dashboard, which became reptilian in texture and formed two indented cones with lavish details of her cleavage, areola, and nipples.

Johnny gasped, "Lucy, this ain't your Uncle Vanya's[50] Oldsmobile[51] . I'm not driving this car! Look!" He spun the wheel like a barker at an amusement park concession. "Step right up. Step right up. Nothing to win. Nothing to lose."

A moment later, the passenger compartment flexed back to normal. As they were racing down a main thoroughfare, a bicycle messenger darted out in front of them. Mr. Funk attempted to slam on the brakes but he felt no pedal. Miraculously there was no collision: the car seemed to go airborne over the

[46] A series of classic science fiction outer space movies with state-of-the-art visual effects by George Lucas beginning in 1977.
[47] Carl F.Gauss, Mathematician (1777-1855). Gaussian Optics influenced development of Topology, also known as rubber-sheet geometry.
[48] A surface with only one continuous side and only one continuous boundary.
[49] In Space by Nikolay Morozov (1913)
[50] Play of words on the play by Anton Chekov, Uncle Vanya about a professor and his young wife.
[51] American brand of automobile (1897-2004).

cyclist. He looked at the floorboard and only saw the enormous accelerator.

Lucy dug her long, blood-red, raptor nails into Johnny's left arm. "Joe-knee!! You run-ed over di by-zicle boy. Oh, *beh-o-zheh-yeh moh-ooo*[52] . For sure, he iz dead, no? Oooh. Oooh. Zis iz terrible."

"Hey! You're gonna draw blood, Lucy. Let up already! We didn't hit nobody. We flew over him," Mr. Funk shouted and he turned to the closed window behind his head. He hit it several times with an open palm. "We got no brakes! All for a lousy C-Note and I'm trapped in this misguided Munstermobile[53] ."

He looked in vain for a switch to open the window. Then he tried to bring the car to the breakdown lane: he turned the wheel to no avail. Nothing. The car was unresponsive. He yelled again, "Is this for real?" His eyes were drawn to the instrument panel and noticed there was only a speedometer the size of a dinner plate. The needle's vermillion center kept darkening as the needle rose: seventy, eighty, ninety, one-hundred. He looked right as trees in a field of yellow shoots and brown cattails zipped by. The needle pegged at one-hundred twenty miles per hour in a solid Chinese red and the limo continued to go faster.

Lucy's mind was in a blur. She breathed heavily as the white lines raced toward her recalling snowflakes falling into formation in the intensely bright, top mounted xenon light bars and xenon headlights of GAZ Tigr[54] driving through Prislop Pass in the Carpathian mountains protecting the natural pas pipeline as she snuggled up close to Major Dmitri Khayapa of the Ukrainian Army. She had hopes for Dmitri, the son of a Russian general, but it was not to be. Dmitri went to work for

---

[52] (Ukrainian) *Боже мой* God; Good God in heaven.

[53] "The Munsters"- a sitcom (1964-1966) depicting the life of a family of classic horror film monsters like Frankenstein (the father) and Count Dracula (the uncle), who had a souped-up hearse for a family car (the Munstermobile).

[54] GAZ-2975 or GAZ-3937 "the Tiger" - Russian light armored troop transport truck.

Laboratory 12[55] and she left for a new life in Midway.

The Rolls Royce was approaching a slow-moving brown sedan in the passing lane. Instinctively, the Silver Shadow flicked its high beams at longer and longer intervals as the distance grew closer. The Rolls swerved at the last moment but the tires didn't squeal. "I may as well be watching TV," Johnny barked out loud as if someone else was listening to him. "I saw the car swerve; make hard turns at a buck thirty. I felt nothing... just waiting for the car to flip over. Yeah, flip over and over and over again. I got nothin': No motion; No sound; Or being thrown from one side then to the other. My guts tightened up. I got nothin'. It was like watching a video game. After a while, my muscles were lulled into serene relaxation. I coulda slept through it."

Back in the vast passenger area, Ernest announced, "Time for pie!"

Vincent sat up and looked eagerly at Ernest, who was getting something from the floor.

Ernest guffawed as he lifted the domed cover off a lead crystal pie plate, "Here, have a piece of this ricotta pie I made. It's a recipe from when we lived in Naples in the fourteenth century. Truly a wonderful time for witches and for pastry."

Dr. Perp sat up straight bumping his head on the headliner of the Rolls Royce. "Y-esss? Y-esss. Xhuljana appears to be helping Daisy purely out of the goodness of her heart. Thus she is not violating the Witch's Solemn Secret. Or would she? Y-esss? Y-esss?" He adjusted his sunglasses carefully then mimicked a laugh from a horror movie. "Y-e-e-h-h-s-s-s! Y-e-e-h-h-s-s-s! Or would she? Y-esss? Y-esss?"

Vincent chided, "Oh, do you think mocking our situation really helps? We're about to lose another one to her and that's the best you can do?"

Ernest snarled, "No! No! No! Xhuljana wouldn't tell Daisy how we turned her mother into Angelina. She can't outsmart us! And risk losing her powers!"

---

[55] Top secret KGB chemical weapons lab. Location unknown.

Dr. Perp made a dismissive gesture and spoke words that crawled along, "Y-esss? Y-esss? Xhuljana is very sly. Maybe too sly for us. Y-esss? Y-esss?"

Ernest made a fist and put his first knuckle into his mouth. He took it out and said, "Xhuljana is not *that* clever."

Vincent added, "Xhuljana has crossed that fine line: she is using her powers against our spells to get Angelina and Daisy for herself."

Ernest caught Dr. Perp's telltale gaze and agreed, "While it is perfectly acceptable for a witch to use her powers to fool a mortal to gain the mortal's allegiance, or try to win a mortal against another witch. That's the work of a bad witch—one of us. To use her powers just to help a mortal elude another witch...whether or not it is for her advantage against us is irrelevant.... That's a good witch. And the only good witch is a witch who has lost her powers and immortality."

Dr. Perp continued, "Y-esss! Y-esss! Of course, we can do something. I was just making light of our predicament. The question is: Is Xhuljana a good witch or a bad witch? Y-esss. Y-esss?"

Vincent recited from memory, "*The Witch's Solemn Secret is to never reveal either the existence of witchcraft or instruct a mortal in ways to defeat another witch's spell for her own personal gain.* That would result in the loss of her magical powers leaving her as hopeless as a mere mortal. Sure, you can conjure up a curse or spell of your own like a tactical move in chess but you can't just break all the rules; a witch can go through all of the motions as though she is helping a mortal, gain a mortal's trust, and then poof-poof-poof take a mortal for yourself. It's such fun, fun, fun."

"I love that kind of fun," Ernest chirped while wringing his hands. "Like back during The Inquisition; when a little torture was useful to loosen the tongue, or sway someone to your side. Hanging some poor girl from her hands in a dark, dank prison cell with squeaky rodents scampering by. Such fun, fun, fun. So much easier than it is today with all the books, movies, and television that make people so much harder to fool. You have to break your back to get a witch these days!"

"Y-esss. Y-esss," Dr. Perp agreed. "If a witch violates the Solemn Secret, the witch will lose her powers and her immortality. We've seen it happen before. Y-esss? Y-esss! And I think we're going to see it again. Y-esss? Y-esss."

Ernest moaned, "It is a very harsh punishment. No powers. I could almost accept that. Oh, dear! I mean, we'd have each other. I could live vicariously: basking in the pure joy of watching you both casting spells, making potions, transforming mortals into witches...ahhhh, But mortality? I'd just die!"

Vincent chastised, "So you're saying Xhuljana revealed the inner workings of witchcraft to those pathetic mortals. That is so, so bad. Xhuljana wouldn't risk doing that!"

Dr. Perp contended, "Y-esss. Y-esss. *To die—to sleep.... To sleep—perchance to dream. Ay, there's the rub!*[56] Y-esss. Y-esss."

"Death," Vincent blustered, "is the happy side of life...for mortals. How trivial: a life that ends! And that's what Xhuljana deserves."

"What if...," Ernest asked, "What if Xhuljana is doing this for goodness' own sake? It doesn't violate the Witch's Solemn Secret: *A witch shall not reveal the existence of witchcraft to a mortal.* She'd be working behind the veil of Reason manipulating the outcome without telling Angelina or Daisy. Her plan would be so very wicked, if it weren't so good."

Vincent belched, pursed his lips, and continued, "Xhuljana is not so sly. Mortals are so gullible. She seduces them. Anyone can see through her: her red hair, mascara, and all! Flaunting her charms before men and women alike!"

Dr. Perp shrugged his shoulders. "Y-esss? Y-esss? Xhuljana has Daisy convinced she is a good witch! Daisy believes Xhuljana is going to help her find her mother. Help them for the glory of goodness. *Surely goodness and mercy shall follow....* Y e e a a h h s! Y e e a a h h s! Only mortals would believe such foolishness. Will the deception Xhuljana has undertaken succeed? Does

---

[56] Shakespeare Hamlet Act III, Scene 1 (incomplete quotes)

that mean all we can do is sit back and watch? Y-esss! Y-esss?"

Vincent insisted, "It was the Evil One himself who created the Counsel of Shtriga. The Counsel can see into the blackest depths of a witch's heart to find out if the Secret was broken. Woe be the witch who violates the Solemn Secret. Satan will use his own Shtriga Serum to take away all of a witch's powers and make that witch mortal."

Ernest agreed, "And you'd know, Dr. Perp. Because you happen to be a direct descendant of Bibbidibobbidibu[57] !" Ernest spoke softly to Vincent, "Dr. Perp quoted from Psalm 23 of David. I think that was a dig at you. You thought you won David over to our side that time, didn't you?"

Vincent snapped back, "So close. So close. What a beautiful man! A trophy! He was...."

Dr. Perp interrupted, "Y-esss. Y-esss? Who are you trying to fool? You never stood a chance with David. Only a fool fights a losing battle. Like what's in store for Xhuljana: Death is the slowest torture of all! Y-esss! Y-esss!"

"Old Beelzebub himself," Vincent chuckled, "will convene an inquisition against Xhuljana—as if he needs to hold one—and fix Xhuljana's little red wagon. To be accused is to be thought of as guilty! When Xhuljana is gone, we'll reign supreme."

"Xhuljana makes me want to scream," Ernest insisted. "Helping Angelina and Daisy is just plain disgusting, if you ask me."

Vincent continued, "As witches we owe it to each other to protect the secrets, spells, and solutions passed down and protected within a clan of witches. If we were not bound by this tradition, witch-on-witch attacks would be the bane of our existence. How else have we survived the millennium?"

Ernest lamented, "This is a dreadful situation when one of our own turns against us!. Let's just have some pie."

Vincent cut a wedge of ricotta pie the size of a billiard rack and picked it up in his hands. He sniffed it delicately and made bite after bite after slobber after slobber after oohhh mama

---

[57] Name of Satan's own daughter.

after oohh mama until the slice was history. His mustache and goatee were frosted like swamp grass on a winter's morning. He breathed out a deep breath of confectionery sugar and said, "Perppy, you're going to give me a heart attack. What are we going to do already?" He gulped, smiled, and asked, "Erniepoo, another slice?"

Dr. Perp shook his head. "Y-esss. Y-esss? Give him the rest of it and be done with it. Y-esss? Y-esss."

O O O

The dog stood convulsing, or shivering, and let out two small, round turds and growled a half-growl.

Ernest exclaimed, "Good, Gup!" He reached over and plucked the turds in his fingers, and rolled them like he was examining pearls for texture, shape, and brilliance. "Your poops are simply divine. They are simply divine."

Vincent moved closer to sniff their aroma. "Perfect poops: a sign it is time for a reading. Gather 'round witches. Gup shall regale us...regale us with canine clairvoyance. We have smelled the sign! When the poops are perfect, the time has come for Gup to read the tarot. Show us the way, insightful Gup, royal tarot reader of the Shang Dynasty."

Vincent lifted Gup, passing dog's tail under his nose for another whiff, smiled the connoisseur's smile of contentment,

and stood Gup near the Braille version of the Book of Troth[58] on the car's floor. The dog continued to convulse and drool a bile green mucus puddle.

Gup keeled over onto his side and flailed his paws opening the book to the page showing the Five of Cups: two dark lily pads floated in the air above an arid chott, their long stems formed an inverted pentacle intertwined through five upright crystal cups. The two stems collected in the crystal cup at the inverted point of the pentacle. The petals of the lily flower hung

[58] A book on the meaning of the Egyptian Tarot by Aleister Crowley and accompanying set of cards illustrated with instruction from Crowley by Lady Freida Harris (1969).

from two centered hooked rods above the cup where the stems began. Two petals are descended from each of the flowers. The symbol of Mars[59] was centered at the top and the symbol of Scorpio[60] was centered on the bottom of the card.

Dr. Perp leaned forward to examine the page. "Y-esss! Y-es-ss? The Five of Cups: the card of disappointment. And the disappointment will not be ours. Y-esss! Y-esss!"

Gup strained to lift his head in vain, and instead puffed out a pungent hiss of gas. As he laid still, yellowish mucus collected in the corners of his sightless eyes, and he made a low, guttural whimper.

"Yes but no," Vincent condescended. "The meaning of the Five of Cups, as my dear friend, Aleister had discussed in Tenochitlàn when he first began working on Egyptian tarot in nineteen aught two: the five of cups aligned Mars in Scorpio. As everybody knows, is a prescription for Disappointment with a capital D. Since we put the spell on Deborah—a.k.a. Angelina—the Disappointment will be Xhuljana's for trying to win Angelina and Daisy over to her side."

Ernest inquired, "Vincent, hasn't the Five of Cups come out nearly every time you've done a reading on this question? And you always see it as Disappointment."

Gup fluttered and the pads of his paw scraped across two paragraphs on the open page of the book.

"Oh, Ernest!" Vincent exclaimed. "How incredible! I remember being on Mt. Popocatépetl with Aleister and eating mescaline, watching the gods of lightning paint the night sky for our amusement, having sex like the Pharaoh Khan and Chioa Khan in the Duat[61] ...."

Vincent began to dance awkwardly like an elephant in

---

[59] ♂ shield and spear

[60] ♏ the symbol of the sun, which is ruled by Mars

[61] Egyptian mythology described a formless region of water where Ra, the sun god, passes through each night beyond the western horizon and enters from in the east each morning.

"Fantasia"[62] on a floor littered with mothballs causing his belly to make him list starboard and port while he danced port to starboard.

"Disappointment!" he continued. "Disappointment! Disappointment to others! How I love the Disappointment of others!"

Dr. Perp made a gurgling sound like water pouring from a downspout onto flagstone. "Y-esss! Y-esss! Boys take a look at the one-way mirror to the driver's compartment. Y-esss? Y-esss?"

"Oh, Vincent," Ernest guffawed. "Mr. Funk looks like he's petrified. He resembles an old Daguerreotype[63] : all smushed up against the one-way mirror."

Johnny had his face squeezed up against the glass trying to peer in at them. His lips quivered but no sound penetrated the glass.

Dr. Perp turned to his right and said, "Y-esss? Y-esss? Don't look at him, It only encourages the mortal fools. Y-esss. Y-esss."

Vincent looked away and asked, "Should I moon him instead?"

Ernest feigned pointing at something out the side window, and Dr. Perp and Vincent pantomimed interest at an imaginary site. Johnny wearily slid off the one-way window and returned to helplessly watching the limousine race through the night.

---

62 Animated movie by Walt Disney (1940) with a scene of bubble-blowing, dancing elephants to *Dance of the Hours* by Ponchielli.

63 First commercially available photographic process (1837) produced a positive on a silvered copper plate.

ननन

Ricardo put dinner together for Daisy while he hurriedly got ready to leave for a meeting at six-thirty. He paused and sat at the kitchen table, pen in hand, to write a note to his daughter. His mind drifted back to teaching Daisy to throw a football early one cold Christmas morning. The two of them on the silent side street beside their apartment building tossing the football, showing her how to stand in a classic quarterback passing stance....

He thought, *I have to write a note to Daisy. She'll come home to an empty apartment, again. I wish I didn't have to leave her here. Adults have to do things kids don't comprehend. What do I say? Will she understand what I've written? Can she understand what I really want to tell her? Can she get over blaming me for everything? By writing down some thoughts, will it create an opening back to where we began...before the upheaval and chaos?*

Little Fuzza[64] -
I have to attend a meeting and won't be back until 9 PM. Supper is in the fridge. Just zap it for 4:30.

Ricardo dropped the pen, which made a tumultuous crash to the table in the empty apartment, and shouted, "¡Ay, Chiapas![65] I don't know why but I just thought about the first time I took Daisy to see a movie. That movie practically mirrored what happened with Deborah!"

Ricardo remembered when Daisy was only five or six years-old, he brought her to the Exeter Street Cinema—originally a playhouse from the 1820s, converted to a church in the 1880s and then transformed into a four screen movie theater in the 1960s—its distinctive high wainscoting, dark wooden moldings, gilding, and two state boxes on either side of the original stage,

---

[64] When Daisy was a baby, she called a flower, "fuzza".
[65] Chiapas is a state in southern Mexico where the calamity surrounding the failed Zapatista revolution by its indigenous people against the Mexican government in 1994 inspired Ricardo to coin this expression as play-on-words on the older Mexican expression ¡Ay, Chihuahua! (A northern Mexican state that fell to US forces in 1847.)

and classic movie posters, paintings, frescoes, sculptures, and high arched ceiling in the concession area always astounded those who entered. Taking Daisy to the movies wasn't easy: Daisy was sensitive to loud noises and she shunned the sensory overload. Ricardo took her several times to the lobby just to look at the posters, or to buy her some popcorn. This time the ticket taker saw the situation and let Ricardo enter without paying. Daisy looked through the little window in the upholstered door to the main screening room and was fascinated by glimpses of the animated movie. So, Ricardo walked into the cinema alone. A moment later, she followed him in. He spotted a couple of open seats in a rear row, so he directed her there.

The movie had already begun but it didn't matter. Daisy had gotten over her fear of going into a movie theater, even though the first scene they saw was a bus turning around a corner and a loud explosion followed. A technicolor nightmare.

The movie wasn't exactly like our situation. Yet, there's a parallel between this very scene and when we saw the bus Deborah got on turn down West Street: enormous black clouds gathered over the buildings, and thunder and lightning followed. Although we missed the beginning of the movie, there was more than an allegorical coincidence. In the movie, there was a bus....an explosion...a corner...treachery....

Daisy saw her mother act like she was all possessed by demons, or something! Deborah ran from the apartment with her suitcase in hand, eyes ablaze, racing around like her hair was on fire, flying down the stairs, stomping madly out of the building past people we knew as if they were strangers, pushing past an old man on crutches in her way, knocking him to the sidewalk before she hopped onto a bus, and, as the bus disappeared around the corner, dark clouds gathered and lightning flashed—as if nature was taking cues off-set for a magical movie scene.

There is a tragically humorous quality to this situation that I might even find funny, if it weren't happening to Daisy and me. A little girl won't accept the idea there's something wrong with her mother. Who knows where she'll place the blame? Yet, a young girl is so vulnerable and could easily blame herself...misconstrue the situation...be taken to a very dark place. Maybe I should talk to Daisy about this? I wonder if she ever thinks about that movie? Or made a connection between it and what happened with Deborah?

He picked up the pen and added,

You're my baby. But you're growing up, too. Sometime, the subtle changes escape my eyes. It has been tough with mom gone. I have tried to insulate you from what I could, even when it broke my heart to do so. Though insulating you from so much might not have been the best thing to do. But I still think we'll get through this.

It's been tough on both of us. Try not to blame yourself for what happened. What went on was unbelievable! It may be something we'll never understand. I promise I will do all I can do to make everything okay. And you know, our word is our bond. It's that important.

What went on was unbelievable.... Now, that's an understatement! It may be something we'll never understand.... Our word is our bond. I say that all the time. And this is the first time I've written it down. How strange. I mean, it is true and it is something I want Daisy to take seriously. The words seem to have more weight when they're written.

Ricardo was uneasy. He shifted in his seat. He looked around the room and saw the mysterious bottle on the bookshelf: *Ilaç Magjistare.* Deborah loved the bottle: its color, its shape, the calligraphy on its label.

Perhaps the bottle is a talisman...a source of good luck? What could Ilaç Magjistare mean?

He recalled Deborah being so cautious, yet excited, when she brought the cobalt blue bottle home and told him about meeting the woman who owned the store downtown which sold potions and magical paraphernalia.

That woman gave Deborah the dark blue bottle and the owl...the stuffed owl...the owl Daisy loved...the one she called Owldoll!

I'll be late and she'll be by herself...and she...she...needs to hear something more personal from me....

Ricardo unfolded another piece of paper from his pocket. He smoothed it out on the table and reread the lines he'd written. He crumpled the original note and left this instead,

Here's a haiku poem I wrote for you.

Baby in disguise
Or have you seen a little
Twinkle in her eyes?

It's tough...there are times I look at my daughter and she seems so grown up. Yes, grown up beyond her years. So mature and clever and capable. Then I look back and I think Daisy is too young. So naïve and innocent and vulnerable.

Daisy, there were times I said too much, and times I didn't say enough. Knowing what to do in the moment is a special talent—sometimes I get it right; sometimes I fall short. Being a father...being a single parent can be like a færy tale with its enchanted joys and exhilaration, and its mysterious twists and turns. All I can do is try to get to you somehow....

Love, Dad

ΟΟΟ

Ricardo stood across the street staring at the ornate lettering on the sign for Witchcraft Heights Potions. He thought, *Witchcraft Heights Potions. Witchcraft Heights? What are witchcraft depths? The lettering is kind of intriguing. This is the store Deborah got the bottle: the deep, dark blue bottle; the one with the cool label and calligraphy; its hefty feel; And lettering like this sign; And the stuffed owl in the fancy wooden box—the one Daisy found in the closet and started to play with. The one I named Owldoll. Owl-doll...Owl-doll. Witchcraft Heights Potions. I must go inside. I must find out more. Maybe they have a potion to unravel the mystery Daisy and me have to solve? Maybe I'll find what I was looking for inside?*

He crossed the street and approached the front door slowly.

Each step forward was weighing on him. Was he about to do something to change the course he was on? Should he stop or should he go? He grasped the handle and opened the door.

A bell attached to the door jingled when he opened it but no one seemed to take much notice. At the counter was a tall, pale-skinned man dressed in a black tuxedo carrying a silver-tipped black walking stick. He appeared to cut off his conversation with the red-haired woman behind the counter as Ricardo entered. The man rapped his walking stick smartly on the floor and began an elaborate exit. His movements seemed designed to draw attention, make a statement, or were part of an intricate choreography.

The man spoke a little too loudly given the store was largely empty. "Y-esss. Y-esss? Interest is picking up, don't you think? I'm sure you'll take full advantage of the situation. Y-esss. Y-esss. We'll have to continue our discussion next time. Oh, we must. Y-esss! Y-esss!"

The man paused in front of Ricardo, looked him over like he was about to make an expensive purchase, cleared his throat as he opened the door, and exited with a slam of the door that jangled the bells violently.

¡Loco! Ricardo thought about the man who just left. *All these bottles look like a bunch of snake oil. What a rip-off. All of this paraphernalia to look so mysterious...and the chick with the long red hair. Probably a dye job...no. It's too beautiful and flowing.*

The woman looked at Ricardo and he was suspended in space and time: his vision focused directly on her soft green eyes, which were comforting and enticing. He sensed a tinge of excitement and magic as he watched her feline movements accentuate her feminine qualities. His imagination drifted. Thoughts of her face captivated him and, before he knew it, she had walked along the backside of the counter to where he was standing.

Ricardo was caught off-guard when they were face to face across the countertop. The woman stooped down to put something back on a lower shelf, slowly stood up, and looked right

at Ricardo. He felt a sudden warmness and he looked dreamily
into her soothing green eyes. He was tongue-tied and smiled
awkwardly.

"Welcome to my store," said the woman. "I'm Xhuljana. I
don't believe you've been here before."

Ricardo looked at Xhuljana and had a strange sensation he
could only describe later as a subtle magic. He felt so at-home
around her he decided to level with her. "Xhuljana. You have a
nice name and I feel like I already know you. But that can't be:
I'd remember you. I mean...you're very attractive. I mean, if I'd
met you, I'd surely remember it."

Xhuljana leaned in closer and touched his hand lightly for
a second. She thought, *Curious development. He wants to know
about the Ilaç Majistare and Owldoll. I don't know why but I sense a
strong connection. But how can this be? Is he one of us?*

Ricardo began, "You have an interesting shop. I don't mean
'interesting' in the way you say...like I don't have anything else
to say, so I said it's interesting. My imagination is fascinated by
the elaborate variety of bottles on display and the decorative
fonts of the labels. I'll admit I don't put much credence into
witchcraft. But I am attracted to the stories and the tales."

Xhuljana answered coyly, "There is always something to be
learned in these tales. I like færy tales very much: the allegories
are so insightful."

"I guess, you're right. And the fantasies underneath the stories, too," Ricardo grinned then recomposed himself. "The reason I came here is because...my wife came here one day six years
ago. She brought home a beautiful blue bottle and a stuffed owl
with huge purple eyes. Now, I'm not inclined to have stuffed
birds...or stuffed animals of any kind in my house. That's an
old *bubbe meise.*[66] Stuffed animals, and especially birds, bring
bad luck. Well, she had this look about her when she brought
it home. How could I say no?"

"You must be Jewish," Xhuljana interjected. "That's a Yiddish expression and your pronunciation is very good."

---

[66] (Yiddish) באבע מעשה old wives' tale; superstition

"Pretty keen of you to notice," Ricardo replied. "Most people don't...notice that is. I guess I don't look Jewish. Or Mexican for that matter."

Xhuljana looked a little amused. "You do have an accent. I have an accent, so I pick up on that. I have had people from many nationalities walk through my door."

"You probably don't remember giving her the blue bottle. It was a long time ago. She kept the blue bottle on a bookcase shelf but the owl she put away in her closet. It wasn't until years later when Daisy...." he faded off at the mention of her name. He thought, *I feel like I can open up my heart to her. Does she really care to hear about Daisy and me?*

Xhuljana caught his gaze. He wondered if she was reading his mind and he snapped back to what he was talking about.

"Excuse me," he interrupted himself. "Daisy is my daughter. She is fifteen. When she was *una bebé*, she was hunting through her mother's closet and discovered the fancy wooden box buried near the bottom. She poked and prodded and, ta-da, she opened the box. Inside, there was a good-sized stuffed owl."

"I do remember the day Deborah came in," Xhuljana exclaimed. "We hit it off. It was a sort of spur of the moment exchange. I had a premonition. Call it women's intuition."

Ricardo continued, "Daisy investigated her mommy's closet and noticed a fancy wooden box on the floor under an old blanket. She was intrigued by the design across the box. Her fingers felt along the edge and somehow she managed to open it. Under the cover was a strange, interesting looking bird with big, sparkly purple eyes. It looked like it knew what she was thinking.

"I remember being confused; 'What are you doing?' Deborah snapped at her and grabbed the stuffed owl and hustled to get it back into its box. She didn't want Daisy to play with it."

Xhuljana nodded sympathetically. "Perhaps," Xhuljana supposed, "Deborah was trying to cling onto what she thought belonged to her, even though it didn't. And what Daisy wanted wasn't part of her equation."

"Years later Daisy found the box in the closet. I liked to watch Daisy playing with the stuffed owl. She'd say: it's an owl but I want it to be my doll. *Florita mia*, I told her. It is okay. You can call it Owldoll."

Xhuljana thought, *What would he think if he knew Deborah was now Angelina? And her exit was not as innocent as it looked.*

Ricardo contemplated what Xhuljana had just thought. *What if Deborah's disappearance was not just out of the blue? What if it only appeared that way like she was staging an act? Were there telltale signs I missed?*

Xhuljana marveled, *See he does suspect it!*

Ricardo began, "You probably won't believe this. I sometimes don't believe what has happened to me...to Daisy and me...was as innocent as it appeared. One day—as if in the middle of a dream—my whole world changed.

"My wife was in our room while I was in the living room. I heard all of this commotion like books or boxes were falling from the ceiling in my room. I went in and *mi esposa*[67] was rapidly moving about the room from one spot to another. She was throwing things into a small suitcase. I asked her: What's going on? She ignored me and zoned out, or something.

"Then she closed the suitcase and ran out of the apartment past Daisy and me! Daisy pleaded: Mommy where are you going? You said we were going to the park.

"*Mi esposa* looked past Daisy like she wasn't there. *Mi florita*: heartbroken, mystified, rejected. I kept calling after her but my words went nowhere. She raced down the walkway, up the sidewalk, pushing her way past an old man using a cane. ¡Dios mio[68] ! But look at me...talk away to you like you have all the answers. What happened to my family was beyond words."

Xhuljana had a knowing look in her eyes as though she could answer his question. She shrugged her shoulders gently, "Some people expect I have a connection to the unknown. That

---

67 (Sp.) wife
68 (Sp.) my God

Witchcraft Heights Potions contains real magic. I really wish I could tell you things but...I..just can't. And look at me, too. I've gotten used to running my mouth—as the kids like to say."

"Oh, yeah. You got that right," Ricardo agreed. "Daisy and her friends say that all the time. You know something, Juliana? I appreciate what you said. Maybe more than you think."

"It's Dg-yule-ee-ana," she replied.

"Didn't I say Juliana?" Ricardo asked.

"You did," she answered. "But it is pronounced Dg-yule-ee-ana with a Dg like in edge."

"Okay, Xhuljana. It was quite fortunate we met today."

Xhuljana looked at him straight on. "You might not think so, but it wasn't completely by chance we met here today."

Two women entered the store. "Oh, Miss," one called out. "We need to get that Mystery Potion #9 for a birthday gift."

Xhuljana added, "It would be nice to talk again. The store tends to get busy right about now."

She extended her hand and he shook hands with her. When they touched this time, he felt something like static electricity. He watched her walk to the other side of the store then he walked outside with a smile on his face.

○○○

The girls left the train, walked from the platform to the stairwell, giggled their way across the massive station, and made their way out to the street level. A thunderstorm rumbled in the distance over Midway. Dark clouds were visible above the buildings downtown.

Siobhan observed, "At least the sky was clear in our neighborhood. I don't remember seeing clouds this dark since I was..."

"Five," Daisy broke in and exclaimed. Her face took on a sad look. "It looks like the clouds..."

Siobhan continued, "...when your mom disa...a...went awa...went mih...mih...mih...when she..."

"Left me and my dad," Daisy finished. "Isn't that what you were trying to say? You think she did this on purpose, huh? I'm telling you: that's not what happened."

Amanda placed her hand on Daisy's shoulder. "Siobhan didn't mean to say somethin' mean or make you upset, you know."

Daisy barked, "I am not upset! We're just bringing up bad memories. I mean, the dark clouds and thunder and lightning have nothing to do with anything. And now you're trying to bring up what happened back then. Dark clouds and thunder and lightning don't signify something terrible is about to occur."

Siobhan lamented, "Sorry, Daisy. I wasn't thinking. But you must admit you can see the storm more clearly from this distance."

The girls kept walking and arrived at their destination: De-Quincy Market, an historic marketplace for selling slaves, livestock, rum, and tobacco from the colonial era. Present-day, it is a huge tourist attraction restored, spiffed up, and filled with eateries, bars, and gift shops that had become a popular hang-out in the city for teenagers and college kids in the area.

The noisy crowd inside DeQuincy Market had them looking all over the place. There were all of the well-known stores, restaurants, and kiosks vying for their attention with neon lights, attractive displays, and popular music. But what caught all of their eyes were two kids from their school: Matt and Kaylee. First, Matt and Kaylee were there together. Second, they saw Matt and Kaylee holding hands.

Amanda tapped Daisy on her arm. Daisy looked back as if Amanda was restating the obvious. Then Amanda tapped Siobhan and whispered, "See?"

Daisy turned so she wasn't facing Matt and Kaylee, then said, "Let's get something to eat. I'm getting hungry."

Siobhan sarcastically licked her lips and puckered.

Amanda kept up razz. "She just wishes she was here with Danny. She thinks he's smart...and cute. Don'tcha?"

Daisy looked a little embarrassed and walked into the market away from where Matt and Kaylee might see her. Amanda and Siobhan caught up.

Amanda noticed a bakery and suggested, "Let's split a giant chocolate chip cookie at Rebecca's Kitchen over there. They're three bucks: that's a buck each, 'kay?"

"Yeah," Daisy agreed. "I'm hungry. Here's my dollar."

They walked toward the bakery/cafeteria and ordered a giant cookie.

"That will be three dollars and nineteen cents," said the young girl behind the counter, who flicked her hair behind her ear with a finger as she made eye contact with a boy wearing a football jacket standing near a woman in her thirties, who was making eye contact with the boy, too.

Amanda asked, "Huh? It says they're three dollars."

The girl snapped back, "Three dollars plus tax. That's three dollars and nineteen cents."

Amanda turned around and Daisy pleaded, "That's all I got. I need the rest to take the commuter train back."

Siobhan started, "Well..."

Daisy exclaimed, "Oh, snap! I just made a connection: a text to self connection."

Amanda prodded, "Not a Mr. Brooks seeing mathematics in real life connection."

Siobhan laughed, "We divided the giant cookie into three equal pieces. One third plus one third plus one third equals one whole cookie. Ooooo, I smell extra credit for the teacher's pet."

Daisy shook her head no. "Quit bein' a doob[69] . You know our teachers are always pushing text to self, text to text, or text to world strategies. It's just a habit they've got us into. Some teachers don't give full credit unless you write the text to *something* connection was why you think it's the answer."

Siobhan continued, "You're bein' a Herb[70] . Whaddabout

69 Youth slang for an idiot.

70 (H□r-b) Youth slang for a know-it-all, or someone socially awkward.

three dollars plus a six and a quarter percent sales tax equals three dollars and nineteen cents." She rolled her eyes. "You just nailed yourself a homework pass!"

Amanda laughed, which made Siobhan laugh, too.

Daisy looked at them from the corner of her eye. "Errr...it's about the first movie I saw! I told you, remember? Dad took me to the Exeter Street Cinema when I was six and a half. And the first scene in a wicked scary movie was a bus turning a corner between tall buildings...dark clouds floated overhead...thunder crashed...lightning flared...and a huge explosion...exploded.

"That's almost what happened with mom! So, I see this connection. This is like a sign.... Well, not really! But the connection is more than what we do when we're in school. The connection I just made is bigger. It's real! A life connection is more real than a movie! I can't just close my eyes and make it go away."

A booming voice came from behind them. "Oooo, how adorable! How positively adorable! Look at this! Three little urchins trying to scrounge up pittens for their sweet treat. Have no fear, young damsels in distress."

The large man dressed in black with the loud voice stood closer to the counter. "Such a delectable cookie." He made a circular motion over the cookie with his hands as his fingers fluttered. "So big! So round! Möle keqe."

The rotund man shoved his hands into his pants pockets briefly, pulled them out, and tossed a bunch of coins haphazardly onto the glass counter of the pastry display case. "Take this, young lady. And keep the rest as a gratuity."

The girl scooped up the roughly one dollar and fifty cents in change and mouthed, "Thanks."

He joined his two companions behind him and the three men in dark apparel walked into the crowd between the vendors' stalls in DeQuincy Market. They blended into the moving mass like a shadow in the rain.

"Y-esss. Y-esss? Back in an earlier day...I don't recalled if it was just before or after the War of Independence. Y-esss?

Y-esss?" Dr. Perp reflected. "William Gribble, tobacconist. His establishment was located over there beyond where the Starbucks Coffee is now. Those splendid Partagás cigars from Havana. Y-esss! Y-esss! And a little further was At Last Liquors, purveyors of Olde Medford Rum. Y-esss. Y-esss. A pint of rum and a fine cigar. Y-esss? Y-esss."

Ernest concurred, "Oh, yes. We'd find our recruits and celebrate with a ho-ho-ho and a bottle of rum! Those were the days. Such fond memories, Dr. Perp. You know how to bring up these pleasant reminders of days gone by."

Vincent added, "Mmmm. Remember the slave auctioneers over there across from At Last Liquors? Forrester, Farquhar, and Hubbard? Hmmm? And the dark chocolaty slave named N'gulafak? She looked very much like Cleopatra. Hmmm. I do declare!"

Dr. Perp stated, "Y-esss. Y-esss. You managed to flub that one. You tried to change her name before we gave her the Shtriga Serum. Then her pride was raised and it acted like a shield against our efforts. Y-esss! Y-esss!"

Ernest looked up and grinned, "I recall those lavish days in Cleopatra's Court. Now, could she lay out a feast. Sooo glorious. Golden goblets. Golden plates. Golden utensils. And buff male servants! Too bad they were eunuchs! Such a waste! But let me see...N'gulafak was a lot darker than Cleopatra. Her Highness was almost pale olive. Kind of masculine looking...but she did have large nay-nays."

Vincent pouted at Ernest , "I'm disappointed. You didn't even notice what I did back there."

"Vincent, that was a nice thing you did at the market," Ernest said acrimoniously. He paused. "Ha! You haven't done anything nice in a century...literally. I think it was around 1908: we were in Milano and little Benito Mussolini had just been deported for rabble rousing in Switzerland and he missed the train to go back to Lausanne, Switzerland. He was screaming about the trains not running on time. So, you gave him a gold piece to buy a cooked goose."

Dr. Perp reflected, "Y-esss? Y-esss! At least that deed was for a purpose. Benito remembered you and gave us positions of prominence. He left it to us to make sure the trains ran on time in Milano and later run on time in all of Italia. Y-esss? Y-esss? What do we want here? All we want here is Angelina. Y-esss? Y-esss. And Daisy! Y-esss! Y-esss!"

Vincent corrected, "Dr. Perp, you never recognize the genius that is me. I'm not just another pretty face, you know." He batted his eyes, interlocked his fingers, and rested them under his chin.

Ernest looked at Dr. Perp and concurred, "He's got a point. Give him a chance to explain."

Dr. Perp turned away as he responded, "Y-esss? Y-esss? When we lose one, Xhuljana gains one. When Xhuljana gains one, we lose one. We cannot afford another moronic scheme to placate his savage amusement. We need to stick to the plan! Y-esss? Y-esss!"

Vincent smiled a Cheshire smile. "Dr. Perp get a grip on yourself. When have I failed?"

He didn't wait for a response.

"I was laying the bait for Daisy." Vincent mimicked the voice of Dr. Perp. "What *leetle girl* can resist a giant chocolate chip cookie? Especially one laced with the secret ingredient of *Bobësi*[71] *Serum?*"

Ernest rejoiced, "How diabolical! Now, we got a four-fer: Angelina, Daisy, and her two friends with the serum of weakness!"

Dr. Perp turned his gaze on Vincent with a wry smile. "Y-esss. Y-esss. Vincent, my prodigal companion, you have served us well. Perhaps, I have spoken too harshly of your misdeeds. Y-esss? Y-esss?"

Ernest answered immediately, "Dr. Perp, your gruff interior and acrid comments are your most endearing charms. A compliment from you is anathema to the toils of witches everywhere. Our predecessors plus our own contributions to the

---

[71] DOE-bes-ee

Fjalë Dëmtues[72] of spells, curses, and serums from the Ages have provided an arsenal for Vincent to win the battle.

"Vincent, just accept my praise and appreciation for the terrible things you do." He walked over to Vincent and jiggled his belly with both hands. "Good baby!"

Dr. Perp added, "Y-esss? Y-esss. Sometime, you amaze me. The Serum won't work on her friends. Have you forgotten everything about witchcraft? We don't get her leetle friends, too. They would have to feel the electromagnetic pulse of the *Bosh Zakon*[73] . Y-esss? Y-esss? But Daisy is who we want. Y-esss? Y-esss!"

Vincent pointed at Dr. Perp sternly, "Don't talk to us like we're children!" Then he stuck out his tongue. "We can feel it whether those children have felt the Missing Dimension."

Ernest agreed, "It's like cosmological feedback. How delightful! A warm oil massage on high-voltage! Oooo, just makes me tingle all over."

"Ernie," Vincent cooed. "You put it so...so descriptively. Your artistic tendencies put me in Hades. Mmmmm: darkness, brimstone, and sulfur. Paradise."

Daisy walked ahead as they returned to the station. She felt an electric vibration pass through her as she walked into the busy complex. She needed to stand a moment. Amanda and Siobhan looked at each other.

"Daisy felt *something*," whispered Amanda.

"Look!" squealed Siobhan as she pointed to the blank giant train schedule display board.

"Yeah, it's been out for over an hour. They say the storm in Midway caused it. Who knows?" said a uniformed woman cleaning off a table in front of the Terminal Coffee Shop.

Amanda asked, "How we gonna know which train to take?"

Daisy looked at the billboard. "That's weird! How does

---

[72] *Fee-ya-ye DEM-boo-ezz*
[73] *Bŏsh Zăkŏn* – roughly translated as The Missing Dimension. An esoteric precept in sorcery: Sorcery is only possible when this dimension is missing.

anyone know which track their train is on? What time it arrives? What time it leaves? I mean...does anybody really know what time it is?"

Siobhan replied, "Does anybody really care?"

Amanda moved closer to Daisy, "You just got to remember which train you took and take it back."

"It looks like our train over there," Siobhan pointed.

A silver train with its bright beam from an ocular chrome housing came in the station as they looked out to the tracks. Daisy stared right into its headlight and exclaimed, "Now this is a sign! You can go back but not the way you came." She thought, *There is a connection....*"

The girls raced to a middle platform along with groups of other anxious travelers. As the train pulled into their platform, Daisy looked it in the eye and spoke softly toward Amanda and Siobhan, "The train down might not be the train back."

IV

Amanda, Siobhan, and Daisy walked past Madame Zhang's Chop Suey Sandwich Shoppe feeling like they've avoided running into the two tuxedoed men they hoped to dodge. Amanda looked ahead and noticed the two wino women across the street they had seen in front of the Pizza Pad.

Amanda quietly complained, "Look it! It's those two wino ladies from the other day, you know, at the Pizza Pad. They're so weird."

Amanda and Siobhan slowed down when the women crossed to their side of the street a short distance away. Daisy turned around when she noticed her friends stopped walking with her. She went back to where her friends were standing.

Amanda mouthed, "Those weird ladies are coming this way."

"What did you say?" Daisy questioned quietly. She couldn't make out what Amanda tried to communicate.

Amanda just raised her eyebrows intensely in a forward direction. Daisy stopped, looked back, and recognized the women dressed in winter coats.

Daisy thought, *I remember the woman in the black coat. I felt something was familiar when I saw her the last time. Maybe I met this woman before, and sensed she wanted to tell me an important message. Don't know what but there's something strange about her now. Something has changed, I think.*

Mary guffawed, "Angie, ain't that those three little snots we saw d'other day? Bet we could scare the bejeezus out of 'em." She coughed a deep rattling cough and spit out some thick phlegm.

Angelina laughed, "Bet they think they're better than us. See 'em whispering. They're talkin' about us. And it ain't good stuff neither. How 'bout if you hawk another lungy. Make 'em run home cryin' to their mommies. Boo, hoo, hoo...."

"Ha! Ha! Ha!" Mary coughed as she stepped in front of Angelina to make sure the girls got a clear view. Mary spoke boisterously, "Got a big lungy here, girls?" She did an obscene pantomime, bobbing her head in the girl's direction while parting her lips to resemble the letter O, and then spat a bile green, protozoa shaped projectile on the sidewalk.

Mary laughed with a hoarse, smoker's cough as she staggered toward the girls. Angelina watched with delight as the girls recoiled at the slippery sight in front of them.

Amanda and Siobhan made horrified faces before they hid their eyes with their hands. Daisy had turned around and missed the show.

"Gross!" Amanda remarked. "I'm gonna barf."

Siobhan cautioned, "Don't give them the satisfaction."

The sun came out from behind a cloud and the bright light bore down on the women's faces just as they approached the girls. The woman in the brown coat shielded her eyes from the blinding sun. But the woman in the black coat was unphased and let the sunshine bathe her eyes.

Siobhan wondered, "How messed up is this? That woman looked at me all strange; her eyes were mad crazy. When she looked into the direct sunlight, her eyes looked like the pond water at Playsteady Park when the frogs lay their eggs. I never saw eyes like that before. I can't imagine what things look like viewing the world through a watery surface covered with frogspawn. Would it be like looking through a kaleidoscope? A fractured image repeated in mosaic tiles; beautiful but untrue."

Daisy thought, *I saw it in the lady's eyes, too. A watery surface covered with frogspawn like at Playsteady Park. I didn't think the lady was up to no good but she can't see what's really here. My friends could be right. What she sees might look beautiful to her but what she saw was untrue.*

Daisy looked into the woman's eyes, which reminded her of a mirrored surfaces in the bright sunlight. She expected clarity but the image in the mirrors became cloudy. The mirrors transformed into a watery surface covered with small, translucent bubbles. Distorted images floated across the surface of the bubbles, which made Daisy want to see a meaning locked within. The images didn't have enough detail to identify what was being viewed. The more the images replicated in multiple bubbles the more tempting it was to fill in the missing details. She could guess, or accept, that the image was what she imagined, but she was left even more confused.

Moments later, they were in Playsteady Park. Amanda said what they all felt, "I always feel safe in Playsteady Park. I'm glad we lost those wino ladies. I mean, yeah, they were creepy."

Siobhan echoed her sentiment, "Especially the one with the weird eyes. When she had the bright sunlight in her eyes, I could see her eyes weren't eyes at all. Eyes are for seeing and I couldn't see how she saw anything. Right?"

Daisy guessed, "Dunno. I don't know what we saw. I just dunno." She paused as she walked in one direction, "I'm goin' to head home."

"See ya, Daisy," Amanda cheerfully replied as Daisy walked away. Siobhan simply waved.

Daisy walked along the pathway looking back and forth at the tree limbs. Then she felt a warm pulsation and clearly heard the voice of Owldoll, "W-issh. One illusion does not make a complete picture. One illusion does not make a complete picture. W-issh."

She looked one way then the other but saw nothing. Her mind raced forward, "Owldoll? Where did you go?" she whispered. "I heard your voice. Where are you? What illusion are you trying to warn me about? Maybe it's an illusion someone else wants me to see? How will I know when I've seen the complete picture?"

Daisy kept walking until she reached her building. She climbed the stairs and reached her door. Once inside, Daisy went to her room and got ready for bed. Her father called to her but she was lost in her own world and did not reply. She felt a little guilty for ignoring him but replayed the words Owldoll said: *W-issh. One illusion does not make a complete picture. One illusion does not make a complete picture. W-issh.*

She looked out the window for her secret companion but saw nothing. Daisy was extremely tired and was thinking about Owldoll as she fell asleep. She rocked back and forth and began to dream:

She saw a lush, tropical area with palm trees and mangroves. Her father was in a small canoe floating down a series of tributaries into a tropical landscape. It was nighttime but the full moon—*el luna del lobo*, the wolf moon—produced enough light to navigate the currents, which grew increasingly rapid. The canoe suddenly took on an unfamiliar look. It seemed worn with splotches of green and red moss. Its seat had broken rattan reeds weakening the weaving. Ricardo could not find the drawing Daisy made on the floorboards or the notches he'd made in the gunwale to show Daisy where oar cleats could be installed.

An arrow struck the starboard side from out of nowhere. Ricardo looked back to his right but saw no one. A second arrow hit the portside with a sharper thud.

"¡Ay, Chiapas! Qué de la...," he yelled out loud. His words stopped midstream when a large boulder fell into the water close enough to touch. The boat rocked and he held onto the tops of the gunwales. Then he heard a strangely sinister voice, "Y-esss? Y-esss? Not what you expected? Rough waters? Not so smooth? Y-esss! Y-esss!"

Four larger rocks crashed close to the canoe and swamped it. Ricardo was thrown into the moving water and the canoe was swept away. He bobbed up and down, swallowed some water, and gasped for air. Laughing voices were heard from behind the trees. They were talking but the words weren't clear. Ricardo regained his breath and used his arms to maintain balance.

Daisy saw the same pool but no one else was there. She heard a piano playing a tune, which she liked and almost instinctively sang the lyrics and counted the ¾ time: We'll have fun. (2-3, rest) We'll have fun. (2-3, rest) We'll have fun. (rest) We'll have fu-uh-uh-un. (Full rest) We'll have fun. (2-3, rest) We'll have fun. (2-3, rest) We'll have fun. (rest) We'll have fu-uh-uh-un. (Full rest)

Daisy remembered her father teaching her to play the piano. The joy of making music. Was this a song he had played for her?

Daisy saw her father being carried downstream. The stream dipped sharply and he fell helplessly with the powerful waters into a large pool that seemed to extend to the horizon. As he moved into the pool, the waters calmed. But it was only a temporary stillness. He lifted his head and saw the stream continued on an unknowable course. He tried to swim to one side hoping to reach land. Then he stopped. Something was drawing him to the opposite direction. He heard a soft voice, a girl's voice, "You can make it. Keep swimming."

Daisy mouthed again, "You can make it. Keep swimming."

A shadow blocked the moonlight. The pool and stream became invisible. A low voice spoke, "Raquim, if you cut the rope, it will unleash a pile of boulders to finish him off. He is our enemy. He keeps you from the world of beauty. You're almost there, Raquim."

Daisy screamed, "No!"

She was in her bed sweating. *Oh, my God,* she thought. Then she spoke out loud, "That dream seemed so real. I coulda cut a rope that coulda released a pile of boulders to rain down on dad. The voices were calling me...calling Raquim. Why did I wake up? Who yelled no? I wouldn'a done it. Would I? Maybe that's why I woke up."

O O O

Ricardo and his neighbors, Mr. Harris and Mademoiselle Lapin, sat around Ricardo's kitchen table on a Saturday morning waiting for a surprise birthday party for Daisy to begin. Some of Daisy's friends had arrived and were in another room out of sight. Ricardo was staring at the calendar. Mademoiselle Lapin looked at Joel Harris, he looked back at her.

Joel joked, "Are you just waiting for the date to change, or something?"

After a moment, Ricardo answered, "Just the date: seven eleven. It used to mean something; Daisy's birthday. The seventh day of the eleventh month. I always made a big deal out of it with Daisy. Lucky seven eleven. Pointing out the convenience stores, 7-Eleven[74] like they were hers. She thought it was funny. But then all this stuff with Deborah.... Daisy hasn't felt very lucky since Deborah left. She's taken too much of what happened personally, like it was her fault. Or that she was responsible for taking care of her mother. She hasn't gotten the same thrill about her birthday for a couple years; now she focuses on what is missing. Why can't a birthday just be a happy occasion? I mean.... I've been hoping a big birthday party—her *quinceañera*[75] —will help Daisy get some childhood happiness back....return to being a regular teenager again.... Be more like...Daisy used to be."

"Everything will be fine, Ricardo," Joel reassured him.

Ricardo continued, "I hope today goes well. She'll be back soon with her friends: Amanda and Siobhan. The other friends are here on time and they're hiding in the other rooms to surprise her. That part has gone okay. And....what if..."

Mademoiselle Lapin spoke up sympathetically, "Oh, Ricardo. You're being such a worry wart, no? *Zees* party you made for Daisy will be *magnifique*."

"Yeah," Ricardo muttered. "Her *quinceañera* only comes around once. What if she doesn't like it? It's only being given here at home. And these kids see the mega-parties on MTV[76]

---

[74] International chain of convenience stores with extended hours from 7 AM to 11 PM seven days a week. Some open 24-hours seven days a week.
[75] (Sp.) fifteenth birthday; a girl's fifteenth birthday often celebrated elaborately in Hispanic cultures
[76] Music Television – a unit of Viacom Media Networks

held at a five-star hotel with a hundred kids where the party girl gets a four hundred and fifty thousand dollar Lamborghini and cries at the end of the night because one of her friends got one with way more bling[77] and a better sound system."

Joel Harris added, "Ah! The worries of the idle rich! Ricardo, don't set yourself up for failure. You're planning a super party for Daisy and I just love the birthday song you composed for her. Your gift from the heart surely outshines and shall outlast an Eye-talian, custom, hand-built—albeit half a million dollar—fire-breathing dragon."

"That's very kind of you to say," Ricardo acknowledged. "In addition to the party, I wrote this song to bring some joy into her life...to let Daisy know she is special.... Maybe she'll hear what I want to say to her through the music?"

Joel interrupted, "Daisy knows she's special to you. Everyone knows that. She just has to know. It is as plain as day." He looked over to Mademoiselle Lapin. "We should rehearse the song again, though."

Mademoiselle Lapin motioned for Ricardo and Joel to follow her to the other room. "Play it once more, s'il vous plaît."

An eleven by fourteen inch mahogany frame sat prominently on a stylish baby grand piano with a small crayon drawing of a horse with remarkable detail for one by a kindergartener to have done. Along the bottom of the drawing in block letters with backward Ss: DAISY LOVES DADDY. Two perfect heart-shaped sand dollars Ricardo found on the beach with Daisy adorned the bottom, and Ricardo's handwritten sheet music of the Happy Birthday Song provided the backdrop.

Ricardo sat at the piano. As he played and sang, Mademoiselle Lapin and Joel Harris sang in harmony:

Happy Birthday
Happy Birthday to you
I'm glad to share it with you...

---

[77] Term referring to precious metals, jewels, jewelry and jewelry related items.

"Shhh...," someone says. "They're coming. Everyone be quiet!"

The apartment door opened and in walked Daisy, Amanda, and Siobhan. Fortunately, they did not hear the muffled giggling.

"Daisy," called Ricardo from the living room.

"I'm with my friends," replied Daisy. She turned to Amanda and said in a lower tone, "It's like I'm a little kid! Errr...a little privacy, please."

After a few moments, he called again. "Daisy. Come here, please...*ahorita*[78] ."

Siobhan encouraged, "Just go. It's no biggie. We'll wait here. What the heck are we doin' anyway?"

Daisy made a face and went into the living room.

"Surprise!!" rang out from the other friends, Mademoiselle Lapin, Joel Harris, and her dad, who was grinning from ear to ear.

"¡Feliz *quinceañera*! ¡*Florita mia*[79] ! her dad beamed.

Mademoiselle Lapin caught the embarrassed look that flashed across Daisy's face. Then she spoke abruptly, "Daisy, 'appy birthday. Such a nice party, *mais oui. Ah!* When I was growing up, my family was quite poor. We all lived in Rouen...a medieval village in Normandy. When I was your age, I only dreamed of birthday parties. Or read about them in books. Oh! And here you have such a pretty one. I am so 'appy for you. *Joyeux anniversaire! Joyeux anniversaire!*"

Siobhan and Amanda walked into the room smiling.

Amanda elbowed Daisy. "Gotcha! You had no idea, huh?"

Daisy turned, walked closer to Siobhan, and said softly, "I am so embarrassed. Danny is here. He must think I am a dweeb[80] . Why didn't my dad just hire a pony and clowns... uhhh!"

Siobhan's eyes widened, "Daisy, lighten up. I think it's

[78] (Sp.) a little minute. Equivalent to just a minute in English.
[79] (Sp.) my little flower
[80] Teen slang for someone who is not cool.

thoughtful. Your dad told us keep it a secret. Who do you think invited Danny? Even after he caught you two making-out. He wanted it to be a nice party for you. Come on, have some fun. Beside, I want some of the French pastry Mademoiselle Lapin made. It's the bomb[81] ."

"Yeah," Amanda chimed in. "Pastry! Yum!"

Ricardo walked to the piano and pointed to the picture frame holding Daisy's kindergarten drawing, the heart-shaped sand dollars, and his handwritten sheet music. "Daisy has always been very special to me. In so many ways, I see things in myself that I see in her: her sense of humor; the way she smells food before she eats; things she says and does. Ah, Daisy. You make me a happy father.

"So for your *quinceañera*, I composed a birthday song. The old standard, *Happy Birthday To You*, needs to be replaced by a twenty-first century one. And I wrote it in honor of your *quinceañera*.

"Listen. I will play the melody a few times and then I'll play the refrain. My good neighbors, Mademoiselle Lapin and Mr. Harris will join me on the refrain. Then I'd like it very much if you would all join in on the next refrain for the next two verses. Thank you."

"Dad...," Daisy started to say but he began to play.

The rich sound of the baby grand filled the room. Then he and Mademoiselle Lapin and Joel Harris sang, "We'll have fun. We'll have fun. We'll have fun. We'll have fuh-uh-uhn."

Ricardo's playing was nearly flawless and their singing was in tune. He thought she'd treasure this moment as much as he was wrapped up in the music.

Ricardo continued, "Happy Birthday...."

Daisy wanted to be a million miles away and made her way to the door. Amanda and Siobhan coaxed her to stay.

Amanda sang off-key, "We'll have fun. We'll have fuh-uh-uhn."

---

[81] Teen slang for something fantastic.

○ ○ ○

As Ricardo approached the Pizza Pad, he decided to get a bite. He saw Butchie, the owner, behind the counter staring out red-eyed.

Butchie spoke up in the friendly way of a TSA[82] inspector at a mobbed terminal at 6:30 in the morning, "What it'll be, Ricardo?"

Ricardo responded, "Just a slice."

As he finished slicing up a pizza from the oven, Butchie asked, "No drink?"

Ricardo nodded no.

"Oh, yeah," Butchie acknowledged. "You usually don't get a drink. My bad...as the kids say."

Mr. Brooks walked in and stepped up to the counter. "A slice to go, Butchie. And I'm in a hurry today. So, whatever's hot."

Butchie slid another slice onto another plate. "Everybody's in a hurry. Hang in there. A hot slice in a nanosecond."

Ricardo and Mr. Brooks made eye contact as they shared this piece of *cinéma vérité*.

"Small world," grinned Mr. Brooks. "Good to see you Mr. Villanova."

Ricardo added, "This place is like the crossroads of the world sometime. Lemme ask you something. Have you noticed any changes with Daisy since last year?"

Mr. Brooks replied, "You mean since the thing with her mom."

Ricardo nodded, "I try my best. But when I grew up, I only had brothers. And most...actually, nearly all...my cousins were boys, too."

Mr. Brooks turned to Ricardo. "Let me be frank, Mr. Villanova. It's not just with girls. When a family is disrupted for whatever reason—death, divorce, relocation, family services

---

[82] Transportation Security Administration exercises authority over public transportation.

get involved—a childhood gets disrupted and most children, it seems, don't take it well.

"There's an anger or anxiety and it gets focused on something else...or on someone else: Parents, one parent, or even teachers are on the receiving end of this redirected frustration. It gets acted out in many ways. It could be yelling, arguing, getting into trouble, emotions in turmoil."

Ricardo thought about what he'd just heard. "You make sense. As a teacher, you see students with their peers. They must tell each other the unvarnished truth every once in awhile."

"Oh, yeah," Mr. Brooks concurred.

Ricardo made a gesture by lifting his chin toward Mr. Brooks. "I'm sure you're busy. So, good to see you. And thanks for what you said. A single dad to a teenage girl needs all the advice he can get. And by the way...Daisy has mentioned you teaching in her classes and she feels she's learned interesting things from you...."

He said, "Hang in there. Time tends to heal all wounds."

O O O

As the party was winding down, Danny approached Daisy's father. "Cool party, Mr. V. I had an excellent time. Thanks again for inviting me." He turned to wave to Daisy. "Happy birthday. Or should I say, ¡Feliz cumpleaños!" He smiled broadly as he left.

Daisy turned to hide her face and muttered something. Amanda put her arm across Daisy's shoulder and nodded to Siobhan.

"Nice party, Mr. Villanova," Siobhan remarked. "I think Daisy is just too overwhelmed to show her true emotions. We're gonna take a walk outside for a while."

"Zis is probably a good idea, no?" said Mademoiselle Lapin seeing Ricardo was the one who was overwhelmed. Ricardo nodded yes automatically as the girls started for the door.

The girls walked up the sidewalk after leaving the birthday

party. Daisy kicked a discarded soda can.

Amanda spoke, "Geez, Daisy, you're in a pissy mood. Your dad threw you a birthday party. I thought it was sweet. Come on, he tried."

Siobhan added, "Yeah, and Mademoiselle Lapin's French pastries...ooo, la la." She spun around and kicked up her heels. "You know, she said she never had a birthday party in France 'cause her family was real poor."

"I'm so embarrassed. Did you see the look Danny gave me?" Daisy grumbled. "How'd you like your folks to invite your steady over behind your back and sing kiddie songs. Who does that? He'd want me dressed in a *huipil, quechquemitl,* and *rebozo*[83]. My dad is so...so...so...Mexican! ¡Ay, Chiapas! See! He's got me sayin' his dumb expression instead of *¡Ay, Chihuahua*[84] ! I mean, I'm normal. I should be sayin' O-M-G!"

Amanda tried to console her. "Everyone had a good time, even Danny."

Daisy sobbed a little. "You don't understand. Remember the rumor how my dad and his cousin from Guadalajara had arranged a marriage for me and my cousin, Alejandro? Danny had a nutty. He thought Alejandro slipped me a Mexican aphrodisiac so I'd get pregnant and *have* to marry him for the family honor. Now he's gonna think my dad is planning my whole life."

Siobhan exclaimed, "Daisy, he's the one who invited Danny and made sure he'd be there on time. I was there when he offered Danny money for cab fare so he'd be here early after practice. Is that the sign of someone who doesn't care?"

Amanda agreed, "She's right. I was there, too."

Siobhan added, "Don't get all bent out of shape. Your dad is who he is and all he wanted was to make a nice party for you. He asked us for suggestions. I didn't know what to say but telling him anything would be fine."

[83] Elements of traditional Mexican dress: tunic, dress, and shawl.

[84] Mexican expression of shock or surprise. Attributed to the execution of Miguel Hidalgo, Father of Mexico, by Spain during War of Independence in the city of Chihuahua in 1811.

Amanda agreed. "I mean, yeah. He asked me, too. When he asked, I thought, he's so nice. Then when he asked us to help make sure Danny was gonna be there.... Can't be much nicer than that."

Siobhan turned to Daisy. "I said you'd be surprised and love it. He knows it's tough for you with what happened a few years ago. He's a single dad tryin' to...."

Daisy interrupted, "Always the same lame-o excuse. He's a single dad. He didn't have any sisters. It's all about why it's so hard for him. What about me?"

Siobhan answered, "Hey, he's just explaining why things are hard from his side."

Daisy continued unabated, "He's not the one who who saw her mom walk out...walk away...go onto a mysterious bus and disappear under clouds with thunder and lightning!"

Amanda attempted to agree, "We know, Daisy. We're as confused about all this as you."

Daisy snapped back, "I'm not confused! She'll be back and then you'll see."

Daisy got silent. Siobhan and Amanda looked at each other.

Amanda mouthed, "Just let her be.... Eventually, Daisy will be Daisy again."

O O O

Ricardo left the apartment after the *quinceañera*; disappointed this special fifteenth birthday party didn't turn out as miraculous as he'd envisioned. Daisy didn't feel all the love he had for her and wasn't taken up in the moment her dad worked so hard to achieve. Ricardo walked and walked in a melancholy mood. He ended up at the Midway Amusement Park by the marina. Sunshine tried to work its way from behind the clouds.

He thought, *What the heck?* as he spied Madame Zhang's Chop Suey Sandwich Shoppe.

"Long time, no see you," smiled Madame Zhang from behind her chrome and glass counter under ultrabright fluorescent lights.

"Hǎo jiǔ bú jiàn[85] ," replied Ricardo. "One chop suey sandwich and a cup of tea, please."

Madame Zhang flipped a swipe of margarine on the grill and a split hamburger bun on top of the bubbling liquid. She lifted the glass cover from a pot of chop suey on a gas burner and a thick cloud of steam rose to the ceiling. She spooned a healthy ladle of chop suey onto the bottom bun and capped it with its toasted mate.

Ricardo looked on half concentrating and half thinking about what may have happened at the birthday party.

Madame Zhang ripped a piece of waxed paper from an industrial-sized roll, smoothed it onto a cutting board and folded the sandwich into an origami-cocoon. She placed an insulated paper cup with several Chinese characters written along its side under the spickett of one of the twin 5-gallon percolators and filled it seven-eights full of oolong tea. She slid the wrapped sandwich and the tea into a white paper bag with the prestidigitation of Ching Ling Foo,[86] whose portrait adorned a place of honor near the entrance.

Ricardo walked out of the sandwich shop into a low lying fog back brought ashore off the water. He spied an empty bench along the deserted waterfront. He decided to have his sandwich there instead of going home. He carefully removed the cup and cracked the flap on the cover. The amalgamation of the steam and the fog made both indistinguishable. A golden beam of sunlight cut through the fog and opened a clearing in the center of the harbor.

The water was tranquil and he heard a chugging motor. The bow of a mahogany boat slowly moved into the clearing. Its graceful movement, almost in slow-motion, took its time as the frothy, gray-green water peeled off the bow to oblivion.

More and more of the boat came into view revealing a strikingly attractive, red-haired girl in a white bikini lying on the

---

[85] (Mandarin) 好久不见 Hau jiu bu jian
[86] Famous Chinese magician (1874-1926)

polished wooden front deck propped up on her elbows. A few teenage boys appeared to his right by the water's edge hooting out cat-calls. The girl disinterestedly looked past their waves and focused over toward the benches. Ricardo made eye contact and he felt like she was drawing his thoughts out through a straw. And in his mind he heard a soft feline voice clearly annunciate, "I am Xhuljana."

Ricardo took a sip of his tea, which was still piping hot, and he noticed no one was at the controls of the boat. He took another sip; the familiar flavor; comforting and contemplative.

He heard her voice again, "I need to talk to you before it's too late. Be cautious, Ricardo. There are those who mean you harm close by."

A rat-tat-tat sound came from behind. It startled him and he turned around and noticed a black silhouette. When Ricardo looked back, the boat and the girl were gone.

"Y-esss? Y-esss. Tea is such a fine beverage. It makes you think, doesn't it? Y-esss? Y-esss?" said a tall, thin man dressed in black. He had very pasty looking skin offset by his very dark, round sunglasses.

Ricardo thought the man odd. He reminded Ricardo of Aschenbach, a sad character in <u>Death In Venice</u>, who wore heavy make-up and tried vainly to blend in with young people, especially a young boy, over twenty years his junior.

Ricardo nodded to the man's inquiry without saying a word.

Dr. Perp walked around the bench, pointed to where the slow moving motor boat had been with his black cane and said, "Y-esss! Y-esss! You know, she can't win. She may try to use her charms on you. She may even try to seduce you. You are a man after all. But don't be fooled. And don't give in. This will be your only warning, Mr. Villanova. Xhuljana won't win. Trust me. I know what I know. Y-esss! Y-esss!"

Ricardo narrowed his eyes. "Sir, I'm sitting here enjoying the afternoon. I don't know you, or have any idea what you are talking about. Why don't you go on your way and leave me in peace?"

Dr. Perp cupped the rounded top of his walking stick and make a tight circular motion. "Y-esss? Y-esss? You only think I don't know what I know. But I do know. You're concerned about Daisy. Y-esss? Y-esss? She seems torn between two worlds. Y-esss? Y-esss? You know she won't choose the world you are in. Y-esss? Y-esss! I know what I know! Mr. Villanova, don't ignore my warning. Y-esss? Y-esss?"

Ricardo was distracted by the noise from the motor of the boat, which he could not see due to the fog. He could not tell if the boat was changing direction or docking. He peered into the haze but saw did not see the boat.

He thought, *This strange man just mentioned Daisy! I'd never seen him before. How could he know her name? What did he mean she was torn between two worlds? Ignore his warning? Where did that beautiful girl go? I wish she'd talk to me.*

Ricardo turned back to the paperbag and removed the sandwich. He studied the wrapping while he unfolded it. When he looked up, the tall man was gone without a trace. Then he heard a different voice in his ear, although he sat alone. It was a low voice with a whimsical overture. "He's right, you know. Xhuljana will try to seduce you. She knows how to hypnotize men, especially. Though, she has wrapped many a woman around her little finger, too. Hmmm."

The fog rolled on shore. It was so heavy he could not see the ground in front of him. Ricardo was lost in his own thought and soon he was somewhere else: He heard Daisy's friends talking like he was secretly with them.

Siobhan asked, "Why do you put your dad down? You try to hold him to double National Honor Society standards. No dad is perfect."

Daisy scuffed her feet. "My mom was."

Amanda pointed a finger, "So perfect she ran off? Left you? Left your dad? Without a word?"

"You don't understand," Daisy loudly replied. "And when she's ready, she'll come back. He's the problem: he's Mexican and he's...."

"Daisy," Siobhan uttered sharply. "I can't believe what I'm hearing. Don't you remember Mr. Brooks' class about desegregation? What caused racism? You're like the angry crowds in Little Rock! You're sayin' Mexican and they were sayin' nigger."

Daisy defended herself. "I'm not a racist."

Amanda looked at her sternly. "You talk like one when you talk about your dad or his family. Siobhan is right. It's not cool."

Daisy teetered back and forth. "Fo'get about it. See ya later."

Daisy walked away with deliberate strides. Siobhan and Amanda watched her leave.

Daisy climbed the stairs to her floor and opened the apartment door.

Ricardo saw himself call from the kitchen, "*Florita. ¿Qué tal?*"

"Errr. Just leave me alone," Daisy said under her breath as she closed the door to her room firmly.

The evening went by without a word. She refused to have dinner or leave her room. He attempted to coax her out of her room but the closed door remained silent.

Ricardo went to bed. He was restless and rolled in his bed.... The night sky was clear. Stars shined brightly and an occasional wispy, silver cloud floated by. He detected a sweet floral scent and felt a light touch on his shoulder.

"I need to talk to you," the same soft female voice whispered.

He turned and looked into the enticing, feline eyes of the red-haired woman sitting on the bench next to him. He felt an instant connection that bridged a wide time span: old, yet something new.

"You look familiar," Ricardo spoke as he turned his head at an angle. "You're the girl from the boat." His eyes widened as he took her in. She was now wearing a white summer dress.

Xhuljana looked inquisitively at Ricardo. "Something's happening here. Really. I can't just say exactly what. I can't. I had to...reach you."

Ricardo confirmed, "You reached me for sure."

"I'm Xhuljana. You happen to be in the intersection of an old conflict. Time was running out. You were at Madame Zhang's. And my arch enemy was on your trail. I was trying.... I've said too much. Just listen, please."

Ricardo inquired, "Does your arch enemy have a name?"

"Oh, him...," Xhuljana held back a laugh. "Since he already told you my name, it is only fair that I tell you his name. He is Dr. Perp. At least, that's the name that he answers to."

Ricardo countered questioningly, "Doctor Perp? Yes? Or should I say: Yeh-ssss? He talks like he has a load in his shorts."

They chuckled.

"Don't take him lightly," Xhuljana placed her warm hand on his. He soaked in the soothing feeling. He felt at-home and relaxed.

Ricardo inexplicably recalled an image of the strange man saying her name. It made him shiver. He quickly turned away trying to escape thinking about the strange man. He looked down at their hands then back into her eyes.

Xhuljana continued, "Sometime you're so close you cannot see the end until after it's gone. I don't like saying this but you deserve better. Daisy deserves better."

"Daisy!" Ricardo desperately yelled and he tore himself from his dream. "Doctor Perp mentioned Daisy, too. Why is she mixed up in this mess? Haven't we been through enough already?"

He was drawn back to something in the harbor. The mahogany boat passed in the opposite direction it traveled before. This time the woman was at the helm wearing the white dress. Their eyes locked and he heard her voice: Hang tough, Ricardo. The keys to the future are the keys to the past.

O O O

Mademoiselle Lapin was strolling in a park downtown. It was one of those days when the weather was just so; not too cool; not too windy; not too sunny. She had been enjoying the deep blue sky when a large gray cloud rolled in. Some birds nearby took flight and a cold breeze weaved around the trees.

Rat-tat-tat-tat sounded behind her. She turned around and saw a tall man in a dark suit with pasty skin wearing deep, dark, round sunglasses.

"*Oooo!* You seems to be here from nowhere," Mademoiselle Lapin gasped in mock surprise.

"Y-esss? Y-esss?" Dr. Perp spoke slowly, "from nowhere indeed. This park is so delightful, don't you think? I occasionally walk here to have a word with myself. And answer my own questions. Y-esss. Y-esss."

Mademoiselle Lapin shook her head. "Monsieur Dr. Perp, what unanswered questions could be in the vast vacuum in your head? *Sacre Couer!*"

Dr. Perp slammed the tip of his walking stick to the sidewalk with a loud snap. "Y-esss. Y-esss. Mademoiselle Lapin, we know what is inside your head. So many deep thoughts. So much French wisdom. Y-esss? Y-esss?"

They faced off silently with tension in the air the way tendrils of breath stream from two rams squaring off to settle a long standing score on a cold mountainside.

Mademoiselle Lapin broke the silence and answered, "Let's not beat around the bush. You know Xhuljana will not be denied. She seems to be...*une longuere d'avance*...or how you say: one step ahead, *non?* And your feeble plot to win over Deborah...or Angelina as you renamed her...and Daisy to your side is futile. It is doomed to fail. *Ah, oui.* It is doomed to fail."

Dr. Perp said, "Y-esss. Y-esss! Ye of little faith. Have you overlooked triumphs like Mussolini, Stalin, Pol Pot, Miloševiⅼ? Didn't you think Xhuljana was one step ahead then, too? Y-esss? Y-esss?"

Mademoiselle Lapin answered, "You might fight for every win as if it was an end in itself; as if no day exists beyond today. After making it through these combative and torturous millennia, you should know better, *mais non?* Monsieur Dr., you can be such an *enfant terrible*. It's a little childish, *oui?*"

Just as two rivals in the forest primeval inexplicitly back down their conversation ended. Each feeling the battle was won but in an empty way as disappointing as a loss.

V

Amanda texted Daisy and Siobhan: "A fancy letter addressed to me was on my door mat! OMG!!"

"Me2[87]" was texted back by both of them.

Siobhan added, "I opened mine. It's an invitation to go to the Midway Arcade 2nite."

Amanda replied, "Just opened mine. me2 "

Daisy texted back, "Me3. Meet u@parking lot@7:30"

The girls met at the parking lot. Each had an identical invitation: the chocolate brown envelopes had each of their names done in beautiful calligraphy. The invitation read:

You are cordially invited for a one time only evening at the Midway Arcade as our special guest. Be sure to try out the coin operated Gypsy Fortune Teller. It is an antique from the 1950s. Arrive at 7:30 and don't be late !

"What do you make of it?" Siobhan asked..

Siobhan and Amanda saw Daisy walking toward them. They made their way to the Midway Arcade.

"Kinda funny when you think about it," Siobhan said. "The Midway Arcade closed down a long time ago. All of the amusements were way old, no video games, no wifi[88] , no food court like in the malls...so no one went, and it shut down. So we each get an engraved invitation like they want to start it up again. I didn't look online or on FB[89] to check out the buzz."

ꗍ ꗍ ꗍ

Amanda, Siobhan, and Daisy walked to the amphitheater on a small bluff overlooking the harbor. They walked onto the stage matching step for step with each other and came together center stage.

Siobhan yelled out to the seats, "Must be nice to have the

---

[87] text for me, too

[88] wireless frequency - a wireless signal for electronic devices

[89] FaceBook® a trendy so-called social media originally created as a dating venue for socially awkward students at MIT.

bright lights shining on you." She stepped forward a step and looked out on adoring fans beyond the imaginary klieg lights.

Then they imagined it was nighttime and the band struck a chord. Siobhan, Amanda, and Daisy extended their right arms with palms facing the crowd.

"Stop!" They sang in unison. "In the name of Love! Before you break my heart."

The three girls pantomimed a 60s girl group performance with sparkling gowns shimmering under the bright lights.

They continued, "Think it over: think it oh-oh-ver..."

The real applause of a single pair of clapping hands broke their imaginary setting.

"*Bravisimo! Bravisimo!*" Vincent loudly declared. "You girls got game. Don't you think so, Ernest?"

Ernest concurred, "Most certainly. It is so refreshing to see three girls who are not so inhibited. Too many people—young and old—cave into traditional conventions. They never open up to what is all around them. Girls, don't you feel freer when you're in the moment? When you're captured by your performance?"

"How true," Vincent insisted. "The artiste captured by her performance! How enticing! How *bon vivant!*"

Amanda whispered to Daisy, "What's he sayin'? Bon Reebok[90]? I'm wearin' Jordan's[91]. You're wearin' Converse All-Star[92]. Reebok is so last century!"

Daisy said, "I think he said: *bon vivant*. It is a French expression for a free life-style...like most artists live."

Vincent was suddenly exceedingly close to Daisy. "Well...! You know something about artistes, don't you?"

Daisy shifted back after being startled by the rotund man wearing a tuxedo on a warm spring day.

Vincent displayed an uncular look as he stared into Daisy's eyes much like a sad eyed cow. "Don't minimize your gift, Daisy. You have a commanding presence on stage. Take it from

---

[90] Reebok – a brand of sneakers
[91] Air Jordan – a brand of sneakers
[92] Converse – a brand of sneakers

me: My name is Vincent." He bowed ceremoniously. "I have performed before kings and queens, sultans, despots, and maharajas."

Ernest courtsied. "I'm Ernest. I can attest to what Vincent has told you. You should be extremely flattered that a legend...a man of renown from the performance arts, Vincent, has taken notice of you and your nascent talents. Ah! To be so young and with such obvious talents."

Before Vincent had a chance to add another word, Siobhan spoke out, "Daisy, we gotta get going." She motioned with her eyes and her head.

Vincent carried on without a comma, "Daisy...hmmm. Daisy is too mundane. We need something better. I'll give you a stage name: Raquim. Indeed, Raquim. A name with style and grace. A little piece of teenage heaven right here on earth." He laughed a deep belly laugh as if it were he who had taken center stage.

The girls turned and scampered off toward the heart of the amusement park. Daisy looked back and Vincent caught her gaze. Daisy heard Vincent's voice like he was whispering in her ear though he was over fifty feet away: Go with the flow, Raquim. Your artistic instincts will lead you where you should go."

They went over a small hill and continued down to a parking lot. Nearly straight across the parking lot, they saw Madame Zhang's Chop Suey Sandwich Shop. They entered the store mesmerized by the sweet fragrance of cooking bean sprouts.

A stately, dark haired, oriental woman spoke in a heavily accented voice spoke, "Girls. What you want? Chop suey sandwich to go? Three to go? No drink?"

"Yes, please," Siobhan replied.

Amanda whispered, "It is almost like she can read our minds. Freaky!"

The Chinese woman shot three swipes of margarine to the hot grill from her shiny metal utensil then three split hamburger buns took their positions on top of spattering pools of boiling liquid. A second later each bun had been assembled with a heap of chop suey from a steamy pot, wrapped securely in waxed paper, and loaded into a white paper bag.

The girls sat on a curbstone and unwrapped their sandwiches.

Amanda said, "That was weird back there. The creepy fat man was talkin' all mad crazy stuff. *Bon Reebok*...or whatever!" She made a circular motion with her index finger around her temple. "He's the whack[93] !"

Daisy retorted, "You're jealous. The other man said he was famous. I believe him. Danny thinks I have a nice voice."

Siobhan added, "Danny would say anything to flatter you. He likes you."

"Nuh uh," Daisy answered. "He wouldn't neither."

Amanda teased, "Daisy likes Danny...Daisy likes Danny."

Siobhan pointed at Daisy. "You know? I think they were two of the three men we saw near the Pizza Pad talking to the two drunk hobo ladies."

Daisy disagreed, "Nah uh. The guys by the Pizza Pad were taller and spoke differently. They had an English accent. Especially, the tall one with the ultra-dark sunglasses. And they had black canes, too."

O O O

The girls heard soft guitar music and noticed two lanky, long-haired young men approaching. One wore white muslin trousers with thin red, black, and blue stripes running down the legs and bunched up at his ankles. He had on a worn out canvas colored peasant shirt. He was barefoot and banging on an old tamborine. The other troubadour wore something similar but he had a large dark-purple brimmed felt hat, a colorful vest, and dark, oversized sunglasses.

The young man with the tambourine clanged and banged out a beat. He sang in a Cockney accent to the slowly strummed song: *Who-ooo-ooo are we? / Are we just / Who we want to be? /*

---

[93] Colloquial for bad or bogus

Who-ooo-ooo are we?

The guitarist harmonized with the singer emphasizing the melody. Both appeared mesmerized by their performance.

The girls applauded at the conclusion of their song. They looked at each other half-daring the other to say something to the boys.

Amanda went first, "How nice!"

The guitarist remarked casually, "Thank you, girls. Much appreciated."

Daisy cleared her throat and spoke up, "What are you doing here in Midway? You have an accent. English?"

The tambourine player answered, "Right-o. We hail from London Town. We're troubadours from old SoHo."

Siobhan noticed they both had a lot of glittery eye make-up. She must have been staring when the guitarist turned to Siobhan like a suspicious security camera.

He said through a laugh, "It's part of the Show—the makeup, the costumes, the trance, the dance, the dreams, the schemes."

Amanda, Daisy, and Siobhan giggled as the two troubadours continued down the road laughing and carrying on with each other.

Amanda looked at Daisy and Siobhan, "They had sparkly eye makeup. I think I'll just call them the glimmer twins. Yeah!"

"You just think they're cute," Daisy teased.

Amanda blushed a little. "Yeah, guess so. I liked the song..." She sang off-key, "Who are we supposed to be...."

"That's not it," Daisy interrupted. "It's Who are we? Are we just who we want to be?"

"What do you think it means?" asked Siobhan.

Daisy answered, "Aren't we just who we think we are? That's what I always thought. You are who you think you are. What we think makes reality what it is.... *Are we just who we want to be? Who-ooo-ooo...ooo-ooo....*Oh, whatever."

Siobhan disagreed. "That can't be true. Remember Mr. Brooks told us about the Native American story in ELA[94] ? The

---

94 English Language Arts

Gold-fish. He said it was 'an allusion of an illusion'. He said he would bring in copies of the story some time. Betcha it'll be interesting. He likes to bring in really cool stuff."

Amanda told them, "He mentioned it in my class, too. He said the Gold-fish was looking for a world of beauty. But she was deceived into believing an illusion."

"Yeah but," Daisy protested. "She *did* think she was seeing a world of beauty. And to her it was a world of beauty."

The girls paused. They heard the troubadours in the distance: *Who-ooo-ooo are you? / Can you do / Just what you want to do? / Who-ooo-ooo are you?*

Siobhan said, "What they're singing is right. We're not just who we think we are. There's much more to it."

The girl heard the troubadours singing softly in the distance, *"Who-ooo-ooo am I? / Does ev'rything work out / And I don't even have to try? / Who-ooo-ooo am I?"*

"We better get to the Amusement Park. The invitation said don't be later!" Amanda reminded them.

Siobhan agreed, "Yeah, it did say: don't be late. Ya know, like we might miss something important that'll happen at the beginning of the night."

The three girls walked toward the Amusement Park with a sense of anticipation. Each felt it would be an exciting night. One they'd remember.

Daisy thought about the Frozen Words: *They are the clue. If can unlock their hidden meaning, I'll find my mom.*

Daisy couldn't figure it out but she knew Owldoll would be there to help her. She wanted to be confident and strong but youth extended doubt when the world looked at her.

O O O

At the entrance to the Midway Arcade was a coin-operated gypsy fortune-telling machine. An older looking female mannequin encased by yellowed and scratched plexiglass wearing a white turban was sitting behind a crystal ball. The mannequin had pale green skin and pale green eyes. She seemed to be look-ing directly at the girls.

"Truth or dare?" said Siobhan as she took a selfie[95] with the gypsy mannequin.

"You're not gonna waste your money on this old thing," Daisy said as she rolled her eyes.

Amanda stepped up and added, "I think it's cool, Daisy. What's the harm? Beside, the invitation said not to miss the antique gypsy fortune teller. It's like a connection to the past."

Amanda gave Daisy a quarter and she placed in the coin slot. A mechanized sound commenced, lights went on, and its plastic hand hovered around the glowing glass globe.

"Let me look into your future," the gypsy woman an-nounced. Her eyelids closed and opened and closed and opened. Then her eyes closed a long while as soft music played. The lights lowered and a blue light shined from below to exag-gerate her facial features. The mystic mannequin pronounced, "I am Madame Buzorkan[96] , Gypsy Fortune Teller. I know all. I tell all. Your past was poisoned by a wing-ed[97] witch and your future will be saved by wing-ed words."

Siobhan looked astounded and managed to utter, "Whaaa..."

Daisy wiggled her fingers in front of Siobhan. "Spooky, spooky. Come on. It's just a recorded message."

Madame Buzorkan raised her hands palms out, turned to look directly at Daisy, and spoke, "Is that so Daisy?"

Then she faced each of the girls and addressed them each by name. The girls froze and turned pale. They looked at each other with an expression of shock.

Madame Buzorkan continued, "You are here about your future but first you must hear about your past. You're all here because of Daisy.

"The origin of the tale will take too long to explain. In fact,

---

95 a digital image of someone by him or herself at arms length chroni-cling mundane activities

96 Buzz-orkin

97 wing Edd

Daisy, it started before you were born. The trouble began with a wing-ed witch and the answer to the riddle you seek will come from a wing-ed word."

The machine clanked and rumbled as its lights dimmed.

"Huh?" Amanda cried. "I'm scared. This is way too weird."

She and Siobhan looked at Daisy.

"Don't look at me," Daisy declared. "I don't know what she means. Do you?"

Amanda looked blankly back and Siobhan shrugged her shoulders. Then Amanda suggested, "Put another quarter in. See what else she says."

Before Daisy could say anything, Siobhan put a quarter into the slot. The machine hummed back to life.

Madame Buzorkan cupped her hands over the crystal ball and stared at Daisy.

Daisy stammered, "Ca-ca-can you tell us more?"

Siobhan asked, "What did you mean it started before Daisy was born? What started? What riddle? What...."

Madame Buzorkan interrupted, "The time is near. Listen to me: You must go to the House of Mirrors. Next go to the Wilde Mouse. And after that go to the Whirl-Ye Twirl-Ye. And all of your questions will be answered. Remember, go to the House of Mirrors. Next go to the Wilde Mouse. And after that go to the Whirl-Ye Twirl-Ye. And all of your questions will be answered."

Madame Buzorkan's booth filled with green smoke and soon she was hidden from view.

"You can't get away with that," Daisy barked as she tried to put another quarter in the slot. But when she pushed on the slide, it wouldn't move. She shoved it again and again. Nothing.

Amanda shoved up to the machine. "Lemme try." Amanda banged it with the palm of her hand. Nothing.

"We're getting nowhere fast," Siobhan noted. "We may as well go to the House of Mirrors."

O O O

Ernest skipped into the House of Mirrors announcing, "Mirrors are so much fun. Only an artist can see the beauty that's there...."

Vincent interrupted, "Ah hum...We artistes are the avant-garde: Only an artiste sees his own beauty! And sees it first!"

Ernest agreed, "Very true, Vincent. The plebeians need us to brighten their sorry lives. I'm so glad we got here before the crowd."

"Ordinary people miss everything. How tragic. We're first... again," Vincent mocked crying as he rubbed his eyes with closed fits. "Let's see what a real artiste looks like, hmmm." They walked over to the large mirror in the foyer and took their position.

Vincent rested as he admired his reflection in the full-length mirror. As he moved closer, the image distorted. "Look at me," he cried out euphorically. "True beauty!"

"No, no. Look at me," yelled Ernest as he bumped his way in front of the mirror. "Don't be such a hog for the limelight, Vincent. Just look at me in comparison! How wonderful am I?"

Vincent moved in front of Ernest, "No, me first. Just wait. Who could be more wonderful than I? Remember Phillppe I, duc d'Orleans? Hmmm? And those magnificent mirrors in Versailles! He adored my reflection. Remember?"

Ernest heard something and cautioned Vincent to stop by raising his index finger to his lips. "Wait. They're coming. The girls are coming. Quick, let's hide."

○ ○ ○

Amanda, Siobhan, and Daisy entered the House of Mirrors to the prerecorded creek of a rusted hinge and door slamming shut behind them as the reinforced cardboard flap swung closed by a spring-loaded attachment. The black walls and dim lighting added to a spooky air about the place.

In the back of the foyer stood a tall mirror in a dark wooden

frame. Just ahead of the mirror was a chrome stand with a placard that read: One At A Time, Please. Above the mirror was
a sign that read: Who are we? Are we just who we want to be?
Who are we?

Daisy looked into the mirror. The full surface transformed
into an image of a raging storm: dark clouds of grays and blacks
and whites, whirling winds, flashes of thunder and lightning
in the distance. Daisy stared at the images in the mirror and
wondered why there was no reflection of the room.

The storm clouds parted and revealed a city from above
with streets crisscrossing between rows of buildings. The scene
telescoped into an apartment and there appeared to have been
some commotion during this brief glance. People in the apartment moved about frantically. The image shifted back out to
view the whole building from above it. Birds flew away in a hurry just before a person rushed out of the building and moved
quickly down the front walkway. Two figures came out of the
building a moment later. One of the two stopped short and
the other continued to follow the first person. That person
stopped, went forward briefly, and stopped again; then turned
around and return to the other figure by the entrance. Then
the two of them huddled together.

At the same time, the person who left first continued at a
deliberate clip careening off people on the sidewalk toward a
bus stop up the street.

Siobhan uttered, "Look, it's your building. And that's you
and your dad. That must be your mother."

"Oh, my God!" sputtered Amanda. "She's right. Look it!
That is your building...and that is you, Daisy!" Amanda pointed to the figure at the entrance to the building.

Daisy shook her head, "No way. You're just buying the
illusion."

"Shut the front door," Amanda let out in a loud voice. "See
the walkway, the trees, the side street. That is your building,
doofus."

Daisy didn't want to believe it but it was her building. She looked closer. She saw herself and her dad standing in front of the building that day. She was frozen in time and frozen in the present: she was somewhere and she was nowhere.

Then Daisy watched in amazement as the scene unfolded. A line of people were boarding the bus as the first person approached. The girls watched half amused by the collisions—it was like watching a video game—until they could see a person in line was knocked over. The image was too real to ignore. Some of the people in the line clustered around someone who looked like he or she had fallen and could not get up. A few people helped the individual back up.

Siobhan added, "Whoa! Mad rude. Look it there," Siobhan pointed to a spot on the ground. "This looks like a crutch."

Amanda continued, ""Yeah! I think it's just a cane 'cause there's only one thing on the ground."

"That was crazy," Daisy said. "Why didn't they wait in line? Who could be so thoughtless?"

The mirror clouded up again and made a clockwise swirl. They stood silently unable to ask each other about what they had seen.

"Let's go this way," Siobhan suggested. "The clouds are rotating this direction. Could it be a sign?"

Amanda and Daisy nodded in agreement and walked toward a long, dark hallway.

Daisy turned a corner at the end of the dark corridor and saw the light outlining an entrance or an exit. She announced, "Here's our way out of the House of Mirrors. Let's take it!"

Daisy proceeded toward the light with Amanda and Siobhan close behind. When she reached it, she began to feel for a handle. Daisy felt nothing at first. It was a situation similar to not recognizing someone you only see at school at a store or in a different city. You look but you don't see. Then you make the connection.

Daisy rested her hand against the smooth surface and as she waited the door knob suddenly was there! She turned it and light flooded in. The girls exited the hallway and were faced with a large archway.

As they walked along, the walls narrowed and the ceiling lowered until they barely squeezed through the space. A distinct scratching sound was audible as they came upon another closed doorway. This time it pushed open easily. A large gymnasium-sized room was on the other side with metal rafters, a smooth concrete floor, and six electric cars shaped like mice.

The girls noticed the cars had wheels and little feet, which were scratching at the concrete rhythmically. Daisy approached a mouse-car that seemed to be calling her. It nuzzled its head against Daisy a few times making mousy sounds.

Amanda made her way to the mouse-car she thought reminded her of the cartoon character Pixie[98] . But it backed away. So, she went to another car that looked more like a real mouse, opened the door, and got it. She asked, "Why d'ya think it's called Wild Mouse? Are these the wild mouses?"

"Mice not mouses! Really! Where are we? In a Looney Tunes[99] cartoon? And you *hate meeces to pieces?*[100] Sometime, Amanda. You can be so...so...," Daisy wagged her finger up at the mouse eyes to Amanda.

"The first one I liked," Amanda insisted and made a face through her mouse eyes. "That one looked like Pixie from the cartoon show, but it moved away from me. At least this one was way more friendly."

Daisy examined the interior of her mouse-car: it was like a fur-lined bathtub with a windshield shaped like two little eyes. There were fur-lined glove sleeves and fur-lined booted pant legs to slip into. When Daisy stretched out, the car spang to life and flew across the floor at a breakneck speed. She was hurling toward a wall but at the last moments she relaxed—contrary to her instinct. This slowed the car to an eventual stop.

Oh, she thought. *I gotta be careful. Hey, I better shout out to Amanda and Siobhan before they...* Daisy shouted loudly, "Watch

[98] "Pixie and Dixie and Mr. Jinx" cartoon series from Hanna-Barbera
[99] short animated films from Warner Bros.
[100] line by the character Mr. Jinx, a cat, who continually was outsmarted by Pixie and Dixie, two mice

it! The gloves and the boots make these cars move. So don't make any movements you don't mean. And when you move, these mouse-cars move mad fast!"

Daisy looked through the mouse eyes and watched. Amanda spun around in place while she laughed hysterically. Then Amanda flew across the room, zig-zagging, racing in wide arcs, and yelling: weeeee! watch meeeee! weeeee! Amanda came within inches of Siobhan's car and skidded to a halt.

Amanda heard Daisy through the mouse ears and felt a vibration rumble along the mouse-car body. She noticed a gray metalac grilled speaker box in front of her that matched the ones where the mouse ears were located.

Amanda replied into the speaker in front of her, "Daisy? You hear me...?"

"Yes!" screamed Daisy immediately.

Siobhan cautioned, "Not so loud. You're hurting my ears."

Daisy answered, "We can hear each other. Let's meet in the center of the room and make a plan."

"Last one there's a big, fat loser," Amanda blurted out as she raced off.

The other girls manipulated their mouse-cars to the center of the area with reasonable dexterity. Amanda kept circling the other two, taunting them with woooos and whoaaas, and screeching stops and starts. While they were preoccupied, they did not observe Vincent, Ernest, and Dr. Perp command the other three mouse-cars, and sneak off to the corners.

Darkness fell over the room and partitions dropped in place from the ceiling and popped up from the floor. Their mouse-cars began to scratch in rapidly and vibrate. The girls saw the landscape had changed before their eyes and were wondering what to do next.

The words Wilde Mouse became visible on what would be the inside of the forehead of the mouse in each of their cars in bright, flowing lettering.

"Hi, girls," said a mysterious voice over all of their speakers. "Now it is time for the Wilde Mouse Ride. You are going on a thrilling ride....uhh huhh. Not like some ride in any amusement park you've seen....oh, no! This is part of an elaborate game designed just for you...hmmm. It is only a game but the stakes are higher than what you're probably used to playing...."

A different voice interrupted, "Don't say too much. You'll ruin everything." The sound of the voice clearing his throat. "You can't control yourself. It happens whenever you...."

"I wouldn't...," the first voice desperately claimed.

"Y-esss? Y-esss! You can't help yourself. Your continual need for self-affirmation. You are never content to be quiet. Y-esss. Y-esss. You don't see secrecy is our best ally. Because what they don't know can trap them. Y-esss? Y-esss?"

I wonder, Daisy thought. *Can the ones who are talking to us hear us through these speakers? Better motion to Amanda and Siobhan to meet up over there.*

Amanda was waving to Siobhan and her to move to their right. And they did and met up on the other side of a partition. Amanda mouthed: we need to keep our silence; like when we're talking in class. She almost giggled but held herself in check.

Siobhan nodded in agreement and mouthed: we'll need to talk in code; I don't like this one bit.

Colored lights blinked on and off in different sections and illuminated the walls of the maze. The cars scratched and vibrated feverishly. Siobhan jerked her head. They took their cue and moved to another spot.

Just after they left another two mouse-cars raced into the space the girls had occupied.

"Oh, darn," the original voice said over their speakers. "But I believe you are getting the hang of Wilde Mouse. Uhh huhh. It is really quite simple. You are either a Wilde Mouse or a Trapped Mouse. Hmmmm. So very simple. Let the Wilde Mouse Ride begin. Hmmmmm. Try to not become a captured mouse. Hmmmmm."

"Flash game[101] mode, girls" shouted Amanda. "Woooo. Woooo."

---

[101] term for old computer games, usually cheap or free

The girls began to work their way separately through the maze. After a few turns, they met up at another spot.

Siobhan said, "We're in an AoE[102] . Wish we could see the maze from above so we'd know where we were going."

Dr. Perp motioned for Vincent and Ernest to come. They drove their mouse-cars to where Dr. Perp was standing in a dark corner.

"Y-esss? Y-esss? The maze is too easy for these girls. We must change things. Y-esss! Y-esss!"

Ernest agreed, "You're right, Dr. Perp. I was thinking...."

"Y-esss. Y-esss. We need to make it more war-like. A battle we will win. Y-esss? Y-esss."

"Oh, how delicious! I love war: it's such good entertainment," Vincent concurred. "I did love the Battle of Bunker Hill and General Howe."

Ernest chimed in, "Goody, goody. We're going to war. All those soldiers in uniform."

"Y-esss. Y-esss!" Dr. Perp replied rubbing his hands together. "We'll surely have the upper hand to win this battle. Y-esss? Y-esss."

The Wilde Mouse lettering flashed again and modulated in intensity. The cars scratched harder. Then the partitions retracted and the room transformed into a grassy hill. Everything seemed over-sized: each blade of grass was just that much bigger, or so it seemed. The blades of grass appeared magnified. They heard a thump-a-thump coming from behind the hill and the sky was an overcast gray with a sharp but enticing odor.

Amanda asked, "What about the stink? It smells like the fourth of July."

Daisy agreed, "Yeah. I thought it smelled familiar."

"Look!" Siobhan shouted pointing at each of their cars. The cars now looked more real and the mouse hair was a darker brown, a more subdued white, and a blacker black. The hair was thicker, too.

Amanda confirmed, "We're outside and it smells industrial.

---

[102] Area of Effect - game term for area where player is vulnerable to attack

It's like when the boys light off firecrackers."

"Yeah," Daisy agreed staring at the outside of Siobhan's car. "Dunno. But the fur is furier."

Right then a group of ten men—or a mix of men and boys—ran past them.

"What was that?" Daisy asked. "A bunch of guys. But what were they wearing? The pants only went down past their knees. And their socks went all the way up. Maybe they were wearing tights?"

"Ewwww!" screamed Amanda. "We're in a different world. Hope they don't have manly-girls."

They saw another group of men and boys to their right. The men were carrying rifles. But old-fashioned rifles and powder horns around their necks.

One man barked, "Tow the line, boys. The Red Coats are o'er the ridge."

"Wow! They talk mad funny. All British or somethin'," Amanda exclaimed when she heard their stylized way of speaking.

Siobhan noted, "But it isn't cold in here anymore. It's kinda warm, don't you think?"

"Yeah. I feel warm actually. Did someone turn up the heat?" asked Amanda.

Siobhan nodded her head in agreement. When she looked over, Daisy signaled for them to get out of there with some urgency. So the girls raced off in different directions.

O O O

"They're using teenage texting lingo. I have no idea what this alphabet soup means," announced the second voice over all of their speakers a moment later.

"Let me see...hmmmm. A. O. E. I think it means An Ordinary...." replied the first voice.

"Vincent!" shouted the second voice. "Put a lid on it! They can hear everything we're saying. If they think we don't understand their code, they'll talk behind our backs. We need the upper hand!"

A bright flash of light went off and their three mouse-cars re-appeared on top of a grassy hillside. There were a few canvas tents behind a covered wooden table. British soldiers were everywhere. Dr. Perp, Vincent, and Ernest stood behind the table dressed like royal tax collectors from the time of the American Revolution.

"Hope you approve of my choice of attire," Ernest inquired as he did a little twirl to display the long tails of his coat and his high buttoned, blue waistcoat.

"Oh yes indeed," Vincent concurred. "You know my fondness of jabots and knickers. Some styles never go out of fashion in my book."

"Y-esss. Y-esss. Time has come to win this battle once and for all. I hope you've not left anything to chance. Y-esss? Y-esss?"

"Like calling me by name. Really, Ernest! And you talk about me! If this isn't the stove calling the kettle black, for sure!" Vincent professed.

Ernest replied, "You're not worried some school-girls are going to outsmart us, do you? Pah-leeeezzz. Just stick to our plan. It will be like it was in June of 1775. It will all be over soon. Remember?"

"Seems like only yesterday...." Vincent answered. "What are they going to know about the Battle of Bunker Hill? And what little they might know will be of no avail. We will follow the plans of General Howe, who overwhelmed the rag-tag colonists. How can you compare the crisp Red Coats to the decrepit, old, smelly, homemade clothes the patriots wore?

Ernest laughed, "Call the fashion police! Call the fashion police! This is criminal! The patriots don't even have proper underwear. They don't bathe. What a stench! No uniforms: just homespun cloth sewn into trousers and shirts. Patches everywhere."

Vincent made a gesture of agreement which could be mistaken as an amorously flirtatious one. "You're so right! Those

Red Coats were so magnificent. This time when the best dressed side wins...and the win will be worth winning."

"Here come General Howe, Vincent," Ernest gasped. "We should go over our battle plan first, don't you think?"

Vincent agreed, "Of course, hmmm." He moved back from the table and spread his arms wide. His eyes rolled back into his head and his mouth opened. Then he stomped his feet three times and spoke the words, *"Möle Keqé."*

General Howe and the other soldiers seemed momentarily dazed.

Ernest turned to Vincent and carried on, "Oh, good. Now we're assured we'll win. I mean, when were here the last time, it was so...so sad. We won but the cost was too great. This time we'll win what we're here to win."

"Y-esss! Y-esss! We are here to win. Y-esss. Y-esss." Dr. Perp emphasized.

Vincent lowered his arms and resumed his earlier position. He faced General Howe but with a dumbfounded look on his face.

General Howe shook his head and cleared his throat. "Yes... left my gob hanging. Sorry Old Chap. Can you continue?"

Vincent gave the General a bewildered look then winked. "Billy, no worries."

"Gentlemen," General Howe continued. "I respectfully appreciate your competencies in the art of war and confrontation. Its order and its manner. I find it refreshing to share your learned conversation. Due continue."

"Well, Billy...General Howe.... Your right flank is exposed. And exposed badly!" Vincent batted his eyes.

The General opened his eyes widely and contemplated his next move. "You do say. And what do you propose we do about my exposed right flank? Fascinating, pray-tell."

Vincent looked at Ernest and back at General Howe. He stared deeply into the General's eyes and said, "The enemy's weakness is in their inexperience and inadequate supplies. If we.... If you pound, pound, pound them day after day after day after day...day after day after day after day...you get it. Their supplies will be exhausted and you just pick up the pieces. You force them to expend resources on meaningless skirmishes. So when the real battle begins, they'll be depleted, and lose, lose, lose. It's done all the time and it's wonderful. Hmmm."

Ernest moved to the other side of the General. "You march wave after wave after wave of those beefy young men in rows of six...chests out, muskets at arms, marching, marching, marching onto Breed's Hill. Pounding, pounding, pounding the patriots day after day after day. Uhhh! They'll use all of their supplies and lose by default. They'll be beaten before they start. And a win is a win."

Either Ernest or Vincent left a microphone on in a mouse-car and a chance breeze opened the door. The girls had heard static over their speakers then they caught the last part of the conversation from Breed's Hill.

Siobhan mouthed, "A win is a win?" as she shrugged her shoulders.

Ernest moved in front of the table and pointed almost directly to where the girls were on Bunker Hill. "The real fight has to be here on Breed's Hill not on stupid Bunker Hill over there!" he continued and seemed to be looking distinctly at Daisy.

"Oh, Ernie-poo," Vincent cooed. "You've hit the nail on the head. Ouch! It is simply a question of breed. Only those of the lowest and I do mean lowest pedigree were shipped off to the Americas. Especially in the northeast with its harsh winters. Brrrr. Not fit for a dog.

"Whereas we nobles and refined families are able to enjoy the fruits of their labors. Why we liberated the serfs I'll never know. Everything went downhill from there, if you ask me."

Daisy pointed to Breed's Hill across the way. The girls followed her lead in the three mouse-cars down one hill and climbed up the next hill. The thump-a-thump noises got louder and the cannon concussions were more noticeable. When they crested the other hill, they stopped to take in the view.

Amanda raced her mouse-car quickly across the tufts of grass, around rocks, under branches, and returned to the spot where Siobhan and Daisy waited. "There's large squads of red coat dudes over there. An' they're shootin'...shootin' cannons. Yhow! Mad cool graphics!"

They watched the battle progress half disbelieving what was in front of them. The smell of camphor clogged their nostrils and sooty residue of spent black powder stung their eyes with each cannon blast. The muskets snapped and smoked. The girls could see the bloodshed and the agony.

Siobhan thought, *Why in the world is this here? We're just children and the arcade is supposed to be for children. Yet all there is is fighting. Doesn't anyone know what they are doing?*

Daisy noticed the other three mouse-cars next to a group of well-dressed Red Coats at a table with a white cloth over it at the top of an adjoining hill.

"Why are the other mouse-cars over there?" Daisy asked looking straight at them.

Siobhan replied, "Does that mean we're on this side and they are on the other side?"

Amanda exclaimed, "Come on! We're in the biggest, coolest, mad realistic video game ever! What we're seeing isn't real. Don't be a scaredy cat. Just enjoy the ride! I'm goin'!"

Amanda raced down the hill toward Breed's Hill. She caught up with a bunch of patriot soldiers ducking for cover behind a small stand of trees.

"Watch out!" yelled Daisy as she saw a cannon fire toward the soldiers.

The heavy projectile barreled through the branches of the trees snapping them in two then striking two soldiers about ten feet from Amanda. The soldier's injuries were sudden and massive. Blood, limbs, bark, and splinters of wood rained down everywhere. Spots of blood were on Amanda's mouse-car and looked as though the mouse was bleeding from wounds. The sounds of men moaning went up and down the hillsides.

"Stay safe, Amanda," cried Siobhan. "Don't move! It'll be

dark soon and you can get back here."

Daisy was horrified and scared. She looked to Siobhan or Amanda for an answer. It seemed as though they were *trapped like rats*. And they looked to Daisy for the same reason: how do we get out of this place?

Siobhan spoke up, "I'm close to you.... So...so close to you. I can count the hairs on your chinny, chin, chin."

Amanda looked around and didn't see Siobhan. *What if I move over there? Maybe I can see her? Uhmmm...better not. She could be making fake moves. Like what her uncle told us 'bout the good old days when he was a taxi driver.*

Siobhan noticed the movements inside Amanda's car. *She gets it! Uncle Rob told us about when he was a taxi driver: they called it* Long Hooding. *A driver calls the dispatcher on the two-way radio and said he was much closer than he really was to the fare. And the dispatcher would give the fare to that driver.*

Siobhan spoke into the steering wheel speaker, "Remember Uncle Rob? And the stories he told us about *long hooding?*"

"Yeah," Amanda replied. "Yeah, yeah! I was thinking about it, too."

Amanda thought, *We'll fool these mad aggie[103] dudes.*

Daisy thought, *Yeah, her Uncle Rob and his funny stories about Long Hoodin': pretending to be where the fare was in the days before GPS[104] .*

Siobhan was thinking, *We're all together now...all together now!*

"Long hooding?" asked the second voice.

The last voice said, "Y-esss? Y-esss? They're taking the bait. It will all be over soon. Y-esss. Y-esss. Don't divert from the plan. Y-esss! Y-esss!"

A gentle tap startled Daisy. She looked to her right and Owldoll was there.

"W-issh. Not all wins are worth winning. Not all wins are worth winning. W-issh."

"What do you mean, Owldoll?" Daisy asked.

[103] aggravating
[104] global position satellite - cerca 2000 system of intersecting satellites triangulating global position

The next few moments lingered in silence. Daisy was confused and relieved at the same time.

"W-issh. One more thing. One more thing. W-issh." Owldoll looked directly at Daisy and added. "W-issh. The solution you seek is wet. A solution you seek is wet. W-issh."

When she looked back, Owldoll was gone.

Amanda's voice came over the speakers, "All of our guys are running away. I don't get it. This is a crappy ending! We should be playin'. There's plenty of daylight left."

Siobhan yelled back, "Amanda, you nearly got blown up. This is no game. The blood is real. You stay put."

"Nuh huh," Amanda replied. "This just mad realistic...even the smells smell real. Aren't you havin' fun?"

Siobhan spoke firmly, "Amanda. Just listen. Stay put."

Daisy looked frantically at Siobhan wondering how Amanda didn't see what they were seeing.

Amanda finally conceded, "Well, the other guys kicked our butts. That's why all our guys fled off mad fast. I am ready to chillax.[105] "

Siobhan added, "Don't you remember? The British won the Battle of Bunker Hill."

Daisy said, "Now I know what Owldoll means: Not all wins are worth winning. Remember what Mr. Brooks told us about the Battle of Bunker. He called it a *pyrrhic* victory."

Amanda laughed. "Teacher's pet. Teacher's pet. You remember all the stuff that gets you brownie points."

Siobhan cut in, "She's right, though. The British won the Battle of Bunker Hill but they suffered tremendous losses. So not all wins are really wins."

Dr. Perp motioned for Vincent and Ernest to join him on the backside of the hill. Vincent and Ernest approached Dr. Perp slowly, nearly dejected.

"Y-esss? Y-esss? All of your best laid plans wasted. Y-esss. Y-esss? No surprise. You practically told them how to defeat you. Y-esss? Y-esss!"

---

[105] chill is to take it easy + relax

Vincent exclaimed, "How disappointing. We find the one middle schooler in a million who knows the word pyrrhic. Damn and double damn."

Ernest commissorated, "You tried your best, Vincent. Regardless, our side won. And a win is a win is a win."

Dr. Perp rat-tat-tatted his cane smartly on a stone. "Y-esss? Y-esss? This win is even more pyrrhic because not only were we part of the pyrrhic victory in Charlestown. Y-esss. Y-esss. But we were in the battle in Heraclia in the south of Italy with King Pyrrhus, the most powerful Greek king. Y-esss. Y-esss. And we failed to learn the lesson in Charlestown again. Y-esss? Y-esss!"

"But," Vincent added. "King Pyrrhus was a king-sized king. Hmmmm. Not a total lose, if you catch my drift. Hmmmm."

Ernest interceded, "Dr. Perp. What Vincent is saying is we'll try harder next time, in own bewitching way. Our plan was foolproof. Who could imagine us being outsmarted by three middle school girls? Unbelievable."

Dr. Perp gave Ernest an unconvinced look as he turned away.

The girls watched the last light of day fade and motioned for Amanda to come back to them. When she got back, they worked their way down the hill to the land bridge the troops had retreated across. When the reached the other side, the space transformed back to the empty building with the concrete floor. The other three empty mouse-cars were there, too.

Amanda bounced out of her car and beamed, "That was sweet! This is the best arcade I ever went to. I can't wait to go to the Whirly-Twirly...."

Amanda was already racing off toward the exit as Siobhan and Daisy looked at each other with unsurprised disbelief.

Siobhan confirmed, "Her pronunciation may be unique but ya gotta love Amanda. Each of us helped win the Wilde Mouse ride. Off to the Whirl-Ye Twirl-Ye."

Ọ Ọ Ọ

The girls walked along a white brick sidewalk and saw an arrow-shaped board tacked to a tree. Its white painted surface was weathered with many dark varicose vein looking cracks and Olde English lettering: Ye Olde Whirl-Ye Twirl-Ye pointing in the direction they were walking.

"Daisy, this is gonna be the bomb!" Amanda shouted. "The Fortune-teller lady said to come here. It's like we're in a real mystery. Maybe these are clues and prizes? It's like we're on a reality show[106] ! And we're the stars of the show! I can hear the music. Tada, tada! Woooo! Woooo!"

Daisy replied, "Madame Buzorkin told us our final destination was Ye Olde Whirl-Ye Twirl-Ye."

"Don't you mean Whirly Twirly?" asked Amanda.

Daisy put her hands on her hip and gave her a look. "No, jerkwad. It's: Whirl. Ye! Twirl. Ye! Don't you follow the-like-old English stuff? It's like all the Ye Olde this and Ye Olde that? And like the Goth[107] lettering? Sometimes I wonder about you...."

Amanda turned her head away and struck a pose. "You're just being a nerd. I still think this ride's gonna be the bomb whatever the ye olde or whirl'n' ye and twirl'n'ye...I'll be whirlin' and twirlin' mad crazy! I wish I had sunglasses...to look ultracool. This is the bomb! Gotta admit it."

Amanda promenaded a little sashay like a tv star on a runway.

Daisy looked at Siobhan and pouted disapprovingly. "Now, everything is a TV show. There's no escape. At least you're not going whack-o."

"After the Wild Mouse," Siobhan added with a bit of hesitation. "I'm a little...little bit scared. I don't know if I want to find out what is there. Beside, I am kinda creeped that there's no one else around. It is just us. The only voice we heard was a mechanical gypsy."

106   a popular genre of television where so-called ordinary people were specially chosen to live out contrived socio-sexual situations.

107   Short for gothic, often signifying someone who dresses in black or sees the darker side of things

Amanda prodded Siobhan toward the ride, "Don't be a scaredy cat!" Then she mimicked a claw and tooth bearing, arch-backed cat.

Siobhan rolled her eyes, "Amanda, you're the one who's always a scaredy cat."

"But now," Amanda countered. "It is you. Come on. Let's go!"

The girls stepped up their pace. The three giggled as they walked.

Anticipation was felt in each step the girls made toward the big and bright merry-go-round. As they stepped onto the polished marble queue cordoned off by thick purple velvet ropes laced through stainless steel stanchions, the air pulsated in time from the throbbing ringing of the carillon and calliope playing a loud swirling melody.

There it was! An enormous spinning, sparkling, mirrored, merry-go-round beyond the images in any of their imaginations. Bright red framing, brass poles, candy-striped poles, and its floor had an hypnotic pattern radiating from its center. Row after row of white light bulbs. Mirrors outlined by white light bulbs. Mirrors reflecting mirrors. Lights shining on lights. Lights shining on mirrors. Mirrored images swirling back from where they came. Mirrors reflecting Ye Olde Whirl-Ye Twirl-Ye spinning like a multi-faceted top; an amalgamation of a Fabregé egg and a dodecahedron. There was a painted pony but it seemed almost an afterthought in a lonely corner going up and down. The other animals and creatures, for lack of a better description, were actually animated and self-propelled. Their movements seemed so lifelike. They almost appeared to be powering the ride with their own strength. It looked, at times, as though they might pull free from the ride and head off into the night. They weren't living and breathing; or were they?

Siobhan looked puzzled. Her head cocked at an angle. "Look over there! That one's an ostrich! Its eyes are blinking. Its head is moving. Whoa! Too much...too much."

The ostrich craned in her direction and shook her body

from side to side.

"Ouch!" Daisy let out. "It looked right at you, Siobhan." She pointed to her left and said, "A nest made out of branches and twigs big enough for all of us. And it is attached to the bird: a hawk or something but it is bigger than any hawk I've seen."

Siobhan took a step back and held her hand above her head to measure a height, "It's as tall as the big slide in Playsteady park. The feathers are way more colorful and nearly metallic looking to be from around here. But..but...I don't see anyone else. Doesn't that worry you?"

"It is weird, but we were specially invited," Daisy remarked. "The invitation coulda been especially for us."

"Check this out," yelled Amanda as she approached a golden chariot. She looked closer to admire its design and gilding.

A polished brass loudspeaker blared, "Welcome. Welcome, one and all. Step right up. Step right up. There is room for everyone for a magical ride on Ye Olde Whirl-Ye Twirl-Ye. Step right up. Step right up. Ye Olde Whirl-Ye Twirl-Ye will take you places you've never seen. Ye Olde Whirl-Ye Twirl-Ye will take you places you've never been. Step right up. Step right up..."

"I've only seen pictures of merry-go-rounds. I've never been on one...." Amanda began.

She was interrupted by the voice from the loudspeaker, "This is not a mere merry-go-round No, no, no. This is the one. This is the only. This is Ye Olde Whirl-Ye Twirl-Ye: It whirls Ye and twirls Ye through a gateway to your dreams. It is not just an amusement ride. No, no, no. Step right up. Step right up."

Siobhan took a deep breath. "The gypsy fortune-teller told us to come here next. We gotta do it. Right?"

Daisy started down the walkway without any hesitation. The gigantic contraption slowly halted as they approached. Daisy got on first and the others followed.

"Your ride begins! Your ride begins! Thrills! Chills! Hey, leader, strike up the band!" announced the loudspeaker. With a *chih-gerk* and ratcheting sound, Ye Olde Whirl-Ye Twirl-Ye went into motion and the calliope thundered the George and

Ira Gershwin song, "Strike Up The Band".

Siobhan pulled on Daisy's arm. "Look around! There isn't anyone else here. Let's get out of here."

Daisy responded calmly, "Just chill. We're on an amusement ride. See..? Amanda is having fun. Let's find a seat."

Amanda sat in a golden chariot behind one reddish brown bull with long horns puffing through his flared nostrils and dragging his front hooves kicking up dust from the floor. "I'm the Leader! I'm the Leader! Follow me! Follow me!" She beamed a big smile.

The platforms motion jerked and rocked. The voice from the loudspeaker called out, "Your ride begins. Take your seats, quickly! Take your seats, quickly! Ye Olde Whirle-Ye Twirl-Ye will take you on a spectacular ride. The path it traverses will take you from where you will be to where you were. And from where you were to where you are! Take your seats, quickly. Take your seats, quickly. We'll be floating through air. We'll be floating through the night. We'll be floating through your dreams. We'll be floating beyond your dreams. Thrills! Chills! Take your seats, quickly. Take your seats, quickly."

"Siobhan! Daisy!" Amanda pleaded. "We're moving and look! We're going up in the air! Grab onto something. Get a seat!"

They noticed the platform was rising up above the ground and spinning. Up and down, and round and round. The girls watched the arcade spinning around them. Siobhan sat in a tea-cup large enough for three, which was drawn by a fluffy white cat the size of a lion. The platform shifted and Daisy stumbled to a Hansom carriage led by two horses. She climbed aboard and sat on an upholstered cushion. A set of black leather reins hung through a brass ring in the middle of the dashboard. When she looked ahead two nubile, bare-breasted women, who were the fronts of the horses, looked back at her. The woman on her left was blonde with light skin and the other woman was brown-haired with dark skinned. Both were showing clenched teeth and were moving as though they were straining to pull the carriage free from the platform.

Amanda let out a scream and yelled, "Giddyap. Giddyap, kitty. Giddyap!" She looked like she was truly enjoying herself.

A loud noise preceded an abrupt rising of the ride from close to the ground to a height of about ten feet. The spinning no longer followed a circular path but seemed to trace a route along the uninterrupted inside and outside of a monstrous rubber band or a Möbius strip. The calliope began playing "The Daring Young Man On The Flying Trapeze."

Daisy grabbed hold of the reins.

"Help me!" Siobhan cried out as her teacup began to oscillate and the cat's fur flared out.

Amanda smiled from ear to ear. She yelled to Siobhan, "Who's the scaredy cat now? Giddyap, kitty! Giddyyap, kitty!"

"Y-esss! Y-esss! Who's the scaredy cat now? Y-esss? Y-esss?" came from within a rectangular black carriage with silver trim and two gray metal staves with a flaming basket on either side of an empty driver's perch. The windows were covered by thick, dark velvet drapes. Distinct laughing sounds could be heard from within the coach, too.

Daisy looked over to Amanda as the platform followed an upside-down loop that made the central hub appear on their right, which had previously been on their left. It was like they had passed through the mirror and were looking back out at the reflection from the other side.

Siobhan called over, "The centaur who had been on the right is now on the left, and the centaur who had been on the left is now on the right. And we're flying upside-down, but I feel my feet are still on the ground...not on the ground...on the platform...not on the platform but in this teacup, which is on the platform, which is on the ground. Or maybe not on the ground?"

"See how they try to make it all fit together?" asked the inside centaur to the outside centaur, who nodded approvingly.

Daisy snapped the rein across the flank of the outside horse, who glared back fiercely. "Sorry," Daisy said quickly. "We're just following the instructions of Madame Buzorkin. She told us to..."

"We know...we know. She told us to expect you. I'm Iris and she is Sibyl. We're your guides," replied the outside horse.

Siobhan asked, "If you're our guides, then this is not a merry-go-round. And...."

Sibyl answered before she could utter another word, "Does it look like you're going in circles? No. Ye Olde Whirl-Ye Twirl-Ye answers the mystery of the Frozen Words. That is why you are here."

Sibyl and Iris spoke together, "Siobhan. Amanda. You are here to help Daisy find the answer she has been looking for...."

"Looking for before...," Iris continued, "Daisy knew she was looking for an answer."

Sibyl looked at each girl a moment then said, "And now the moment is near."

O O O

Vincent stepped from behind the ox drawn black wooden hearse. He flapped his long dark cape, extended his arms to his sides, and let out a low, bellowing, *"Möle Keqé."*

Everything changed: motion slowed, lights smeared from the direction where they were a moment earlier like dripping wax, the calliope and carillon sounded lower, longer tones, and the rushes of air puffed and collided against them like wading in the still water of a warm pond.

"Y-esss! Y-esss! The moment of truth is upon us. Y-esss? Y-esss!"

Ernest argued, "Moment of truth my rosy red..." He was standing in front of a candy-striped tugboat towing a flat barge. Vincent climbed up onto the tugboat.

Vincent moved to the back of the tugboat and declared, "Ernest! They're just children!" He wore a long black cape with a stiff shiny black collar covering about half of his head and its pointed ends occasionally poked into his cheeks.

Vincent stood arms at a forty-five degree angle, took a step onto a plastic footlocker, tripped on some fake fish netting, and fell face first on the floor. "Mommy! My clavicle! My tum-tum! Mommy!"

Ernest snickered, "How gallant. Captain O'Blow-me-down to the rescue! We both know we're here to finish things off."

Vincent looked sharply at the cane Dr. Perp held as he lay in the prone position. "You have your special platinum tipped cane today. How apropo!"

"Y-esss! Y-esss? Made from a twelve ruble coin. Y-esss! Y-esss!"

Earnest continued, "The tip was fashioned from a twelve ruble coin from the reign of Czar Nicholas II. What a fool! He liberated the serfs and began a giant spiral downward. Imperial Russian was such a magnificent time for witches and magic. Each tap-tap-tap just grinds down those awful memories."

Vincent stumbled to his feet. "Dr. Perp, it's time to finish things off and take what is rightfully ours!"

O O O

Thunder sounded and lightning flashed below as calliope music seemed to suspend Ye Olde Whirl-Ye Twirl-Ye as it swirled in the nighttime sky above the clouds. Each measure of music moved it up or down, side to side, round and round.

Daisy looked to her side and saw Mademoiselle Lapin and Joel Harris riding on a canvas covered wooden carriage drawn by chicks and ducks and geese. Mademoiselle Lapin sat smiling on the forward bench seat next to Joel Harris as the white fringe jostled above them.

"Daisy!" Mademoiselle Lapin shouted. "You must be oh-so careful: the closer you get to the beginning...the closer you get to the end. Ah! To quote Alphonse Karr: *Plus ça change, plus c'est la même chos.*" [108]

"Say what?" Daisy shouted back. "*Plus...? La même* ...what?"

Joel Harris looked at Daisy and answered back, "The more

---

[108] Jean-Baptiste Alphonse Karr (1849)

things change, the more they stay the same. A great French saying. Indeed, the more things change...the more they do stay the same."

Daisy looked around Ye Olde Whirl-Ye Twirl-Ye and couldn't imagine anything ever being the same as what she was seeing here. She wondered why words that made sense didn't make sense at the same time and how it was so difficult to tell the difference between what seemed to be true and what is true.

Iris looked back and repeated, "*Plus c'est la même chos...plus c'est la même chos.*"

"Got it," Daisy tried to reassure her. "The more things stay the same."

Sibyl spoke up, "We are trying to help you solve the riddle. Isn't that why we're here, after all?"

Daisy wanted to reassure the centaurs, in part, and reassure herself even more. She wanted to find the answers to the mystery of the frozen words. Maybe the invitation had more to do with what she was looking for than just going to the Midway Arcade?

The chicks, geese, and ducks peeped, honked, and quacked as they moved past Daisy.

Joel Harris waved, "Let me add an English one from John Heywood: Two heads are better than one." [109]

"Y-esss? Y-esss? We have them right where we want them: trapped on Ye Olde Whirl-Ye Twirl-Ye. No way out. Round and round. A captive audience. Y-esss. Y-esss. What unforeseen complications are in our way now, Vincent? Y-esss! Y-esss!"

Vincent shifted in his seat once or twice. "You see...that miserable French madame and her southern gentleman from Georgia are here. You know the rules of witchcraft as well as I do. We can't reveal them to the mortals or risk losing our own immortality. Mademoiselle Lapin and Mr. Harris are cheating but in a good way. I mean, it's allowed."

"He's right, Dr. Perp," Ernest interjected. "We've done it ourselves many times to put another witch at a disadvantage, so

---

[109] John Heywood (1546)

we could strike at another time. Our plans have been short-cir-
cuited by those two. It doesn't look good...for us."

Vincent sprang up and declared, "There will be other opportunities. I'm getting my two-fer. Mark my words."

"Y-esss? Y-esss? That's all I've done. Just mark your words...
and mistakes. Y-esss. Y-esss"

O O O

A fanfare trumpeting from the calliope announced the ride
was ending. Each successive spin brought them closer to the
ground. The carriage with Mademoiselle Lapin and Joel Harris
was gone. So was the gloomy, square, black carriage.

Iris started to sparkle and radiate a rainbow. She addressed
Daisy and the other girls, "Ye Olde Whirl-Ye Twirl-Ye is coming to an end. Ye Olde Whirl-Ye Twirl-Ye has led you near the
answer to the puzzle of the Frozen Words. That is why you are
here. Take what you've learned with you. You're very close.
You're very close."

"Thank you, Iris. Thank you, Sibbyl," Daisy responded.
"We've followed the instructions Mademe Buzorkin gave us.
Each amusement ride was necessary to understand the next.
Mademe Buzorkin told us the order of the rides to take. The
Wilde Mouse prepared us to work together to win. Ye Olde
Whirl-Ye Twirl-Ye showed us the more things change, the more
they stay the same. Like Mademoiselle Lapin said: the closer
you get to the beginning, the closer you get to the end."

Ye Olde Whirl-Ye Twirl-Ye came to a gentle stop just as she
finished saying these words. The calliope exhaled a great gust
of air and carillon unsprung its wound up energy. The bright
lights dimmed.

"Move on out! Move on out! Move on out! The magical
evening at the Midway Arcade has concluded. Move on out!
Move on out! Move on out!" shouted the familiar voice from
the polished brass loudspeaker. "Ye Olde Whirl-Ye Twirl Ye was
the last ride of this magical evening. You've had chills! You've

had thrills! This one time only evening here at the Midway Arcade was presented just for you! Good night, one and all! Good night, one and all! Good night, one and all! Move on out! Move on out! Move on out!"

Amanda jumped up from behind the reddish brown bull pulling her golden chariot. "Crazy, mad, fun. Woooo! Woooo!" She began to make her way back into the amusement park with her typical velocity.

Siobhan peered out from her oversized teacup with a relieved look. Daisy put down the leather reins and dismounted the Hansom carriage.

Sibyl placed her hand on Daisy's shoulder and whispered, "We are trying to help you solve the riddle. Isn't that why we're here, after all?"

As Siobhan and she walked away, Daisy remembered something her father said: Life is not fair. She didn't know why she was thinking about this now. She remembered thinking how it was so difficult to tell the difference between what seemed to be true and what is true. She had just finished an amazing night at the Midway Arcade and had gone on all of these fantastic—really unbelievable—rides bringing her even closer to solving the puzzle of the Frozen Words and finding her mother.

Siobhan caught up to Daisy and spoke softly, "Wow. No one will believe us if we try to say what we did. We'd better keep it a secret...for now. The Ye Olde Whirl-Ye Twirl-Ye was the strangest ride of all. Mad crazy!"

Daisy nodded in agreement. "We have to solve the puzzle of the Frozen Words. My carriage was drawn by two centaurs: Sibyl and Iris. Sibyl told me something before we left. She said: We are trying to help you solve the riddle. Isn't that why we're here, after all?"

"Only one of them spoke?" asked Siobhan.

"No. They both spoke during the ride and afterward," Daisy answered. "The last thing Iris said was, 'Take what you've learned with you. You're very close. You're very close.'"

"Sibyl and Iris knew we are going to solve the puzzle. How

cool is that?"

Siobhan smiled, "Pretty cool. Pretty cool."

"You're tellin' me?" Amanda confirmed as she snuck up on them. "Gotta tell ya...no one and I mean no one will believe any of this. So let's keep it a secret for now. Whad'ya think?"

Siobhan and Daisy nodded yes in agreement.

O O O

Deborah walked around the apartment from one room to another then went back into the bedroom. She opened her closet and chose a different outfit than the one she put on earlier. This time it was somewhat more stylish and haute couture. She recalled something Ricardo mentioned in passing that stuck in her craw; he said Angelina looked loosely upholstered.

She stood in front of the mirror, and admired herself. She thought, *Loosely upholstered, indeed! Look at me! This makes the type of statement I want to make: stylish; chic; approachable but aloof; an artiste—a true artiste.*

There was some hesitation but she resolved to wear this one. Deborah changed shoes a few more times and finally left the apartment wearing high heels. She went downtown and strolled the busy boulevard. She stopped somewhere for an iced tea, or a latte, as she swerved in between and around people on the sidewalks.

She felt the eyes of the world were upon her. And it felt divine. People would wonder who she was and what brought her to a humdrum place like Midway? There was something about admiration from afar from the ordinary people that amplified her existence.

Where had those thoughts come from? Where had they gone? Why only a crowd can make you feel alone? she heard in her head.

Her thoughts were interrupted by an enticing voice, "My... my...my. Don't we look fine today? Haven't seen you in some time. Hmmm. Hmmm."

Deborah turned around and was face to face with Vincent

and Ernest. She wasn't prepared for this but she was relieved to see them. She felt a little flushed.

"I don't know what to say," Deborah finally said. "There have been so many changes! I don't know if I am coming or going. Hope you are both well. I'm...I was just...."

Ernest first looked at Vincent then to Deborah and began, "There...there. You know exactly why you're having these feelings. Once you've lived in the World of Beauty there really is no other place to be. I was just telling Vincent, who has been absolutely apoplectic about your departure, I had this feeling you'd be back soon. Didn't I, sweet cakes? Uhh huh."

Vincent continued, "Apoplectic on steroids is more like it! Ernest was right. He has been trying to console me. No use! I'm tell you, no use! We had done so much...and seen so much. Angelina! You must come back! You belong to us! I mean...you belong with us. All of the Beauty...all of the Beauty is waiting for you."

The three huddled and attempted to relive earlier moments. Visions of Beauty swirled about, and pretty soon they were talking about the Shtriga Serum.

"W e l l...!" Vincent spent what seemed a full minute getting this word out. "You see...the Shtriga Serum is what lets you see the World of Beauty. It is a tradition, of sorts. Artistes must pay a certain price of entry, alas! This is a small price but one we must pay to live as a sybarite. What is Beauty without a little magic? Mmmm? Mmmm."

Ernest nodded in agreement. "He's right, you know. What is Beauty without a little magic? Remember how magnificent everything looked before? How vivid the colours were? Seeing shapes, contrast, themes, negative space, chiaroscuro...."

Vincent mouthed the word chiaroscuro as though he was gobbling an oversized chocolate bonbon then wiped his mouth on his sleeve.

Deborah broke down and sobbed without restraint. Ernest and Vincent supported her weight but needed to release her after a few moments. They wobbled and swayed trying to balance her on her high heels. She listed from side to side then they labored to bring her close enough to lean against a wall.

Ernest looked knowingly at Vincent and mouthed, "A heavy load to bear." Vincent mimicked a strained gesture to Ernest out of Deborah's view. Ernest and Vincent laughed then Deborah joined in. They carried on for a while more.

"It does seem to me," Vincent announced. "Your truest calling is one of an artiste. You don't want to let this go! It is your *raison d'être*. Our meeting again was no accident. Your life with us was calling you...calling you. We must meet tomorrow and administer the Shtriga Serum. You know it, and we know it."

Ernest nodded in complete agreement. "You also know you are Angelina. Can't deny it! Can't deny it! We'll meet at our rendezvous tomorrow, for sure...for sure. Now there is one more thing...." Ernest turned to Vincent and winked. He turned back to Deborah and continued, "Raquim!"

"As her mother," Vincent added, "you must implore the lass about her truest calling, too. You see she is an artiste like her mother...like all of us. Just try once for me?" Vincent batted his eyes several times at Deborah and pronounced the name Raquim several times softly in a pseudo-Gregorian chant.

Deborah was hearing what she thought she was missing in her life. She did not know how things came about when she was living in the World of Beauty, but it was better than Midway. Infinitely better. It was better in ways she could not articulate but she had this gnawing feeling that was truer than how she felt about anything else.

The three embraced like survivors from a shipwreck, or castaways on a deserted island, who just found food. Tomorrow would be the day to make everything alright.

σ σ σ

Ricardo was alone at the kitchen table after Daisy left for school. He took a sip from a second, or third, cup of coffee, and a blue shadow on the floor caught his eye; its shape and its shimmering movements. He trained his eye on the cobalt blue bottle, along its diffused reflection on the floor, and then wondered, *Here's the magic potion! Lotta good it did. Magic! If there really was magic, what we don't like would never happen. We'd use magic and it would be gone. We'd make it disappear like it never happened and we'd go on in our own little world.* Sin problemas[110] *.The magic potion worked but then again it didn't really work. Deborah...I mean...Angelina was saved from being an evil witch by the solution in this bottle. Daisy unlocked the meaning of the frozen words. Well...she and Owldoll did. Maybe I helped, too? I told her solution could mean a liquid....una solución. Owldoll told her to use this magic potion and it ended the curse. Angelina was changed back into Deborah. The magic potion worked! She was here! We were all together and I thought...we could go back to the way we were.... Deborah is back but she doesn't seem to want to be who she was...or who I thought she was. Maybe she'd rather leave her old life behind and be that other character. And now I think magic only works in færy tales.*

Ricardo pushed his chair back and said out loud, "I gotta bring those things back to Witchcraft Heights Potions. They just don't belong here anymore."

He got up, went into Daisy's room, and picked up the stuffed owl. He thought, *Owldoll? You worked, too. Yet everything you did didn't bring a "happily ever-after" ending. How sad. What good is having magical powers when you get nothing? Not your fault, Buhota mia*[111] *. Reality gets in the way.*

Owldoll was looking at Ricardo in a way he'd never seen before. He didn't hear any words but he felt like Owldoll was, in fact, talking to him. There was a sense about hidden dangers, or dangers concealed by darkness, that Owldoll could see and neither Daisy nor he could see them. It would be better for them if Owldoll was here. The hidden dangers were waiting and he shouldn't face them alone.

He shook his head in disbelief. He had lingering doubts. Deborah was back; Owldoll had completed her task. But it

---

[110] (Sp.) without problems
[111] (Sp. diminutive) my owl

might not stop Deborah from becoming Angelina again. This might just be a tease; twenty-first century torture. He was particularly upset about Deborah's callous disregard for Daisy, and her selfish preoccupation.

Daisy was so young when this began, Ricardo thought. *I wish Daisy and I could have flown away just before this all happened to somewhere safe from the onslaught that was coming...to an enchanted medieval castle...when times were simpler and Daisy could see what was in my heart.*

He spoke out loud, "¡Ay, *Chiapas!* Those are things you can do, Owldoll. Not me."

Ricardo whistled part of a tune: But it wouldn't be make-believe / If you believed in me.

Ricardo reminisced about hearing Xhuliana's voice the first time when he sat on a bench looking out at the water. He had not felt anything like that before; perhaps ever. It was amazing; a magic moment.

He was unsure if he had really heard anything about hidden dangers, or were these silent words a figment of his imagination? The stuffed owl had an odd look in its glass eyes like it could see within him. He didn't know how to react to his own reflection in Owldoll. He went back to packing up the *Ilaç Magjistare* and the silver grey owl. So, he put Owldoll back into the wooden box she came in. He cautioned the owl not to speak just before he slid the cover on. Then he put wooden box along with the blue bottle wrapped in a dish towel in an empty cardboard box and tried to stay focused on the task at hand.

Ricardo knew what he had to do next and went to Witchcraft Heights Potions. He stood across the street from the store for a few moments and tried to look through the windows. He only saw the image of his side of the street, although it was distorted.

The door chimes rang their familiar sound. Xhuljana and Ricardo's eyes met. She seemed as though she expected his visit. He walked over to the counter and placed the cardboard box down.

Xhuljana had a disappointed expression, "You didn't have to bring these back, Ricardo."

Ricardo looked at her after hesitating. "They don't feel like they belong any more."

Xhuliana's eyes softened, "Don't you think Daisy still wants the owl? Didn't she call Owldoll her special friend? I remember when I was a little girl. I'd want to hold onto something like this. Little girls are sentimental."

"You have a point," he acknowledged. "She's been through a lot; seeing her mother placed under a spell; having her mother disappear; believing she had to help her; solving the mystery.... Growing up hasn't been easy...for my little girl, has it?"

"No, it hasn't. I'm sure Daisy will want to keep Owldoll. Think about how much time has gone by, how long Owldoll was with Daisy, and how, maybe, they should be together." she replied. Xhuliana paused and added, "And don't you like the bottle? The color. The shape. The weight. It is perfectly fine if you keep them."

"I just felt like they didn't belong with me anymore," Ricardo answered. "I believe they have done all that they can do. They can only bring up bad memories now."

Xhuljana went over to Ricardo and took his hand. "Remember, not all memories are bad. What we can forget can be valuable, too."

Ricardo nodded. "Thanks, Xhuliana. What you've said makes sense. I needed to hear this."

They looked into each other's eyes without saying anything. The moment lingered.

Xhuliana smiled and looked at the cardboard box, which contained the bottle and the stuffed owl he wanted to give back. "Owldoll," she suggested, "told Daisy, and you, the story you needed to hear."

Ricardo smiled in agreement.

She removed the bottle wrapped in a towel and the wooden box containing Owldoll from the box. She slid the cover open and stood the owl on its feet. The owl instantly became animated, which did not surprise Ricardo.

Owldoll bobbed and waited for Xhuljana to tell her what she needed to do next.

Xhuljana began, "Don't be melancholy, dear Owldoll. You have bridged the distance between victory and defeat. You enabled Daisy to undo the curse, which could have captured her, too. Many will face the same challenge as Daisy: to be yourself, or to be an illusion. But you saw the hidden dangers. What you told Daisy about them was instrumental. You were in the right place at the right time. Daisy ultimately could be herself."

"W-issh. Now we can turn the page. Now we can turn the page. W-issh."

Xhuljana walked between Owldoll and Ricardo where a beam of light came through the window and her red hair glowed. "After a story ends, it continues somewhere else in a different setting. Sometime soon you will be needed as a special friend. It is who you are, Owldoll."

Owldoll remained stoic and looked back and forth from Xhuljana to Ricardo and back to Xhuljana.

Ricardo squeezed Xhuljana's hand. "I don't want our story to end. Not here. Not now."

When he caught her eye, the light intensified her gaze and he felt the warm glow.

"It won't," Xhuljana assured him.

"Good," Ricardo confirmed. "I thought the look in your eyes said what I wanted to hear."

O O O

Xhuljana walked to the front of the store taking in the city night through the window from inside the store. The outline of the buildings appeared to almost spell out something: Was it something Xhuljana wanted to remember or something she wanted to forget? She lowered the window shade, went to the front door, flipped the sign to Closed, and turned the store lights to their nighttime setting. She walked through the doorway strung with glass beads. Instead of walking five steps into the backroom, Xhuljana entered a thick fog and the air was noticeably cooler with a wispy bucolic scent. After seven or eight steps, the fog thinned, and she stood before a mighty gray stone edifice stretching out as far as the eye could see, and its fluted walls reached above the clouds. Xhuljana paused to take in its enormity then walked along the base, around a five-sided footing, perhaps, for a turret or watchtower. Owldoll stood across from Xhuljana on a sharp cold edge of the gray stone at the other end of the footing.

Each waited stoically for the other to make the first move.

"Welcome to Thélème[112] , Owldoll," Xhuljana greeted warmly.

"W-issh," Owldoll replied. "The giant Abbey of Thélème built by Gargantua had one rule to be observed: Do what thou wilt. Do what thou wilt. W-issh."

Xhuljana affirmed, "So you know where we are and it's no coincidence why we are here."

Owldoll moved her wings behind her back. "W-issh. I was waiting for you to tell me why we are here. I was waiting for you to tell me why we are here. W-issh."

Xhuljana looked discernibly at Owldoll. "Why did you come to a place that is so hard to find? Why did you fly to this very spot? Why are you here at Thélème? Why? You're here because Thélème and Gargantua hold a special place of honor in our hearts. We can speak at Thélème without risk of being overheard in keeping with a long tradition of hidden meanings."

Owldoll agreed, "W-issh. I am only here because I sensed you wanted me here. I am only here because I sensed you wanted me here. W-issh."

Xhuljana noted, "Owldoll, you have an important role. Adolescence is blind to what can be seen. I, for one, am grateful for all that is taken in by your magic eyes."

Owldoll looked deeply into Xhuljana's eyes, looked skyward, and without a word sprang into flight. She quickly flew

---

[112] T-ay-lem

above the clouds.

Xhuljana whispered, "See you soon."

Xhuljana pulled her arms to her side, closed her eyes, and began to elevate. She did not fly like Owldoll but rose steadily in a gentle reverse trajectory of a perfectly shaped crystal clear raindrop taking in more and more of an expansive view of the landscape, passing through the damp, airy clouds into the bright sunlight above the wall of the Abbey, and floated down into the large courtyard. On either side were tall green topiaries making up a labyrinth in the style used in Crete to trap the Minotaur.

Xhuljana and Owldoll landed at different ends of the labyrinth. They negotiated a deliberate route to reach each other. Each saw different shapes in the hedges; almost a living mosaic accompanying their journeys. Xhuljana turned onto a very long, straight avenue and paused. Owldoll rounded the bend on the other end a moment later. Owldoll stood her ground, too. Their keen eyes locked onto the other's gaze.

Xhuljana spoke loudly, "Owldoll, how has your time gone with Daisy?"

Owldoll replied with equal amplitude, "W-issh. Time for a teenager is tricky, especially for girls. Time for a teenager is tricky, especially for girls. W-issh." She unruffled her feathers, settled back, and continued, "W-issh. As you should know. As you should know. W-issh."

Xhuljana conceded, "Touché. But you've also revealed yourself to Mr. Villanova. How did that happen? You know the dangers of disclosing immortal secrets to mortals."

They walked toward each other and met in the middle of the path.

"W-issh. Mr. Villanova is trying to help Daisy just like we are trying to help Daisy. Mr. Villanova is trying to help Daisy just like we are trying to help Daisy. W-issh."

Xhuljana went closer to Owldoll and said, "I, too, have spoken with him and looked deeply into his eyes. He is truly a kind person, dedicated to Daisy, and had his world completely overturned by the effects of the Shtriga Serum."

"W-issh. A stain bleeding through many layers. A stain bleeding through many layers. W-issh. "

"He seems to be almost like us," Xhuljana added. "He is aiming to reach Daisy while keeping her youth insulated from the corrosive poisons of the adult world. But you must be careful not to say too much when you're helping Daisy find the solution to her dilemma."

"W-issh. The solution to the riddle might not be the solution to the serum. The solution to the riddle might not be the solution to the serum. W-issh."

"You are a wise owl," Xhuljana noted. "No wonder I was so confident you'd succeed in defeating the Shtriga Serum by helping Daisy solve the riddle. I feel like I'm the daughter of my own work. Now you're telling me about the intricacies of spells and their limits."

Owldoll moved up and down as her feathers moved slightly in the breeze.

Xhuljana nodded sympathetically. "Use good caution, Owldoll. What you say can be more dangerous than what you don't say. And if you don't say anything, you won't say something that will jeopardize your immortality."

"W-issh. You were going to tell me why I am here? You were going to tell me why I am here? W-issh," Owldoll asked.

Xhuljana began, "I put you here as a voice for Daisy; to think the thoughts no one else would think; say the words no one else would say; to raise the questions no one else would raise. You are a lone voice speaking with clarity about what only you can see under the cover of darkness—and hidden from what Daisy can see."

Owldoll replied, "W-issh. Sometime, Daisy can hear my words. Sometime, Daisy cannot hear what I see. Sometime, Daisy can hear my words. Sometime, Daisy cannot hear what I see. W-issh."

Xhuljana agreed, "Owldoll, your task is not an easy one but I have faith in you. There is no question it is better to try to help save Daisy from the evil spell foisted on her family than to remain silent for all eternity. While words can disappear into oblivion, words can do amazing things."

VI.

Good Reader, we have reached a point where you are deserving of mild caution—as the often ill-informed hawkers of doom & gloom say—The End Is Near! You surely can tell by the thickness of the preceding pages we are approaching the end of <u>Owldoll</u>. This is no grand revelation. What I will tell you, Good Reader, the encroachment of the twenty-first century makes the ending of this færy tale unlike ones from yesteryear the way tea infuses itself into your drink.

Read on to find out how Owldoll helps Daisy solve the mystery of the Frozen Words and undo the curse placed on her mother.

Have no fear! Daisy will be okay! Yet the modern world will take its toll on her. What child would be immune to the ravages of witches, magic, spells, and the mysteries of the adult-world? Isn't being a teenager in the twenty-first century difficult enough?

But this caution is one of melancholy. I lament when <u>Owldoll</u> concludes you will be left in a state such as when dear friends depart. I cannot help this but felt obliged to place a gentle hand on your shoulder, figuratively speaking.

— Author

Daisy hadn't been home since she left the *quinceañera* in a huff. Ricardo was becoming impatient. He walked drearily from the living room into Daisy's room, looked right at her pile of dolls under the window, and half smiled at the way each doll stared back at him. He thought, *Daisy is not here but at least I'm not alone.*

Ricardo noticed the I-Don't-Know-Turtle by the lamp on the desk looking up at him. He felt silly but picked up the carved rosewood turtle. He asked it a silent question remembering the way Daisy used to ask it something, rock the turtle from side to side, stop, turn it on its back, wait a moment, and say, "Duh, I don't know."

He looked at the turtle in his hand and it felt different. The turtle suddenly twisted its wooden head and craned its neck skyward toward Ricardo.

He flinched and thought, *Is this really happening? What's*

going on?

The turtle in his hand began to speak and asked itself the question Ricardo had been thinking a moment earlier, "Why shouldn't Daisy understand how her father feels about her?"

The turtle rocked from side to side lifting its now flexible wooden legs from his palm muttering a contemplative chant for a moment or two. Suddenly, it flipped onto its back and answered predictively, "Duh, I don't know."

He gingerly placed the turtle back on the desk next to the lamp. He heard a small voice. It was barely audible.

At the bottom of the pile of dolls was an all white doll that looked like a baby lamb. He picked it up and was going to ask it if it was the one he just heard. Then he heard the pretend voice Daisy used for Lambsy, "Bahhh. How could you not see things through Daisy's eyes? Bahhh. Bahhh."

He responded, "I didn't mean to let Daisy down. I only wanted to try to build her up."

An older looking doll whose silver-gray, curly hair was thin and white dress was worn through in a few spots seemed to be staring at Ricardo. Daisy called this one Mamma Sedona, which reminded her of pictures of her grandmother, added in the accented voice Daisy used for Mamma Sedona, "Why didn't you just leave her alone? Anyone could see she wanted to be alone."

Ricardo felt affronted and quipped back defensively, "¡¡Es *florita mia!!* Don't I have to try something? Something to reach her? Something to show how much I care? How can you find fault with what I did out of love for Daisy? I was trying my best. I really was trying my best."

He addressed the pile of dolls, pleading his case, "Can't you help me? You all sit here and talk to Daisy in her room. You share what she says to no one else but you. What does she say? Tell me...."

The dolls looked back unsympathetically. *No wonder Daisy spoke to you like old friends. You all look so serious. Maybe the answers to all of her problems are here with you! And not me.* "Answers can be found in the most unusual places, don't you think?" he asked out loud rhetorically.

A miniature teddy bear at the bottom of the pile spoke to the other dolls, "He's just trying to figure this out."

"*Gracia*," Ricardo answered to the teddy bear Daisy named Erica-A-Weiner, after Erica Weiner, who gave the teddy bear to her. Erica had gone to the chain-store, Make-A-Bear, where children fill his or her partially sewn teddy bear with shredded polyfoam and choose from an array of accessories to personalize the creation, so many times that she began calling her friend Erica-A-Weiner. The teddy bear continued to drum up support among the other dolls.

A chorus of yes he is, isn't it a tragedy, why do things always happen this way, and murmurs of agreement and disappointment cascaded round the pile of dolls. Every doll seemed to have something to say about the *quinceañera*, parenting, or adolescence. Every doll but the stuffed owl, who remained motionless, was involved in this episode.

Did I just see a pair of suspicious eyes move? He thought, *They're just a pile of dolls! I'm trying too hard to understand Daisy...or to make her understand me!*

"Owldoll, don't you have anything to say?" he asked feeling foolish. "All of your other friends seem to have opinions. What about you? Don't you want a chance to criticise me and tell me everything I did wrong? How trying to protect Daisy from all the evil things that happened, or to let them hurt me instead, was such a bad thing to do? Here's your chance; go ahead."

Then he noticed it again: the oversized purple eyes of the stuffed owl—the one he named Owldoll for Daisy—blinked. Its eyes were bright; concentrating all the light in the dark room within its vision and back directly into his own eyes; penetrating; mesmerizing; touching his very core.

This was very different: he could half write-off the dramatic scene that was staged for his benefit but Owldoll was really real. Her voice. Her penetrating gaze. The way she touched his mind.

"¡Ay! Are you...are you really there?" he pleaded. "Don't mess with me. I came into Daisy's room to try to figure this out. I came hoping to see what she sees. I came here to find out what's going on. Talk to me. Tell me what Daisy needs to hear to make her hear my voice!"

Ricardo looked at the stuffed owl and it puffed out its chest. The faint light in the room reverberated in its eyes—brightening those purple eyes—and touched Ricardo's inner thoughts.

"¡Ay!" Ricardo yelled out. "*Diablo.*[113] " Then he became mesmerized by the intense gaze of the owl.

Ricardo reflected on this: *Maybe that's how owls can see in the night! Maybe the owl sees more than I can see!*

He sensed this connection to the owl again and it startled him. Ricardo felt he was with an old friend; someone familiar. He asked out loud, "Are you really there? Are you trying to tell me something Daisy wants me to know? Did Daisy send you here? Talk to me? Please, talk to me. You can tell me so much. Maybe you see things the way Daisy sees things?"

The owl bobbed up and down, and spoke, "W-issh. Daisy cannot see what I saw. Daisy cannot see what I saw. W-issh."

"¡Ay, Chiapas!" Ricardo said out loud. He looked at the owl and asked, "Owldoll? You've been with Daisy since she was *una bébé*. Daisy always loved to play with you in her room. I heard her having imaginary conversations with you so many times. I've often wondered what she said...what she confessed to you. What secrets she shared with you. What thoughts she told no one...thoughts she told no one but you. Did she send you here to talk to me?"

"W-issh. Daisy is why I'm here. Daisy is why I'm here. W-issh."

Ricardo spoke directly to Owldoll, who moments ago was just one stuffed animal in the pile of other stuffed animals, but now spoke in her true voice. "Owldoll. It's really you! You are not speaking in one of Daisy's make-believe voices. The words you are using are your own."

Owldoll moved up to the top of the pile methodically and turned her gaze on Ricardo. She looked intensely at him half

---

[113] (Sp.) the devil

waiting to say something and half waiting for him to speak to her.

Ultimately, Ricardo broke down and sobbed, "I wish I could have told her...maybe some of what you told her. Reached out to her when she was so vulnerable. Perhaps preventing what did happen from happening. I wish I had had the words to make everything alright.... But things got too out of control so quickly. Her mother ran off right before her eyes! There was thunder and lightning. It was almost like the scene she saw the first time she went into a movie theater...." He looked sadly off into space and thought about the upholstered door at the Exeter Street Theater, "It was dark inside the theater. Daisy walked into the theater with the movie playing up on the huge screen with its larger than life characters in action. Daisy came in right behind me and sat down next to me in one of the back rows. Daisy watched wide-eyed at the giant animated images on the screen. Like a page from a bad dream: the bus turned the corner and disappeared just out of view behind the city buildings...then...B O O M ! Life can be very strange. The movie was almost a recreation of what Daisy had just seen when Deborah rode off on the bus. The significance didn't dawn on me until later. How utterly ironic to bring Daisy to conquer her fears of movie theaters and the first scene she watches mirrors the greatest tragedy in her life."

Ricardo reflected inquisitively at the ironic juxtaposition of the scene he found himself in and the one he was recalling.

Ricardo waited wondering if Owldoll ever made mistakes like he had done, and added, "You are a little like me, Owldoll; You tried to tell Daisy what you knew but she could not see what you've seen or understand what you've understood."

Owldoll answered, "W-issh. I am a little like you. I am a little like you. W-issh."

Ricardo watched Owldoll meld back into the lifeless stuffed owl Daisy played with all these years. He thought, *Something magical just happened. I got so close to finding out how to reach Daisy. Yet I still don't know the answer.*

Ricardo turned his back, and walked slowly to the living room.

Owldoll hesitated until after Ricardo left and spoke in the presence of the other dolls in Daisy's room, "W-issh. Helping Daisy will help him. Helping Daisy will help him. W-issh."

O O O

The girls gathered around the cobalt blue bottle with a silent reverence in Daisy's room. They stared at it taking in the power of the words: *Ilaç Magistare*. The calligraphy, the worn texture of the label, and the weight of the bottle all collected in their minds elevating the importance of this moment. They were looking at the solution that was the answer to the puzzle they had been chasing.

"Owldoll told me to be sure to spray the potion directly into Angelina's eyes. That's how it works!" Daisy explained.

"Whoa!" Amanda shouted. "It's like Visine[114] for evil potions."

Siobhan laughed. "Yeah. Take Visine to get rid of the redness in your eyes from evil potions."

Amanda countered, "Yeah. Remember the song Daisy's dad played for us? 'The Monster Mash'! Take the Eel-Eee Ash to get rid of your monster mash[115] !"

Amanda picked up a hairbrush and held it like a microphone. She counted to three, turned, and began singing, "They did the mash / They did the Monster Mash/ They did the mash / It caught on in a flash...."

"Quit jokin' around. It won't be that easy," Daisy told them. "I can't just walk up to her and ask if I can put some eye drops in her eyes. We gotta come up with a plan."

Siobhan walked over to the sink and pulled out an empty plastic spray bottle. "This is the bottle you use to spray water on the Jade plants, huh? It'll work."

---

[114] an over-the-counter eye drop medicine
[115] "Monster Mash" by Bobby "Boris" Pickett (1962)

The girls agreed the spray would get the job done. Daisy carefully opened the blue bottle and transferred some of its precious liquid into the small orange plastic bottle in Siobhan's hands. Amanda twisted on the atomizer spray top while Daisy pushed the cork of the glass stopper back into the antique, hand-blown, cobalt blue bottle.

The girls agreed Daisy would distract Angelina by showing her a video of the noisy lunchroom on her cell phone. While she was concentrating on the confusing scene in the video, Amanda would approach her from behind and spray the *Ilaç Magistare* right in her eyes.

They were excited as they walked to Playsteady park where Angelina told Daisy to meet her. But they could not see Angelina as they approached the playground. Before any of them could ask about it, the girls heard the sound of the tip of the walking stick striking the pavement behind them.

"Y-esss! Y-esss!" Dr. Perp announced. "Our little friends have returned. This could get interesting. Y-esss? Y-esss."

Daisy broke away from the group and walked to a different part of the playground away from the baseball diamond. She turned around and looked right at Angelina, who was momentarily paralyzed.

Vincent nudged Angelina. "Shoo. Shoo. Go get her. Go get Raquim. She is ready to join us. Go get Raquim!"

Angelina stepped clumsily and waved with an unsteady hand. "Raquim, I'm coming. Just wait...right there. You'll be able to fulfill our dream...join our World of Beauty...fulfill your dream to be more. It won't be long. Just wait...right there."

It seemed to take an eternity for Angelina to walk the short distance as Daisy's heart pounded. Angelina put her arm across Daisy's shoulder and the acrid smell of her clothes nearly made Daisy run for the hills.

Daisy stood her ground and counted silently to ten. "Oh, Angelina. You gotta see this! It's the boy at lunch today sayin' there ain't no world of beauty. I tried to tell him he was wrong. It was makin' me wonder if I was makin' a mistake. Uhh! Look it, here."

Daisy produced her cell phone and punched up a video clip. The raucous lunchroom blared through the phone's speakers. Daisy pointed to a small spot on the screen. Angelina scoured the images and tried to find the boy who was undermining all she had done. Daisy handed the phone to Angelina and she held it up to look more closely.

Amanda had circled around and stepped from behind them with the orange spray bottle in hand.

Ernest screamed, "Ahh! Those rotten little.... They did something. Quick! Let's get them."

Amanda moved in and sprayed the *Ilaç Magistare* directly into Angelina's eyes before Vincent and Ernest got much closer.

Dr. Perp pointed at Angelina and Daisy with his walking stick and Vincent moved quickly in that direction. Ernest followed.

Perhaps there should have been a fanfare but there wasn't. Joel Harris and Mademoiselle Lapin appeared on the path.

"*Bonjour, Daisy! Bonjour,*" Mademoiselle Lapin trumpeted. "I was hoping to see you today. I have made *kwa-sohn* and I want you to come and get some to take home, *s'il vous plait.*"

Vincent and Ernest stopped in their tracks. Vincent whispered, "Drat and double drat! We can't reveal the secret of witchcraft to the mortals. We're blocked by the fickle finger of fate!"

Joel Harris stepped up to Daisy and added, "There is nothing so fine as one of those freshly made buttery delicacies. And Mademoiselle is a world-class baker, if I do say so. And I do. Walk with us. And Amanda and Siobhan, too. I'm sure Mademoiselle has plenty for them, too. Come along, girls. Don't dawdle."

Daisy motioned for Amanda and Siobhan to come over and they all walked away.

ooo

Somewhat blinded to Vincent, Ernest, and Dr. Perp's departure, or even their presence, Angelina succumbed what she began to see again; for the first time in a long time an ordinary setting emerged. She recognized the spreading chestnut tree at Playsteady park. The *Ilaç Magistare* began to take effect and her eyes didn't see things the way she had been seeing them. As each successive moment past, Deborah began to reappear and Angelina began to vanish. The excessive tension between the two—Angelina and Deborah, or Deborah and Angelina—expended a tremendous amount of energy and left the emerging Deborah fatigued. She collapsed into a deep sleep right there in the park under the tree and slept until sunlight woke her up the next morning.

Deborah looked around and couldn't believe it. She knew who she had been but only in a cursory way. It was like a drunken episode left discarded when the next day resumes. Deborah had a lingering feeling like a ringing in her ears following a loud concert. She could not believe the awful smell of the clothes she was wearing; or perhaps from the noxious perspiration from yesterday's life.

A bird dropping fell to the ground close by and motivated Deborah to get up. She was a little unsteady on her feet but managed to walk along the path and out of the park. She kept walking and came to her old apartment building. She stopped and looked at it. Deborah was happy, sad, and confused.

"*Oh, Mon Deiu!*" Mademoiselle Lapin shouted as she walked out the front door of the building and saw Deborah standing there, albeit, wearing raggedy clothes. "*C'est toi! C'est toi!* Deborah! Deborah! *Ça alors! Ça alors!* I am so dumbfounded. You are here! Come, come. *Vite!* Vite! We must go to your apartment *tout suite! Oh, Mon Deiu!*"

Mademoiselle Lapin grabbed Deborah by the hand and pulled her along into the building. They literally flew up the stairs as though their feet never touched the floor. She rapped at the door excitedly while she sang out flurries of French so rapidly they were indiscernible. The door opened and Daisy stood with her mouth wide open.

Deborah and Daisy were motionless. Mademoiselle Lapin pushed Deborah into Daisy and they embraced. Tears began to fall and their words were as indiscernible as the French from moments ago. It didn't matter: Deborah was finally back.

"Oh! My! God!" Daisy yelled when they settled down and stood apart again. "The magic worked! It really, really did! Mom, you're back! Wow!"

They spent the next several minutes talking about what had happened and how Daisy never let up, never stopped trying to find her mother. Deborah, on the other hand, was unclear about her other life. Daisy did not care whether or not her mother could tell her about the world of beauty, witchcraft, or what Angelina saw through her eyes. Just having her mother back was all that mattered.

Mademoiselle Lapin stayed a while longer before she excused herself, and let them be together. She was happy to see Deborah but said something Daisy found odd when she departed.

She said in her heavily accented voice, "Dis weel be good while Deborah was back. *Mais oui?*"

The word "while" stuck in Daisy's mind as though Mademoiselle Lapin was predicting another departure. Daisy held on to her mother as if it would stem the tide from turning.

Deborah told Daisy she needed to shower before her father got home. She said he might send her packing because she really smelled bad. Deborah waved her hand in front of her nose and made a funny face. It seemed like old times. They both laughed.

O O O

Good Reader, we have come to another twist in the journey now that you have read how Daisy has solved the puzzle. The solution was the Illaç Magistare—the secret potion to remove the curse placed on Deborah—and how it changed Angelina back into Deborah. You might think we've reached the conclusion, the færy tale would be over, and your humble author would be tying up any loose ends with pithy verbiage and obligatory praise for the moral framework you, Good Reader, had supplied to support this færy tale.

But this is a Twenty-First Century Færy Tale and it will temporarily be eclipsed by the sixteenth century. Don't worry, Good Reader, like a lunar eclipse, this won't be permanent.

You will recall, Deborah had been placed under an evil spell, was transformed into someone else—a witch no less—with a new name, and no association to her past for several years. Xhuljana gave Deborah the magic potion to undo the curse and the stuffed owl, who would become, Owldoll back at the very beginning when Deborah was pregnant. Thanks to the efforts of Daisy, and the guidance Owldoll provided, the Striga Serum was defeated. Family life did not return to normalcy quickly or seamlessly.

— Author

Daisy woke up to the sounds of chirping birds, a cool breeze, and sunshine. She stretched: warm and snug in her bed. A pile of teddy bears and dolls rested motionlessly on the floor beneath the window.

Rap-tap-tap on the door preceded Deborah as she it opened, "Good morning, Daisy, another beautiful day. After breakfast, let's go for a walk downtown. What do you say?"

"That'll be fun," Daisy replied basking in the sunlight.

"It's such a perfect day," Deborah said.

A smile on your face but not in your eye, thought Daisy. She got dressed and had breakfast. Then she got ready to go.

In fact, it was a wonderful day: The temperature was very mild. They would not even need a coat. Deborah looked at Daisy warmly. They laughed like school girls; acting silly. They were lost in the moment going this way and going that way. They walked past Playsteady Park and the fragrance of flowers was reminiscent of earlier days.

A short while later they were downtown. Deborah caught

sight of the Pizza Pad and remarked, "I have a craving for pizza. How about you? Maybe we'll come back this way and have a slice?"

Daisy nodded yes but at the same time she felt three pairs of eyes looking at her—feeling as though her soul was almost being sucked right out of her. She turned away from the open front of the Pizza Pad and looked at her mother. "Later might be better," she answered. "They've got the best pizza in town."

Deborah and Daisy proceeded along the rounded corner in front of the Pizza Pad. They strolled down State Street still giddy as they soaked in the sunshine. They turned left, turned right, and went past several funky shops. Then Deborah and Daisy stopped and stood still like statues. The building where Witchcraft Heights Potions stood was now a vacant lot filled with trash intertwined and scattered among the overgrowth.

"Hey, mom," Daisy gasped. "This is right where Witchcraft Heights Potions is located. Or was located."

They looked at each other confused by what was before their eyes. Something familiar was no longer there and in its place the past had been obliterated.

Deborah added, "You're right, Daisy. Maybe it was torn down while I was under the evil spell? Though, I wasn't gone *that* long. Look at the weeds...look at the scrub pines. And that trash. It looks like this spot has been unkempt for years."

Daisy exclaimed, "But I was here...well, not here...yeah, here at Witchcraft Heights Potions just a week or two ago. I'm not crazy: the store was here."

Deborah walked to the spot where the stairs were and looked around. "The stairs were here and the dark oak door...." She spied Daisy walking toward the vacant lot where the building had been. "Daisy, stop. Don't go in there!"

Daisy continued unabated.

"Daisy, don't ignore me. We don't know how safe this area is," Deborah scolded.

"Chill. Don't be a witch...again," Daisy snapped back with attitude.

Daisy walked onto a spot in the lot like she was being drawn by an unseen force: a space without name; a space without sound. Daisy instinctively knew where to look among the garbage and the flowers. She reached down and felt something in her hand.

Deborah looked on curiously. Daisy appeared to be picking up an object but there wasn't anything in her hand. "Whatcha find there, sweetie? What are you holding?"

"A...It's a...There is a...," Daisy replied as she seemed to be turning over something make-believe in her palm. The air in her hand corrugated with a crumpled up Mylar-like[116] refraction and, as if in the middle of a dream, Daisy manipulated something visible out of thin air. She was holding a tarot card like what Xhuljana had shown them: bigger than an ordinary playing card. But it was a tarot card neither of them had seen before.

The card pictured a regal, silver-gray owl with oversized purple eyes staring out hypnotically perched beneath a Gothic archway with chevron molding with a thick, blood red outline that tapered off with wispy red lines. In the upper left and right corners of the card, a sultry green eye engaged the viewer knowingly as if these eyes had been spying on the viewer. On the top of the card was a Roman numeral one and on the bottom the title *Magistar*[117] .

Daisy exclaimed, "Mom, what does this mean? The card says Magistar. What's a Magistar?"

Deborah pondered the tarot card examining its details: The owl had a wand with green buds in the talons of its right foot, a globe of the world locked in the talons of its left foot, on the left side of the card outside of the archway was a golden cup, on the right a silver sword. The owl stood on an open book half covered by a translucent purple cloth. Over the archway was a gold coin with an infinity sign[118] and a black Roman numeral one at the top of the card. The perch the owl stood on was also

---

[116] trade name for BoPET

[117] mahj-ee-star

[118] ∞

the title box: *Magistar*. Along the outer edge of the perch was a snake that appeared to be eating its own tail.

Deborah enunciated, "*Magistar*: it almost sounds like magic...or magic-er."

Daisy added, "Maybe it's the word for magician in another language?"

"Could be," considered Deborah. She noticed the eyes in the upper corners. "I know these eyes. They look so familiar. They're European eyes..."

"Xhuljana," Daisy interrupted. "I know the eyes, too."

Deborah nodded yes. "And it's the owl she gave me.... Well, the stuffed owl."

Daisy lost hold of the tarot card and began to look but the card disappeared. It was as if it landed invisible side up.

"Was the owl in a wooden box, mom?" questioned Daisy. "A beautifully decorated box?"

Deborah nodded again as she began to help Daisy look for the tarot card. Their hands searched the ground and they looked intensely at the same time. They got up and moved to near the spot where they thought the card had landed.

Daisy and Deborah took two steps toward each other. When they realized they were standing on the invisible side of the tarot card, they recited the name in unison, "O-w-w-l-l-l-d-o-l-l-l-l" as they fell through a gray cloud without a falling sensation, and landed softly in another land.

Where are we? We're not in Midway any more, They each thought.

Deborah and Daisy stood before a gargantuan stone edifice. The sky was dark and cloudy. A cold breeze blew dust and dirt swirls here and there.

"I'm cold. Let's look for a door or something, mom," Daisy suggested.

Deborah took her by the hand and walked to their right around an edge of the building. There did not appear to be any windows just a cold stone wall reaching above the low-hanging clouds.

Deborah observed, "This is like the cathedral in Rouen, France but on a more massive scale. Perhaps, the stained-glass is above the clouds."

"Maybe...," Daisy remarked as she stared up into the clouds. "It is like what we did in class with Mr. Brooks on proportions. He told us the ratio, or proportion, of the circumference of *any* circle is the number pi[119] times the radius squared."

"What if what we see is only a small proportion of the whole thing, mom?"

Deborah beamed, "Very good, Daisy. You see, math can be useful in real-life situations."

They walked along and came to a rounded corner, where the flat side walls curved outward. They followed the curve for what seemed like an hour then were on a different the side of the building. It seemed as though this side of the building extended to the horizon; or into more dense fog.

"O-M-G. This is mad crazy! It goes on forever!"

Deborah continued, "Let's go a little further. Who knows what we'll find?"

Deborah and Daisy continued as a cold wind howled. The top of the structure was blotted out by a silver-gray fog with white streaks of clouds and swirling gusts of grit and sand. They kept close to the building to block the wind and continued for almost another hour until they reached a doorway made with heavy wooden planks the height of a tunnel.

Carved into the stone above the arch were the words: *fay çe que vouldras*[120] .

Deborah spoke, "My French is a little rusty. Let's see.... It says: You do...um...Do what you want. I think that's what is says: Do What You Want. Wait. I remember something your father said one time when he was talking with Mademoiselle Lapin. He said, although pronounced the same, the French words *fay*, spelled ef-ey-why, is an antiquated form of *Fais*, spelled

---

[119] π approximately 3.14159

[120] Fay seh kay vouhl-dhra

ef-ey-eye-es, and both words mean do.

"You know her," Deborah continued as she stiffened her face and narrowed her eyes. "Mademoiselle Lapin said, 'Mais oui. Monsieur Villanova. That is how we spoke back in the days of Louis Douze.[121] *Mais non.*' And that means the word above the archway—vouldras—is old French. So, the other words—fay çe que vouldras—say: Do what thou wilt."

Deborah and Daisy walked into the huge castle and marveled at the massive fountain foyer. Before they could speak about where to go something caught their attention.

"W-issh," came from on-high in the vaulted ceiling. "Welcome to the Abbey of Thélème. Welcome to the Abbey of Thélème[122] . W-issh."

Daisy asked, "Where are we?"

"W-issh. The Abbey of Thélème was built by Gargantua for a monk in Thélème by the river Loire in France. The Abbey of Thélème was built by Gargantua for a monk in Thélème by the river Loire in France. W-issh.

Deborah asked, "Owldoll, how did we get here from Midway?"

"W-issh. Travel is an impossible fiction. Travel is an impossible fiction. W-issh."

Daisy shook her head. "Whadda you mean? We were in a vacant lot where Witchcraft Heights Potions was! I've walked to Witchcraft Heights Potions tons of times. We get there today and it's like nothing was ever *there*. The whole building was gone. Buildings don't just disappear."

Owldoll flew closer and landed on a low stone barrier. "W-issh. The road up and the road back are not the same road. The road up and the road back are not the same road. W-issh."

Owldoll led them down a hall into a great hall. Deborah was captivated by the enormity of the situation. Once inside, they gazed at massive room that seemed to extend for miles. The gray slate entrance way had led to smooth white stone floor.

---

[121] Louis XII (dooz) King of France 1498-1515
[122] T-ay-lem

Owldoll flew off without a word.

"Hello," cried out Deborah to the vast empty space.

Daisy said, "The inside of this building is like a sphere whose center is everywhere and whose circumference is nowhere."

The silhouette of a woman appeared from the shadows and was walking toward them.

Daisy thought out loud, "My! People come and go so quickly here."

Xhuljana spoke, "You see, you entered through the South Gate. It is called the Gate of Thoth. Thoth was the Egyptian Messenger god. Some say Hermes, the Greek Messenger god, was a metaphorical incarnation of Thoth. You made a good choice for your place of entry. Had you chosen a different gate, your journey would have had you wander a long, complicated route before you got to where you are right now."

Daisy asked, "Is that why we saw Owldoll? And why she talked to us?"

Xhuljana smiled slightly and looked directly at Daisy and Deborah. "Why, yes. Owldoll can say the things you need to hear. Without her words, you would be in a world of silence. You'd have no signs to navigate your way through this labyrinth."

Daisy and Deborah paused and examined the enormous room they were standing in. The darkness in the distance made it feel as though the expanse was endless.

Xhuljana continued, "The labyrinth within the Abbey Thélème is the key to the Book of Thoth. What is the Book of Thoth you might ask? It is a key to the future, if you will. In ancient Egypt, Thoth, their Messenger god, wrote down the secrets for the initiated ones of the Alchemy of Physics and the Alchemy of Spirit in a secret book.

"Later, Moses became initiated by the High Priests of Ra, the sun god, in the teachings of the Book of Thoth on astrology describing a huge dodecahedron mapping out the cosmos. The twelve faces of the dodecahedron correspond to the twelve faces of Physics and the twelve faces of Spirit. Some say it is not coincidental there are twelve tribes of Israel."

Daisy countered, "What about the Ten Commandments? Why not twelve commandments?"

Xhuljana smiled wistfully. "Tarot can be spelled t-a-r-o-t or t-a-r-r-o for the Egyptian words *Tar* for road and *Ro* for Royal. You shouldn't be surprised that there is a cryptology embedded in tarot cards. The twenty-two trump cards plus the four suites of fourteen cards are the Royal Road to the Book of Thoth."

Looking around the dark, vacant hall, Daisy wondered, "Are we on the royal road to the answer of another puzzle? Is that why Owldoll sent us into this room?"

Xhuljana turned her head and her thick red hair concealed her left eye. She looked straight at Daisy with her right eye, which nearly glowed. Her voice was subdued and only Daisy heard her. "You should consider this a prequel to things to come."

Deborah blurted out, "This can't be a royal road. Where is the beauty? Where is the art? This is just a dank, old church filled with centuries-old smells of people and animals urinating on the floor. Besides, we're not in the room where we entered. Owldoll pointed us...well, not exactly pointed us...motioned for us to go in the direction that brought us to this chamber."

"Everything is so dark. I don't see where it stops or where it began," Daisy gasped. "Mom, the inside of this place is more enormous than it looked like from the outside. Now that we've gone through a few sections, it appears to have been laid out like a mad mystery."

Deborah agreed, "Yeah...mad mystery...a deceptive design...a puzzle."

Daisy thought a moment. "You know, when I was trying to find you...trying to get you back...when you got turned into a witch, I had these frozen words. The frozen words turned out to be a puzzle that told the way to defeat the evil spell put on you."

Xhuljana made a gesture to the abyss before them and numerous glowing globes appeared in two vertical columns joined by interlaced silver pathways. "Behold the Sephiroth Tree of

ten luminous spheres connected by twenty-two paths. Ironical-
ly, there are twenty-two trumps in a deck of tarot cards—just like
there are twenty-two letters in the Hebrew alphabet."

Deborah remarked, "This sounds like the Qabbalah: where
there is a numerical value for each letter of the Torah to decipher its hidden meaning."

"Xhuljana," Daisy said. "your descriptions paint a beautiful
picture of geometric shapes, colors, space. Everything moving
around: choreographed dancers in zero gravity."

Xhuljana added, "Owldoll and I can only provide an outline: something like a silhouette to you. Like me, what Owldoll
can share is limited in space-time. We're an allusion of an illusion to what happened or things to come."

Daisy cried out, "I want to go home. I'm getting scared.
One mystery just got solved...not another one!"

Daisy looked sad and Xhuljana wanted desperately to help.
Daisy looked into Xhuljana's eye for some consolation.

She took Daisy's hand and spoke softly, "Don't worry about
another mystery. I am here to show you what you already know
and bring you home. I must go now but I will come back when
you need me."

Daisy mouthed thanks then stepped back and ran her finger under her nose.

Deborah pulled Daisy to her and remarked, "You make it
sound so simple but it can't be. Xhuljana, I'm the mother. I'll
tell Daisy what to do."

"She's tryin' to help," Daisy whispered.

Xhuljana extended her arm to Daisy. "Please, give me the
tarot card you found."

"I lost it," Daisy answered. "It dropped from my hand and
it seemed to land with its invisible side up. I could no longer
see it."

"You see the clear glass plate on that table?" asked Xhuljana
as she pointed to her left.

The missing tarot card was on the plate. Daisy stared at it as
though it might tell her something but she did not approach it.

Deborah said, "It's okay, Daisy. Xhuljana is here to help us."

Xhujana faded into the darkness and was gone.

Deborah was overcome by things lost in the twilight world where perception was as real as it felt. She turned to her left and asked, "Daisy, is something bothering you? It's okay. I'm right here with you."

Daisy listened to the sound of her words and thought, *My mother's voice: Where had it been? When you were gone...not gone-gone...I knew you were somewhere. Now that you're here...it doesn't help. Not now....* "Oh, mom. I just want to go home. I wish things would be normal again. Why is everything so screwed up?"

"I don't have an answer," Deborah replied.

Daisy yelled, "You never have an answer."

"W-issh. Drizzle, drazzle, druzzle, drone. Time for dis one to come home. Drizzle, drazzle, druzzle, drone. Time for dis one to come home. W-issh."

Deborah recognized the line from *Tutor Turtle* on Cartoon Network. "How can we get home, Owldoll? Please, help us."

"W-issh. Light without end. Light without end[123] . W-issh."

Owldoll flew to a nearby desk and walked over to the clear glass plate. She reached over and took the tarot card in her beak. She flew to the floor, tucked the card under her wing, and waddled several steps away from them.

"W-issh. Walk this way slowly. Walk this way slowly. W-issh." Owldoll clasped the card in her beak and took flight. She circled above them a few times. Then she made a figure eight, swooped down, and tossed the card face down. Its visibility vanished into thin air.

Neither Deborah nor Daisy knew where the card hand landed. Daisy and Deborah stepped slowly toward the invisible hole as instructed: one step, two steps, three steps, four steps...."

"W-issh. Say my name. Say my name. W-issh."

Daisy and Deborah recited the name in unison as they stepped onto the spot where the card landed, "O-w-w-w-l-l-l-d-o-l-l-l-l-l-l"

---

[123] Kabbalah: אור אין סוף (*Ohr Ayn Sof*) - Light Without End

as they vanished into a gray cloud, falling in suspended animation, down, down, down, and landed softly on the vacant lot where Witchcraft Heights Potions had been located.

Deborah looked at Daisy and Daisy looked back at her; both only half-believing what had happened.

O O O

Daisy looked out the window at the billboard on a building downtown. It displayed a rolling highway floating through a rich, blue sky with puffy clouds. The copy was the words of the big local radio station's jingle: It's smooth sailing with the highly successful sound of wonderful radio Midway.

Daisy sighed, "I wish I could fly away and leave all of this behind. If I were someone else, I could fly away! Maybe...if I became someone else...if I chose to be Raquim, my life would be like riding along a highway in the sky. It would always be sunny! I'd be above it all. All the little people would be down there in places like Midway. I'd be up in the clouds with the heros! Superpeople like Vincent, who perform before kings, queens, sultans, and maharajas! And at night I could play among the stars! No wonder mom changed. Midway is soooo boring! I am Raquim! I am someone else!"

Daisy thought about living another life as she closed her eyes. It all seemed so close; close enough to touch. Life as Raquim might solve all her problems, especially if she was above the clouds.

Two oversized purple eyes illuminated in the darkness from the other side of her room. Daisy gulped audibly. Owldoll took flight and lited upon the end of Daisy's bed.

Owldoll tapped her beak on Daisy's shoulder. Her beak had sharp point but she touched Daisy very lightly. Daisy was startled and quickly turned around.

"Hey," Daisy winced. "I was deciding to live among the stars people looked up to and make life worth living. " She shook her head and preened her face forward. "Up there...among the stars! You could fly up to see me once and awhile, right?"

Owldoll gently rose and fell in place. "W-issh. The light you see is from another time and another place that no longer exists. You cannot live in the past! The light you see is from another time and another place that no longer exists. You cannot live in the past! W-issh."

Daisy thought out loud. "Life used to be simple. I could go out and play. And when I'd come home everything was right. Everything had a place. Then Vincent and Ernest became part of mom's world. I wanted to be with mom. It's only natural. I thought I was an artiste. I was Raquim.

"Now I don't know who I am? Am I me, or am I Raquim?"

Daisy looked back to the window and was surprised the billboard light was out. Instead of the view of the highway in the sky, she saw the outlines of the panels and the buckled skin of the covering in the moonlight.

"Oh..." And Daisy remembered the song her dad sang to her as a child, *Say it's only a Paper Moon / Sailing over a cardboard sea / But it wouldn't be make-believe / If you believed in me.*[124]

Daisy had a tear in her eye when she looked over her shoulder. Owldoll was gone. "What did you say?" she asked the empty room. "Another time...another place. I should not live in the past."

Daisy looked out the window and sobbed, "¡Papa! ¡O, Papa! ¡Lo siento mucho![125] Why did I turn my anger toward you? Why couldn't I hear what you were saying all along? What did I do?"

O O O

Deborah and Daisy strolled along the tree-lined street. There was an abundance of sunshine and the sweet smell of spring in the air. Daisy was beaming to be with her mother; just walking; doing plain things; that you don't know what you've got 'til it's gone. The whole ordeal seemed so far away.

[124] "Paper Moon" - Harold Arlen (music), E.Y. Harburg and Billy Rose (lyrics) 1933

[125] (Sp.) I'm very sorry

Deborah suggested, "Let's cut through the park. The sun is shining. It'll be a little quicker going this way."

Daisy replied, "Kay, mom. Guess you're finally going to keep your promise."

"What promise do you mean?" Deborah asked sharply.

"Ya know," Daisy smiled. "You promised to take me to the park just before all of this craziness happened."

Deborah made a face. "You don't expect me to remember something like that do you? I just thought we'd cut through the park...and save some time. Beside, it is a beautiful day. You don't have to be so critical."

They walked into the park and Daisy asked, "Will you make a whole turkey for when Tio Roberto comes over this weekend? You know? With mashed potatoes and cranberry sauce like you used to do?"

Deborah looked to the sky, smiled and answered, "If you'd like that, I'll do it. We'll go shopping tomorrow morning. I think Uncle Rob is planning on coming over this weekend."

While Deborah was looking upward, a plump moth buzzed by. The moth flew a circular pattern and seemed to squeeze a capsule-shaped tumor with its legs. The tumor sprayed a discharge that sounded like words. Deborah knew she had received the Shtriga Serum. She didn't need to hear the words.

Daisy looked at her mom and thought about what had gone on for the past few years. "I knew I'd find you. I'm so glad to be with you. A big turkey dinner like we had before this whole nightmare ever happened. It can be a special celebration, ya know, like 'cause we're all together now."

Deborah added, "I think Uncle Rob is coming over to talk to his brother. He might want to take you and him to a baseball game, or something."

"Tio Roberto is the bomb," exclaimed Daisy. "He knows me so well. He could almost be my brother, too."

Deborah scratched her chin, "What else should we have with the turkey? Mashed potatoes, of course, cranberry sauce in a can, of course. What else?"

Daisy smiled, "Jalapeño peppers...and black bean soup. Yum!"

Deborah looked sternly at Daisy. "Hold on there! It is only going to be four people. That's a lot of food. I don't think we should mix traditional food with...Mexican food."

"We could...," Daisy hesitated, "invite Mademoiselle Lapin and Mr. Harris?"

Deborah looked inquisitively at Daisy. "And if Mademoiselle Lapin brought pastries, who'd be surprised? Why not? Turkey, mashed potatoes, and cranberry sauce. Together with fattening French pastries, and Mexican beans and hot peppers."

They walked a bit further through the park along a winding paved path. Deborah continued while Daisy looked back from where they came. Deborah stopped by some hedges and notices the remains of a baby bird on the ground. She studied it smiling as though something was funny. She looked back at Daisy, the bird, Daisy and the bird.

"Whatcha looking at?" Daisy asked. "And what's so funny?"

Deborah did not answer. She looked at Daisy and then the baby bird.

Daisy took another look and saw a new scene. Her mother...well, not her mother...she saw a different woman standing there. Her posture somewhat slouched; her eyes somewhat watery—not teary.

"Mom? Why you lookin' at me funny? Did I do something wrong?" Daisy moved next to her but Daisy felt something had changed the way you sense you're being ignored.

Angelina thought a moment, motioned her head toward the carcass of the baby bird, and turned quickly to Daisy. "You see this fledgling? Once...so full of potential! She did not follow her mother's lead. What happened? She perished. A lesson for you to learn: listen to your mother. No matter what! It could happen to you!"

Daisy thought, *Why didn't the baby bird listen to her mother? Now look: it lays there dead with its sunken eyes and little tongue hanging out. Yuk!* She felt nauseous and looked away.

A large gray cloud blocked the sun. The air became noticeably cooler. When Daisy looked back, she saw her mother.

"Looks like rain," Deborah cautioned. "We should duck over by the big shade tree over there until it passes."

Daisy and Deborah huddled close to the mighty tree truck. Then they heard a snapping noise. Then again a moment later, the piercing noise was louder.

Deborah looked nervous. "It sounds like lightning."

"Y-esss. Y-esss," spoke a very tall, thin man in a full-length, gray raincoat wearing deep, dark, round sunglasses. His features were difficult to make out in the shadows. "So, we meet again? Y-esss? Y-esss."

"Who is this man, mom? We don't know him, do we?" asked Daisy.

Dr. Perp rat-tat-tatted his walking stick. Vincent and Ernest came out from the other side of the tree.

Ernest sneered, "Yes, Daisy. We do know each other. Don't we, Angelina?"

"He called you that other name...the one when you were.....," Daisy cried out.

Vincent coughed and broke into her conversation, "And should we say Raquim? Don't you remember who you are? All artistes...all great...truly great artistes have a *nom de plume*; a stage name. Your mother's is Angelina. Your's is Raquim. Isn't it the dream of every little girl to be someone else? Someone more glamorous; more enchanting?"

Vincent paused a three count. "Just MORE," he boomed. "No one is satisfied with a humdrum, work-a-day, ordinary life. We...we artistes are MORE. More, more, more."

When Daisy looked at her mom, it was the other woman again, her mom's eyes looked like pond water with floating larvae. Daisy felt like she was being viewed from across a parking lot by a thousand eyes.

Angelina looked mesmerized at Dr. Perp. "Oh, you found me!" She breathed deeply. "Midway is so ordinary. And..."

Daisy grabbed her mom by the arm, "Mom! These men are

creeping me out! Let's go! Let's go now!"

Angelina pulled back her arm from Daisy as the transformation became complete. Neither recognized the other for who they were. Both saw what they wanted to remember.

Dr. Perp appeared to grow taller—or, perhaps, Daisy appeared to grow smaller—and spoke words that echoed, "Y-esss? Y-esss! Daisy, don't you see you're one of us? You were meant to be here, too. You both are one of us. Y-esss. Y-esss."

Daisy began to see someone different. Someone who wasn't her mother. Yet it was her mother. Her hair changed color and texture. Her clothes had an unfamiliar appearance. She turned to Daisy and said, "Daisy, life is a one-way street. You have to grab opportunities when they find you. This is ours. I want you to be more. More than I was at your age."

Daisy began to worry. She said, "I just want to go home. Mom, I'm scared."

Dr. Perp alluded, "Y-esss? Y-esss? Daisy, why don't you ask your mother what you should do? She can tell you what to do. Y-esss? Y-esss?"

Vincent erupted, "Perpy old man, use her stage name! Her venerable *nom de plume*...that was given by *moi*: Raquim! Ra-quim!"

Daisy shrugged, "What-ev-errrr!" She stood hands on her hips and tapping her left foot.

Angelina curled her fingertips within the palm other hand. She moved close to Daisy and spoke softly, "Vincent is one hundred percent right. We are who we want to be. And I want to be Angelina. I could never tell you before. You weren't ready to hear it. I followed you from the shadows; waiting and hoping for a day like today. The world you were in was not right for you. You needed to be more. And the only way you could be more is if I became more. If I became Angelina. That's why you must become Raquim."

Vincent spoke in a deep voice, "We are renowned practitioners of our time-honored craft. Raquim, Raquim. I see that far away look in your eyes. You're going to fritter away a chance of a lifetime."

Angelina pleaded, "I found where I belong. It is where we belong. Listen to me!"

Vincent added, "It is where *we* belong. We are part of a new world: one filled with excitement. Leave the boring life of Midway. Step onto the stage!" Vincent awkwardly executed a pirouette, a plié, and a fouetté. His stomach continued to oscillate to a bah-rump-a-pah rest.

Daisy snapped back at Vincent, "You...you imbecile. You stupid fat-head you. You bloated idiot! Ewww. Leave me alone! Mom! We go to get away! Now!"

Vincent turned one hundred eighty degrees to Ernest. His face got beet red. "How dare she! How dare she!"

Ernest agreed, "You're right. When you're right, you're right. We should insist Angelina discipline her daughter. We are...." He stopped mid-sentence as he watched Daisy..

Daisy rolled her eyes.

"How insolent!" yelled Ernest then he put his arm around Vincent's shoulder as his eyes welled up and softly said, "There...There...There...."

Vincent removed an oversized handkerchief and loudly blew his nose. He looked distraught.

Ernest added, "Let me take care of you, Vincent." He turned to Angelina. "This is all your fault. Bring that girl around; it's now or never!"

Angelina went over to Vincent and patted his back. He looked at her with pursed lips. He paused and whimpered, "You can do it, Angelina."

Angelina breathed heavily and moved awkwardly toward Daisy.

Angelina and Daisy looked at each other. Both pleading silently for different things.

Daisy was witnessing an illusion; a transformation. What had been real was now a mystery. The shape that was her mother was now some alien shape. The voice that was her mother was now some alien voice. The feelings she felt for her mother were now some alien feelings.

Daisy ran off into the park and stopped at the edge of a pond. She began to cry and a teardrop fell into the pond. The water rippled. When it cleared, Daisy saw a goldfish swimming carefree and easy. Daisy remembered "The Gold-fish Story" and how the Gold-fish couldn't see it had left everyone behind.

O O O

Ricardo walked the streets of the empty financial zone. He wondered, *Why did Deborah choose to be a witch? A witch of all things. She had just been saved by Daisy...and Owldoll. Daisy had just reversed the curse and she could have had her life back. Yeah, right. Deborah chose to be with those three clowns? The thin one, the fat one, and the tall, one with skin like plaster of Paris. And Deborah chose to be witch, again! Things could have been like they were before. ¡Ay, Chiapas! That seems like ages ago. Life seemed to be focused on Daisy before...at least my life did. And what about Daisy? How can a mother abandon her child to pursue something so vain...so selfish...so... bizarre.... Sometime, life is stranger than fiction.*

Now, his thoughts were about Xhuliana. After what they said and felt when he tried to return Owldoll and the magic potion, he was bewildered about not being able to find Xhuliana anywhere. They planned on meeting, or so he thought. He was restless and went out to find her. He did not want to wait any longer.

Ricardo kept on walking and found himself facing a building, which used to appear to be mysterious. Now those familiar colors offered a feeling of comfort. He stopped and stared at it like a traveler cresting the last hill on a long journey and seeing his final destination. A large CLOSED sign by the front door was clearly visible from where he was standing. The calligraphy on the marquee—Witchcraft Heights Potions—beckoned him to cross the street. He heard a metallic sound as he approached. The bolt released from the lock and the door opened a crack. The bells clanged when he closed the door but the store was dark and empty. No sounds like he remembered.

Ricardo took a few steps. Nothing. A few more. Nothing. Some lights went on automatically. Nothing. "Hello?" he called out. Nothing. No alarm beeps. Nothing. *Has everything changed? Has Xhuliana disappeared? Has all the magic disappeared?*

He went over to a glass covered display counter and eyed the unusual items: an ivory, or synthetic, mortar and pestle, a crystal ball, and what looked like a magic wand on a purple satin cloth. He looked to his left and Xhuliana was standing there quietly.

Ricardo put his arm around her shoulder and kissed her on the cheek; words escaped him.

Xhuliana whispered in his ear, "I'm glad you're here."

"I had been looking for you," Ricardo answered. "You disappeared. I thought maybe you went away and I'd never see you again."

Xhuljana looked at him warmly and faced him. "Ricardo, I'm not going anywhere. There are so many things we should talk about, but we shouldn't talk here. We need to go somewhere else. Come with me. I want to take you to someplace special...a restaurant I know. We need a break...and...we need somewhere to...be together...."

Ricardo said, "...be together," at the same time as she did.

They went out a back door and Xhuljana unlocked a shiny yellow Jaguar XKE convertible, although unlocking a convertible seemed superfluous. She placed the key in the ignition and pressed the start button on the bird's eye walnut dash. The car purred and soon they were buzzing along an open road heading toward the Benjamin Franklin Building; a twenty-one story concrete building that once typified the Midway skyline. Xhuljana did not slow down as they approached busier streets. The wind rushed by and Xhuljana's long red hair flowed a slow-motion mesmerizing wave as they traversed the city streets. Soon they stopped at a convenient parking space near the Benjamin Franklin Building.

"When Daisy was little," Ricardo said, "she used to call this the John Neighi[126] Building. Don't ask me why. She just did. She had her own names for a lot of things."

Xhuljana asked, "Perhaps, it was the building's famous lightning rod, which extends seventeen hundred seventy-six feet into the air?"

Ricardo shrugged and then smiled at Xhuljana. He held out his hand and she took it.

They walked through the large brass doors into the Benjamin Franklin building to the elevators. She pressed the elevator call button for the fifteenth floor. They went to the left and a temporary sign beside an archway in the middle of the hall read, The Lookout.

A tall black man at the maître d's station smiled as they approached. He spoke in a French-Caribbean accent, "Mademoiselle Xhuljiana, how are you this fine day?"

"Trés bien, Monsieur Züm." she replied.

"Would Mademoiselle prefer indoor or outdoor dining?"

"Outdoor, s'il vous plaît."

Monsieur Züm escorted them into an enormous room: there was row after row of square desks; perhaps fifty desks deep by fifty desks wide.

Ricardo eyed the scene: At each table, a grey or brown suited man wearing a stiff green plastic visor sat behind a black shaded desk lamp. The men never looked up. They kept tabulating numbers by manipulating round keys on antique adding machines, which went ching-a, ching-a, followed by a ratcheting sound, and bing! repeatedly after each entry. The men recorded numbers on ledger sheets in large cloth bound books as the emptying spools of white paper crept along the floor in front of the desks.

They walked between two central rows and made their way past the last row. Cardboard boxes were piled ceiling high and Monsieur Züm walked sideways between two piles of boxes, into a small opening, and a red canvas awning leading to a floor to ceiling glass door covered with long sheets of opaque fabric.

---

[126] Pronounced Ney-Ghee.

He announced, "You are at table seven. Spectacular views! Bon appétit!"

He drew back the fabric and the clear sunlight flooded in. Three tables appeared to be suspended in mid-air on the other side of the glass door. If it were not for the thin silver seams between the glass plates, there would be no frame of reference to judge where the room ended and the sky began.

The maître d' discreetly disrupted their silence and pulled a chair away from the table for Xhuljana. He turned to Ricardo before he walked back into the building, extended his arm, and moved his flattened palm from left to right, "The floor and walls are made of one-way mirrored glass, so nothing is apparent from the outside."

Ricardo took a seat facing her. The view was indescribable: Xhuljana surrounded by glass walls, floor, and ceiling looked like she was floating on air with the greatest of ease. Monsieur Züm said the glass was a one-way mirror, so Ricardo was the only one who could see this beautiful scene.

"Isn't this truly fantastic?" Xhuljana said with a touch of drama in her voice.

Ricardo clasped her hands and added, "I love being with you!"

His words lingered and she picked up on them with the twinkle in her eyes.

Xhuljana let a small smile grow on her lips. She moved her head to an angle and said, "Me, too. But you have no idea how difficult it is for me to say these little words. You know I am a witch and I risk my immortality every time we're together. But I do love being with you, Ricardo. I cannot explain it."

"My world is upside down, too," Ricardo added. "I think it was no accident that we met. Certainly no accident that you gave Owldoll...or what became Owldoll...to Deborah with the magic potion in the blue bottle before Daisy was born. Then Daisy found Owldoll...or did Owldoll find Daisy? Owldoll was always waiting in the wings to steer Daisy in the right direction and ultimately to help her solve the riddle to reverse the curse—as it were—and...I guess, to lead me to you. Talk about strategic planning!" He looked at her slyly.

Monsieur Züm returned unnoticed and poured chilled champagne slowly into fluted glasses. He left the bottle in a glass bucket filled with ice on a small stand next to the table and retreated into the building.

Xhuljana and Ricardo took a sip: it was cold and perfect. They looked quietly at the view before them: blue skies—nothing but blue skies.

"Even though," Ricardo said, "we're floating on air... alone...and everything is as fine as fine can be...." He drifted off not completing his sentence as though the next word was not ready to be heard.

Xhuljana interrupted, "You look like you're miles away. What's on your mind?"

Ricardo answered slowly, half-smiling, "Do you really have to ask? You can read my mind, I assume."

Xhuljana pantomimed by pointing her fingertips to her temples and rolling her eyes back, "I cannot really read minds. Although, many people's thoughts are there for the taking. Being a witch is not like that at all. A lot of books and movies give witches too much credit. There is the thinnest of lines between where magic begins and reality stops."

Several white doves flew by closely and banked off past the building. Their feathers highlighted in the sunlight.

"Okay, Xhuljana. I'll try not to imagine you know everything. I have been thinking about *mi florita*. I wish I knew why things turned out as they did. Why Daisy directed her anger toward me...treat me like I cast the curse...blamed me...shut me out of her life at a time I could have helped her so much. I tried to be sensitive...to insulate her from the crazy world adults live in...yet I was the brunt of her anger. I still sit on pins and needles worrying she could go back to thinking that way."

Ricardo heard Xhuljana's voice in his mind, *Good thing for you I am a good witch. Of course I can read your mind. I just cannot say it out loud. That's against the rules. And it's the reason I can't answer your question. But I can try to give you clues.*

He looked at her. She looked back. They stayed silent. He tipped his cup in her direction before taking a cool sip.

Xhuljana continued in his thoughts, *But who'd believe you heard my voice in your mind? No one, right? But why a teenage girl acts the way she acts; does the things she does; says the things she says...will always be an eternal mystery as long as teenage girls are teenage girls.*

He choked a little on the champagne, cleared his throat, and smiled. He thought, *I'd never want you to break the rules for me. Mi bruja buena*[127] .

Xhuljana extended her slender arm out toward Ricardo and interlocked it with his. She sipped from his glass and he sipped from hers.

Xhuljana was about to speak, but she paused. Then she continued, "You know, when Daisy was five or six, a year was a big percentage of her life. After she was ten, this ordeal was almost half of her life."

"You're right," he nodded. "The impact of everything was magnified."

Xhuljana added, "Disruptions to routines—moving to a new house; big changes in family life; death—are difficult for teenagers and young children. There's no magic solution.... Unfortunately."

"Guess you'd know," he laughed.

Then they both laughed at the irony of each of their statements.

Ricardo continued, "But now, I hope she sees I was the one who stood behind her even when she was trying to get away from me. At least, I hope she does someday."

She took his hand. They looked at each other a moment.

He thought out loud, "I wish you could show me what Daisy thought and her secrets. I just want what is best for her. Tell me what to do. You can see all those things, right?"

Xhuljana sipped her champagne. "Ah...Ricardo. Even Magic cannot undo the past; otherwise, there would be no future.

---

[127] (Sp.) my good witch

Witches would use magic to change the past: forever unsatisfied with the way things turned out; they would continually seek perfection; they would continually remain stagnant; living in the past.

"So you see.... Love is stronger than Magic. Love is what won after all...not magic. Without love none of this would have happened."

Ricardo absorbed what she said for a moment, turned his head to see the view from side to side, and asked, "Can't you just cast a spell and put the odds in your favor? What chance would an ordinary person have against a witch?"

"Once a curse is cast," Xhuljana replied, "it takes on a life of its own. The course it travels is a little unpredictable. A curse is completely beyond our control. So people can outwit witches. It happens all the time."

"You make it sound so good, Xhuljana. You make it sound... beautiful. I mean it. I'm not trying to flatter you. I believe what I said. I'd like to believe Daisy and Owldoll defeated the evil witches, even if no one in the outside world sees it this way."

Xhuljana added, "This will be our little secret. Let's not use the M word or the W word. Those words just get in the way. We have other things to do...."

She kissed him and he knew she understood what each of them was trying not to say. He took the bottle from the ice bucket and refilled their glasses. The foam rose to the fluted edge and settled back. Their glasses clinked harmoniously before they each took a long, slow sip.

"Ricardo," Xhuljana spoke. "The illusion is only real when it reflects what someone else believes it shows."

Ricardo nodded. "If we can just enjoy the mm...mag.... I mean the happiness we have, the story lives on."

"Well said," Xhuljana acknowledged.

W-issh.

W-issh

Owldoll—the character and the færy tale—has an underlying didac-tic quality inherent in færy tales. Yet Owldoll is restricted from being too forthright. Otherwise, you would have been bored before too long and kept these pages from reaching their true ending. The urban legend of Owldoll was not a contiguous unfolding. It developed in bits and pieces, which roughly correspond to the sections of the færy tale. Since you have uncovered the various clues in what you have read so far, Good Reader, you have cleverly arrived at this comment of mine. The greatest magic of this færy tale is you, Good Reader, who has brought this twenty-first century færy tale to life. And I remain forever grateful for your interest as we move along to the final scene.

— Author

Daisy went to Playsteady Park to walk around. The park was a world within itself: playtime made everything make-be-lieve; the way you wanted it to be; a place where problems disap-peared. She wanted to be surrounded by memories of happier days. She thought, had only she and her mother come here that crazy day, none of what happened would have happened and life would have gone on as it did before everything changed.

Daisy walked over near where the pink daisies grew. She was getting so close she could smell their bouquet. The scene made her smile. Then she was unhappy when she thought about how she asked her mother to take her to see the pink daisies that day. She wondered if she hadn't asked so many times would that have changed things? She heard the tune in her mind:

Daisy, Daisy give me your answer do
I'm half-crazy all for the love of you.

Why was she hearing this song in her mind? It wasn't her mother who loved the song. It was her father who sang her the song. He had given her the gift of music. She thought about what she had been putting her father through. He stood by her even when she blamed him for everything. It wasn't all his fault. How could it be? Perhaps there was a connection between music and how she was feeling?

Daisy heard a familiar voice with its southern drawl. "Daisy. How are you this fine day?"

"Oh. I guess I'm okay. I'm just walkin' around...," Daisy automatically replied.

Joel Harris said, "Sometime.... Yes, sometime, it is good to get out in the fresh air to let your thoughts wander free."

Daisy thought out loud, "Yeah. That's what I was doin'. So much has gone on and I don't know.... I am not sure what is real any more."

Joel Harris joined her and they walked further on the path in the park.

"You know, Mr. Harris," Daisy continued. "I never thought things would turn out as they have. What did I do to deserve this?"

Joel Harris gave her a look then smiled. "You didn't do anything. Daisy, you are a fine young girl. And I do know how you've seen some very sad things. Maybe that puts it too mildly. But what I am saying may be a little difficult for you to follow because you are so young. Just take it from me that no one wants to read a story that is all sadness. You need to look on the bright side, too."

Daisy sobbed, "I just wish I had my life back. It wasn't supposed to turn out this way. I could use a story with a happy ending, you know?"

Joel Harris paused then responded, "Not all happy endings are happy the way we imagined. Who knows why things carry on as they do? Sometime the outcome is way beyond our command. Just like parts of life are beyond our control. Sometime, you see, we cannot have the life we had...hoped we had...or thought we'd had...once it has gone away. Even memories lose their meaning after we see things for what they were."

Daisy admitted, "Mr. Harris, I kept waiting for my mother. I waited for her to take me to the park. I waited for her to come back. I waited for her to call. I waited for...something. I didn't give up. I didn't leave. I was left behind."

"I know you didn't leave. Perhaps, it left you living in the past. Not that it makes it any easier," Joel Harris agreed. "Questions? I suppose you have many. Answers? I suppose I don't have many."

They reached a point where the path splits. Mr. Harris continued along one side and Daisy took the other. They waved to each other and went their separate ways. He walked a little down the path and spoke softly, perhaps to himself, "Any of us could find solace in a story placing ourselves somewhere when we're nowhere. Sometime, words on a page make it okay; another voice in your head drawing a blurred image into focus. There are other times when everything in life gets ripped apart. The floor, the walls, the ceiling have no fixed place: Where no words comfort. Daisy is there now."

The path Daisy was on had a stand of trees on both sides and she thought she heard the wind rush by. A curious feeling tugged on her and she looked to her left then to her right. She came to a stop and noticed Owldoll on a tree limb close to where she was standing.

Owldoll dropped a pink rubber ball from her craw. It bounced a few times and rested close to Daisy. They both looked at it curiously.

"Oh, Owldoll. You used this pink rubber ball to make the connection with me that night on the roof. You must-a known my mom gave it to me and how I loved it. Now, you're bringing it back to me again. What are you trying to tell me?"

"W-issh. Memories cannot share what was not there. Memories cannot share what was not there. W-issh."

Daisy agreed, "Mr. Harris was just saying memories lose their meaning after you find out what really happened." She went to a bench and sat down. "It is a hard lesson to learn. Who wants to find out her mother cares more about starting a new life than caring for the life she helped create?" She covered her eyes and then uncovered them. "I guess it is never easy to say goodbye.... Especially to someone who wasn't really there for you."

They sat in silence a while then Daisy looked back at Owldoll and continued, "I always thought memories were to hold
onto and cherish. What do I do now that my memories weren't
really there? It is like the past is gone."

"W-issh. The past can be present but the past cannot return.
The past can be present but the past cannot return. W-issh."

The words echoed in Daisy's mind: *the past can be present;
the past can be present; the past can be present; but the past cannot
return; the past cannot return; the past cannot return. The pink rubber
ball was there. But it probably wasn't the same pink rubber ball. Even
if it was the same ball, it doesn't mean what it did before.*

Daisy asked, "How do I say thank you, Owldoll? You have
taken me from the horrible days when I saw my mother cast under an evil spell. It turned her into a witch. I saw her run away
from me and disappear from my life. You helped me solve the
mystery of the frozen words. You helped me break the curse she
was under. Now, you're helping me see what's going on today."

Owldoll twisted her head around once, "W-issh. I am your
special friend whenever you need me. Just look over your shoulder and I'll be standing there. I am your special friend whenever
you need me. Just look over your shoulder and I'll be standing
there. W-issh."

Owldoll As Advertised

Owldoll (A Twenty-First Century Færy Tale)
As Advertised In Social Media

Owldoll (A Twenty-First Century Færy Tale) is the first novel by Jerry Brooks. It was developed from his short-story "Owldoll", which came from a local Urban Legend about contemporary family life. The story was, as he puts it, *"fleshed out freshly by intensive interviews, dialog, and reflection with those whose character or characteristic were rendered nearly intact—a journalistic cryogenics—for what you are about to read."*

The novel takes place in the fictional city of Midway, which is like a city you may have lived in and unlike it at the same time. The reader will recognize people and places never specifically mentioned in the novel as familiar and analogous to those from her or his own experiences. The protagonist is a complex and precocious teenage girl named Daisy, whose mother ran away abruptly when Daisy was five years-old. Deborah, Daisy's mother, was placed under an evil spell that turned her into a witch and Daisy seeks to find her mother throughout the story with help from her father, friends, neighbors, and the title character, Owldoll.

Owldoll is a magical stuffed owl given to Deborah, then nine months pregnant with Daisy, by the proprietor of Witchcraft Heights Potions. Daisy discovers the ornate wooden box containing the stuffed owl years later in her mother's closet. It becomes a favorite play thing she names Owldoll. When Daisy really needs a special friend, Owldoll becomes animated and speaks to her in cryptic but revealing lines, which ultimately lead her to undo the spell cast on her mother.

The reader will find the places, adventures, and characters engaging and interesting. Copious footnotes lend an air of authority to the book making it suitable for scholarly subjects. The story, being a twenty-first century færy tale, has all of the expected elements like magic, mystery, suspense, humor, romance, and a surprise ending to make this novel one for the ages as well as one for readers of all ages.

About The Writer

Jerry Brooks is a graduate of Boston College. He is a founding member of Red Rock Rewriters, a writers' group, meeting at the Swampscott Public Library since 2006. Living near Boston and the ocean has added a distinct and somewhat salty flavor to his writing, like potato chips, that subtly attract more of your attention. He writes in many genres; impossible fiction, mystery, crime/detective, children's parable, and sci-fi, but has a recognizable voice across all. To quote a character in one of his stories, who is describing the character's anonymously written stories: The cool thing is his books walk the fine line between just god-awful lousy, attractively intriguing, and somewhat scholarly.

Owldoll (A Twenty-First Century Færy Tale) is the first novel by Jerry Brooks. It was developed from his short-story "Owldoll", which came from a local Urban Legend about contemporary family life. The story was, as he puts it, "fleshed out freshly by intensive interviews, dialog, and reflection with those whose character or characteristic were rendered nearly intact—a journalistic cryogenics—for what you are about to read."

The reader will find the places, adventures, and characters engaging and interesting. Copious footnotes lend an heir of authority to the book making it suitable for scholarly subjects. The story, being a twenty-first century færy tale, has all of the expected elements like magic, mystery, suspense, humor, romance, and a surprise ending to make this novel one for the ages as well as one for readers of all ages.

e-mail: owldolltcft@gmail.com